feelin'
the
vibe

feelin' the vibe

CANDICE DOW

GC

GRAND CENTRAL
PUBLISHING

NEW YORK   BOSTON

The events and characters in this book are fictitious. Certain real locations and public figures are mentioned, but all other characters and events described in the book are totally imaginary.

Grand Central Publishing
Hachette Book Group
237 Park Avenue
New York, NY 10017

Printed in the United States of America

Grand Central Publishing is a division of Hachette Book Group, Inc.
The Grand Central Publishing name and logo is a trademark of Hachette Book Group, Inc.

ISBN-13: 978-1-61523-487-5

Book design by L&G McRee

ACKNOWLEDGMENTS

As always, I would like to thank God for this journey; the obstacles and the blessings.

Special thanks to my readers for inspiring me to write a sequel to my first novel, *Caught in the Mix*. This book is for you. These characters seemed to have really resonated with you, and over the years many of you have shared with me your own love stories and the resemblances to Clark and Devin. You wanted to know more about them, and you felt there were unanswered questions. Your excitement kept them alive and made me want to finish their story. I hope that *Feelin' the Vibe* is all you'd hoped for in Clark and Devin's reunion.

Thanks to my parents, family, and friends for supporting me through everything. To my agent, Audra Barrett. To my editors, Karen Thomas and Latoya Smith. Thanks for always making sure the story is all that it should be.

Special thanks to everyone who has offered me advice, encouragement, or inspiration along the way. You are truly loved and appreciated.

With love,
Candice

feelin'
the
vibe

1

DEVIN

After my mother got over the shock that I was getting married again, to a girl she didn't even know, she figured she would do her part and plan the rehearsal dinner. She was all about custom, and she had to do the right thing whether she approved or not. She and my father came into DC three days before the wedding. But judging by the looks of the window-enclosed banquet room at the Mandarin Oriental Hotel, she'd done a lot of planning over the phone. One hundred guests were invited to the rehearsal dinner, and my boys took full advantage of the top-shelf open bar. They raised their cups to me multiple times. *To the rich boy*, they would say. That had been a running joke since we were in college.

Here I was, thirty-two years old, a successful political attorney, and my millionaire parents were still trying to make up for lost time, mend our estranged relationship, do what they assumed good parents do. I know my mother at least regretted that while they were building a multimillion-dollar law firm, I was being nurtured by the nanny, the housekeeper, and even the gardener at times. I was off to college in a matter of minutes, as my mother explains. They had totally missed my childhood and probably knew less about me than they would have liked. The plan was for me to go off to Hampton for undergrad, then on to law school at Columbia and back to Arizona to work my way to partner in Patterson & Patterson, but I diverged from the course. I got married during my second year in law school—big mistake, by the way. And I wanted a real relationship with my daughter and I couldn't allow her to be second to my success. So, I decided to find my own path and stayed in New York after law school to give my daughter the security she deserved, even after her mother and I called it quits.

Despite the awkward relationship with my parents, they have always been my financial backbone, and I plan to follow their professional path. The only thing I'd yet to master was to marry someone who could potentially be my business partner. However, in my relationship, I planned to be the leader and not be like my father, who seemed to be led around like a puppy. My mother was clearly the mastermind behind the Patterson & Patterson empire. My father always seemed to be along for the ride.

I looked across the room at my bride-to-be and smiled, hoping I had found that partner. She had all the checkmarks. She was a successful attorney as well, daughter of a prestigious Baptist minister and effortlessly classy. I walked in her direction and my smile got bigger as I got closer. Her fitted, green strapless dress accentuated her tall, shapely figure, and the color made her maple-brown skin sparkle. She gave me her usual doublewide smile, and her plump lips glistened. Her big eyes squinted and she batted her long lashes as I approached. Long, black, straight hair was weaved into her normally ear-length hair, and it flowed down her back as if it belonged to her.

As I reached for her hand, I couldn't help feeling lucky.

Taylor was the baddest chick left in the game. By thirty, most women were scarred and ruined by the bad selection of men out here, so they couldn't recognize a good man with bifocals. Taylor, on the other hand, was just one year younger than me, but she was uninhibited, carefree, and didn't sweat the small stuff. She was beauty, brains, and bedroom skills all packaged in one. When I met her, I knew she would look good by my side, professionally and physically.

My mother stood up, wearing a stiff baby blue business suit in the middle of June, looking like Hillary Clinton's twin sister, and chimed her glass with a fork to gain everyone's attention. Taylor's parents smiled, anxious to hear what she had to say. I felt a little edgy, because my parents had invited several of their fellow Stanford alumni friends, and she was in her element. Taylor's guests looked around as if to say: Who the hell is this white woman? It wasn't something that I had branded on my forehead—or in my physical characteristics, for that matter—so people were always shocked to discover that I was biracial.

"I must say that this wedding came as a big surprise for me. I mean, I just met Taylor yesterday. Devin called me, it seems like two weeks ago, and said, 'I'm getting married.' I said, 'To who?'" she said, chuckling.

The crowd gasped, and Taylor looked like she could disappear. My eyes shot daggers at my mother, and I held Taylor's hand tightly and apologetically. She waved a napkin at Taylor and me to suggest we not be so sensitive. She continued, "But I'm sure if my son picked you, you're quite a gem. Devin has a heart of gold. I just hope that he is everything you dreamed of, because he is truly a good man."

She doesn't even know what kind of man I am. Hesitant claps trickled throughout the room. Based on people's confused expressions, they probably wondered what was the purpose of her comment, but I knew my mother. She said exactly what she wanted to say when she wanted to say it. The translation for what she was saying was, "I don't even know this ho. Devin, is this just another one of your public-service projects? Well, if it's not, this chick better be good to you."

She'd pretty much made everyone uncomfortable. I wondered if she was plain old oblivious to the way she insulted people or if she was so used to being the boss that she was desensitized. What the hell could I do? She was my mother. As fucked-up as she was, she was what God gave me. Shortly after, the guests began to bail out one by one. Taylor looked irritated, and I held her hand to remind her of all the things I'd warned her about my mother. My parents lived between Arizona and Florida, and with their busy schedules and mine I got to see them a maximum of twice a year, so her personality wouldn't pose a problem in my relationship.

On the other hand, I was glad my mother cleared the room. It was time for the bachelor party. All of my line brothers were already drunk, and I knew it would be off the chain. I gave Taylor a long hug, kissing her bare shoulders. Her ever-glossed lips pecked me on the cheek.

"Baby, I'll see you at the altar."

My hand rested on the small of her back, as I looked her up and down for the last time before she would be Mrs. Devin Patterson. Her height made it appear that she always wore heels, so no one took notice of the casual flip-flops she sported. She claimed she didn't want to tire her feet before the big day. I kissed her again. "I wouldn't miss it, TJ."

I rounded up the fellas and we headed out of the hotel like twenty-year-olds who were on their way to visit a strip joint for the first time. Most of them were married or in long-term relationships, so this would be the first time in a long time that multiple chicks grinded on them at once. I couldn't wait to be where they were: stable. I was tired of the game, tired of dumb-ass girls. Which was probably why I was four months into the relationship and already tying the knot. One thing was sure: My parents didn't raise a fool. I didn't plan on letting a good thing pass me by twice. Taylor was going to be mine against all odds.

And boy, did we have odds. I met Taylor at the Congressional Black Caucus in DC a few years back. We danced at a party and I was feeling her physically, but of course I was guilty of assuming she was a fine chick with nothing to offer. When I found out that she was also a corporate attorney and worked for the Train Workers Union, I immediately thought we could be the next DC power couple. She, on the other hand, couldn't see the possibilities and kept telling me that she had a man. She never told me much about him, just that he existed. A part of me believed he was just imaginary. Still, she wouldn't give me what I wanted, so I laid low for a while, opting for intermittent friendship.

At the time I was between DC and New York, so whenever I came to DC I'd give her a call and we'd hang out. If you want something to happen bad enough, keep checking in. One day, I hit her up and she told me that she had broken up with that nameless, faceless dude she'd been calling her man. I wasted no time making her my girl. It was right around my thirty-first birthday, and I felt like she was my gift. I couldn't wait to have her on my arm at the party I was planning. She and her best friend, Courtney, came up to New York and arrived at the house a few hours before the party.

When we got to the club, all of my boys gave the head nod; she was a winner, and everyone could see. When my best friend, Jason, and his girlfriend, Akua, walked in, it seemed like the entire club stopped moving, the music skipped a beat, and Taylor looked like she'd seen a ghost. Jason scowled at Taylor. I was confused and my eyes shifted from Taylor to Jason to Akua. Clearly, they'd all met before, and this definitely was not a happy reunion.

Taylor had told me that the guy she was seeing while I pursued her was her high school sweetheart and she'd broken his heart way back when. But after running into him at their ten-year class reunion, she'd successfully stolen him from his girlfriend. I'm thinking this dude lived in the Maryland-DC area or somewhere close. Maybe I didn't ask enough questions, because Jason was the guy and he lived in Connecticut, and as far as I knew Jason and Akua had never broken up.

While I was shocked that our worlds intersected in such a crazy way, I was pissed to think that Taylor was dissin' me for a dude who already had someone. I couldn't believe the chick that I'd hyped up in my mind was just another dumb girl. I was mad as shit. I was mad at Taylor for being stupid, and I was madder at Jason, because after all we'd been through he could have told me he had a chick on the side in DC. Had he done that, we wouldn't have had this problem.

Taylor made it seem like she realized Jason wasn't what she wanted and that's why they stopping dealing with each other, but Jason claimed he didn't want to leave Akua. He said that Akua was the better woman and Taylor was crushed when he broke it off. He thought Taylor might have intentionally targeted me for revenge. Jason and I debated whether she could have known we were line brothers and if our relationship was nothing more than an attack on him. I tried to explain that I chased her and she couldn't have possibly known. He wasn't having it. Jason was adamant that she'd masterminded this entire situation.

Momentarily, I wanted to believe that she was a snake in the grass. Then my wisdom kicked in: There was no way possible she could have known we were connected. Taylor was never the type to play the who-do-you-know or what-do-you-do games. In fact, she hated "status probing," as she called it, and avoided it at all costs. Not to mention, at the time I was between New York and DC. Jason and Akua were in Connecticut, and Taylor was in Maryland. What were the chances? Still, my boy looked me in my eye and told me that no matter if Taylor did this intentionally or not, he really didn't want any of his boys with her. Taylor was his girl that got away. So without question or regret, I ended it right there because men don't expose those kind of weak feelings for random chicks. I shook his hand and promised him that he never had to worry. There were too many women out here.

After more bad conversations, more bad dates, more you're-such-a-good-man-I-want-to-marry-you-now chicks, I broke my promise. I could search the whole world, which I had, and never find someone to click with the way Taylor and I did. In the most upstanding way, I let Jason know that I planned to see where it went with her. I told him as calmly and as honestly as possible that he had a good woman and I didn't, so I deserved one, too. Me wanting to be with Taylor should validate our friendship, not destroy it. Hell, it only meant we both had good taste. Initially, he laughed it off and told me to do what I had to do. He claimed his sideline with Taylor only strengthened his relationship with Akua. We danced around the fact that there would be no couples vacations or double dates. That would

be too much, but still we were boys and that took precedence over any soft-ass feelings.

Three months later, my ultimate goal of running for
United States Congress seemed attainable. My advisors told
me that my chances were greater if I were married. Voters
tend to support politicians they see as committed. There was
a part of me that wanted to get to know Taylor better. Then
there was the side that said that I'd seen enough already and
why not. I contemplated all of two days before I drove down
to Tyson's Corner and snatched up a 2.7-karat clear-as-hell
solitaire in a platinum channel-set 2.0-karat diamond band
from Tiffany.

When I asked Taylor, she took nearly five minutes to say
yes. My heart pounded and I regretted it for those moments.
This is too much for her to handle, I thought. *We don't know each
other that well.*

Finally, she shrugged. "Devin Patterson, why wouldn't I
marry you?"

I told her that I wanted it to be done quick and fast. Partly
because I wanted to be married for at least a few months
before I submitted my application for the election and partly
before I came to my senses. After we set the date, it was time
to announce to the world that I'd found the one again and
this time would be for good. That was when Jason lost his
damn mind. He basically called me every bitch-ass, back-
stabbing, no-good-for-nothing, rich-boy, spoiled-ass, selfish-
motherfucker name in the book. It wasn't until that moment
that I realized the extent of their little fling, but I was in too
deep. I was in love, and Taylor was my only serious girlfriend
since my divorce, nearly seven years ago. So I really didn't
have a choice. My only recourse was to get Jason to empa-
thize with me.

I went up to Connecticut and reasoned with him. He hung his head. "So, you really love her?"

Holding my chest up, I said, "Yeah, man. And you know I haven't felt like this for anyone since—"

"Clark. Yeah, I know. So, what about her?"

My eyebrows scrunched up. What the hell was he talking about? "Look, man, Clark is a married woman."

"Nah, I'm saying what would you say if I told you that I loved Clark and wanted to marry your old girlfriend? A chick that you had mad love for."

I gazed off for a minute and then stared him dead in the eye. "Look, man, I would shoot you if you even *thought* about dating Clark." I laughed a little. "If you tell me you feel as strongly for Taylor as I felt for Clark, I'll call it off."

He reached out to shake my hand. "Nah, dawg. It's not that heavy. Do what you have to do. Taylor would probably work out better for someone like you."

"And besides, you got the baddest chick out here anyway," I said, referring to his orthopedic-surgeon, sexy-ass, love-his-dirty-drawers fiancée. We made amends that day, and I was cocky enough to ask him if he'd be my best man. He agreed with a smile.

The wedding had become way more than I expected. Taylor and I wanted something simple, but her father was a pastor of a church with about six thousand members, and her mother was in charge of the bridal ministry. So, in less than five weeks, we had nearly five hundred invited guests, a host of church members who planned to just come see us exchange vows. It was all too much for me. The one simple thing that Taylor and I were able to control was we didn't want a whole slew of bridesmaids and groomsmen. Her best friend, Courtney, the maid of honor, and Jason, my best man, were the only members of the bridal party.

The fellas rented a Stretch Hummer to drive us from the rehearsal dinner to the bachelor party. As soon as we hopped in, we started taking shots, drinking beer, talking loud, and just flat out celebrating the biggest decision a man can make. In the midst of all the noise and the partying in the limo, I didn't pay attention to where we were going. When we pulled up to my condo, I was confused. They started spilling out of the truck when the chauffeur opened the door. I looked at Jason and he said, "The party is here, dawg."

I jumped out and we poured into my bachelor pad. The place was sprawling with sexy-ass chicks wearing skimpy thongs and those hooker heels. They walked around feeding us desserts, kissing on us, and making me question whether I was making the right choice. There were like three chicks assigned to me at all times, even while each girl performed, a girl personally entertained me. In a quick glimpse at Jason, a dark cloud hovered over his dark skin. His forehead rippled like he was stressed, as he stared aimlessly at the dancers. I excused myself from the ladies and staggered over to my boy. His eyes were red and steam was rising from his bald head. The pit of my stomach felt funny as I stood in front of him. Before I could ask what was going on with him, he looked into my eyes and said, "You always got to jump on something before somebody else gets it, huh?"

"Man, c'mon now. Stop trippin'."

Jason was always the one who didn't mind shedding a tear, and it looked like he was about to. I was too intoxicated for that comical shit. I snickered, and he looked up at me like he hated me. His stood up and rammed into me and my back banged into the opposite wall, instantly cracking it. After shaking the shock, I punched him in the face.

The dancers, our line brothers, and everyone else watched on in awe. If they hadn't been so caught off-guard, they probably would have tried to stop it. It was as if everyone's mouth was open, but no one spoke. We trampled over furniture; fixtures and glasses clanked as they fell to the floor. No one even tried to stop me from whipping Jason's ass. They watched like we were scheduled entertainment. He kept calling me a punk-ass nigga, but I couldn't help thinking how much of a punk he was. He would have been better off saying something months ago. I slammed his six-foot-two muscular body around like I was a Marvel superhero. I don't know where the strength came from. Even though we were about the same height, Jason was more bulky than me. Maybe I would have called off the damn wedding if I knew this clown would act like this. Here I was again, like déjà vu. Clark had waited moments before I married Jennifer to profess her love for me and to tell me that I was making a big mistake and that she and I belonged together. Why was I dealing with shit again right before my wedding?

As Jason and I fought all the way into the guest bedroom, everyone shifted from location to location with us. Finally, I threw his bag at him.

"Get the hell out of my house, punk."

He slung his duffle bag over his shoulder and stormed from my house. A part of me was concerned that he was too drunk to drive, but I was obviously not concerned enough to go after him. Everyone was confused, but I wasn't up for explaining. I looked at Brandon. "I hope you can fit that tux in there."

He shook my hand and patted my back. "I gotchu, man."

I walked into my bedroom and slammed the door. During the fight, I was too pissed to rationalize the situation, but the blood stains on Jason's polo shirt and the look in his eyes as I slammed the door haunted me. My mind raced and I really couldn't sleep. I couldn't stop thinking about all we'd been through. With the wedding just hours away, I figured I shouldn't sweat it. I had too much respect for Taylor to call it off now. If this shit didn't work out, I wasn't doing it anymore. I loved Taylor enough to at least give it a shot. I ran my hand down my face. *Taylor J, you better be worth all this bullshit.*

2

CLARK

When are you supposed to come to grips with an anti-climactic life? No one could have convinced me that I wouldn't be jet-setting around the world, in mad, breathtaking love, with a bunch of kids, a nanny to help me, and a bottomless spending account. It seems like all those dreams slipped away in a nightmare nine years ago on New Year's Day. I was just twenty-five years old then, and what should have been a celebration of a new beginning marked the end of my best friend's life. Tanisha and I had been inseparable from the time we were nine and ten. In a crazed state, her then fiancé, Fred, killed her in a murder-suicide after discovering she was still sleeping with my brother, Reggie, her kid's father. I blamed him. I blamed me. I blamed the world for being so cruel, but nothing would bring her back. My life literally spiraled out of control in just twenty-four hours.

When I received the call that she was gone, I was in New York and had just begged Devin not to marry Jennifer. He was the love of my life, and after some ups and downs we had a temporary breakup. In that time, Jennifer got pregnant and Devin decided it made sense to marry her. I pleaded with him, nearly down on my knees with tears streaming down my face. Still, he looked me dead in the eye and pledged his love for her. I felt like I wanted to die, too. The two people I loved the most were gone in a blink of an eye.

My niece, Morgan, was ten years old at the time and she wanted to live with me. My nephew, Little Reggie, was six and he went with my brother. Considering I was forced into motherhood, I knew that I couldn't just die or sulk over Devin. Instead, I sought therapy for Morgan and me. We needed real help. God would have it that Kenneth, my therapist and the director of Agape Mental Health, would fall in love with me. He, too, was a single parent with a daughter, Mia, a year younger than Morgan. We could help each other and we did. We married two years later.

It set out to be the ideal marriage, because he believed in family and human services, and I had evolved to be that person, too. He inspired me to leave the corporate world to pursue helping foster kids. My group home opened five years ago, and Kenneth and I planned to have a home full of our own kids. But shortly after, I was diagnosed with polycystic ovarian syndrome, which can cause fertility issues. My doctor insisted that with fertility drugs, I'd be pregnant in no time. We went from fertility drugs to shots to in vitro fertilization, or IVF, and so far nothing has worked. Our retirement, our savings, all the equity in our home, is gone as we continue to go broke attempting to bring life into this world. After the last cycle, I was tempted to tell Kenneth that we should stop, but I could never find the right time to say it.

In August, we dropped Mia off to college. It seemed like in the two months since we've been home alone, the silence was alarming. It didn't seem so bad when Morgan was the only one gone, but it was clear that Kenneth and I were missing something. We were trapped in a monotone, lifeless marriage, distracted by the kids. So, I decided to try again to give my husband what he wanted and attempted IVF for the fifth time.

I sat up in my bed and looked at the clock: 3:25 a.m. My insomnia had gotten worse several days ago after my eggs were extracted. When the sun came up, I would be going in for the embryo transfer, in which they would insert up to four fertilized eggs into me. The process does not guarantee pregnancy. Trust me, I know. I wondered if this time it would work or if it was even worth it. The damn artificial hormones in my system were driving me crazy. My mind raced with thoughts about bills, needing a new car, and wanting just to be free of the pressure to conceive. I felt trapped.

If the transfer didn't take this time, we would be forced into taking out a loan to do it again. Kenneth wanted to try until the damn fat lady sang. I heard her singing loud and clear, but he was the positive one, the one who believed that your mind predicts your destiny and all that other over-optimistic hoopla he tells his clients. And I didn't want to disappoint him, so I said nothing. I just went along with the program, despite it being my body experiencing all the changes. He was a good husband and this was my way of being a good wife.

Six hours later, we were in the cold, sterile room trying to get pregnant. Why couldn't I be like everyone else and con-ceive in a warm, sweaty, lustful bed? I looked at Kenneth, standing beside the bed. His hair was thinning, and his dark lips attempted to crack a smile. I reached out to hold his large hand, which was about as romantic as my reproductive process gets. I lay back on the table and put my feet in the stirrups. I prayed that it would work this time, because I was tired. I was so tired of my life being on hold. From the dark blotches on Kenneth's once-smooth milk-chocolate skin and the slight traces of crow's-feet around his small eyes, he was tired, too. Maybe it just wasn't meant for us to have kids together.

The doctor inserted the egg and tears rolled down the side of my face. Kenneth wiped them and asked, "Does it hurt?"

I shook my head.

"So why you crying?"

I shrugged. "I just hope it works, because—"

"Stopping thinking negative."

I huffed. You'd think after seven years of marriage, he'd learn to be my husband and not my therapist. *Don't be negative. Be careful what you say out of your mouth.* Kenneth thought he knew me better than I knew myself. Considering he was five years older than me, it often felt like he thought he was my father. Sometimes I just needed a partner to say that everything would be okay, not teach me. But, he'd yet to get it, and when I tried to dispute his teachings, we always ended up in an argument. I closed my eyes, because I knew that I didn't need the added stress. Not now, especially since I'd concluded that this was definitely the last time. I wasn't putting my body or my mind through this shit anymore. It had to work and I didn't want to take any risk. I needed to be as calm as I could be.

3

DEVIN

Shortly after I launched the legislative branch of my parent's law firm in DC, I was quickly inducted into the high-powered political scene in the Maryland suburbs. Most of my clients were there, and many of them believed I could make a difference, and they encouraged me to purchase property in the Maryland area. The Democratic congressman in District 4 had suggested he would retire, making his seat available in the 2008 election. Considering I'd only been in the area a short time, I was surprised the Young Democrats were interested in supporting me. Congress had always been a part of the plan, but I assumed first State Senate and then Congress. I guess when things are meant, they're just meant. Or better yet, when you have the money to pay for your campaign, it's possible to win any election.

The Young Democrats knew that it would be no issue to call my parents and ask them to give me a couple of million. That would seal the election. Right after I purchased the house in Mitchellville, Maryland, I asked Taylor to marry me. Despite the short courtship, I knew she couldn't resist the million-dollar home and the million-dollar man. She accentuated my political résumé. I had set myself up in less

than two months to be the party's candidate if the congressman really decided to retire.

I didn't want to jinx myself by spreading the word that
my plan was to run for Congress if the opportunity arose.
After the wedding, I thought it was the perfect time to surprise Taylor with the news. We were chilling on the beach
in Turks and Caicos for our honeymoon, relaxing in beach
chairs. She read a romance novel, while I read a book about
being an effective leader. It hit me, this was the time to say
something. "Taylor, what do you think about me running for
Congress in oh-eight?"

She lifted her sunglasses. "Oh-eight? Like next year oh-
eight?"

"Yeah. I mean the seat would have to be available and it's
not right now."

"First of all, we just got married. Do you realize how hard
running for Congress will be? Do you realize how much of a
strain that would be on our relationship?"

"But, you know that Congress is my ultimate plan."

"*Ultimate* is the key word. Let's live our lives for a moment,
before we put them under a microscope," she pleaded.

Considering it was only a mere possibility, I decided my
honeymoon wasn't the time to argue about it. I had nearly
six months before any decision would need to be made. I
leaned back in my chair and nodded like I was listening to
her plan. Taylor paused and almost leaned back, too. As if
she had another bright idea why this was wrong, she popped
back up and said, "Not to mention, you're just getting Love
My People going in the direction you want it to go."

I grimaced because I didn't understand what my nonprofit
organization had to do with my possible run for Congress. I
kidded, "You can run that for me. Right, baby?"

Her neck snapped back, probably because Love My People was a concept that Jason and I had come up with in his last year of medical school. He did a medical rotation in Honduras and when I went to visit, I felt compelled to help. In the small village where he worked, the clinic was literally about two hundred square feet. The man running the clinic told us if only he had people to contribute sheets and beds or even to take time to hand out water to the patients that were waiting, things would be better. He asked for so little, but there was so much that needed to be done. I felt it was my mission to start an organization that would take a group of law students twice a year to different South American countries, especially in the areas where black people were. That way the students could experience injustice firsthand and hopefully they'd be willing to fight it when they graduated.

Jason liked the idea, too, and he wanted the other component to be medical students coming to administer health care. Since he had been so busy with residency and his finances weren't actually where they needed to be yet, he hadn't had the time to fully commit to Love My People. And based on what happened the night before the wedding, I wasn't sure he ever planned to join the mission. Obviously, Taylor thought we'd eventually get it right, which is why she was staring at me with a smirk that said she didn't want to work so closely with a guy she used to date.

"I trust you," I said jokingly.

She rested back and said, "Devin. Don't play me. Do you realize if you run for Congress, you may have to give up the foundation? I mean, they're going to be watching your every move, and you'll probably have to expose all your contributors. It's just not good."

Maybe she didn't fully know what type of man she had

yet. I laughed. "Taylor, you do realize that I knew all of this when I started Love My People. I only solicit and accept donations from American citizens."

"So I guess you got this all planned out, huh?"

"No, I thought I should discuss it with my wife first."

She rolled her eyes. This was clearly not going the way I expected. I rested my hand on her knee and looked at her. I said, "Taylor. You make the call. When do you think would be a good time for me to run?"

"After kids, after we explore the world, I guess when we're about forty or so."

I nodded and stared out into the sea. I understood where she was coming from, but I clearly didn't agree. How often do congressional seats open up and you really have a shot? I decided we'd cross that bridge when we absolutely had to.

It wasn't until the end of October that I finally gave up hope and assumed that God had granted Taylor her wish. Congressman Grayford had yet to announce his retirement and was still wavering whether or not he would do it. I mentally began gearing up for the 2012. That would give Taylor the time she wanted to build our relationship. Things were going well so far. This marriage was far better than my last. Unlike Jennifer, Taylor knew how to give me space. She liked her time with me when she liked it, but she knew how to occupy herself when I wasn't around. Still, we always made the best of the time we had. Taylor enjoyed socializing and trying new things, so there was never a dull moment in our house. She couldn't cook well, but she knew how to pick out the best restaurants in the city. So, I couldn't complain.

In fact, I loved coming home to Taylor. She was always so excited and full of life. No matter how drained I was, her personality invigorated me. I came home on the evening train after spending two days in New York with my daughter, Nicole, and I was ready to relax with Taylor. Initially, I suggested we go out to eat, but she offered to cook.

When I walked in the house dragging my bags behind me, Taylor met me at the door. She talked a mile a minute, obviously excited that I was home. I kissed her so that she could stop talking. She tilted her head. "You're not listening to me."

I laughed. "No, baby. I'd rather just hold you."

"Well, hold me then."

We stood in our large kitchen holding on to each other. All I wanted to do was eat dinner and watch a good movie. I raked my hand through her asymmetrical haircut. I liked to run my hand up and down the nape of her neck where the tapered part was. She leaned her head into my shoulder, and I asked, "What did you cook?"

She pulled away and shifted her weight to one leg with her hand on her hip. I laughed and she laughed, too. It had to be one of two dishes. I walked over to the stove and confirmed it was chicken parmesan. I sniffed. "Hmmm. It smells good."

"You're just trying to get me hyped," she said, as she walked closer to me.

Actually, I didn't smell much of anything, but I wanted to acknowledge her effort. My stomach was growling, and I hoped that the lack of aroma didn't reflect how it would taste. "Nah, baby. I'm not trying to get you hyped. I'm ready to eat. Let me go get cleaned up and I'll be back."

When I returned, she had lit an apple cider candle that sat on the kitchen counter. The plates were prepared and on the table. I grabbed a bottle of Shiraz from the wine rack and set it on the table beside the toasted garlic bread. Taylor dimmed the chandelier and sat down. She said grace and opened the bottle of wine. I poured some in her glass and then in mine.

She raised her glass and said, "To being happy."

I nodded. "Yeah."

We both took a couple of sips before either of us tasted our food. Finally, I was the brave one to taste it first. I put a piece of the chicken and a forkful of pasta in my mouth. My face immediately turned up. It didn't taste as good as it did the last time, but for the sake of her feelings I was going to stomach it. She smiled at me suspiciously and then she started laughing.

"It's not good?"

"It's okay," I said, struggling to chew the overcooked, unseasoned chicken.

"You don't have to lie."

"I'm not lying. It's okay."

She tasted her food and pouted slightly. She chewed and her face crunched up like it was sour. She shook her head. "It's not good. You don't have to eat it if you don't want to." Then she laughed slightly, like she was embarrassed, and I started laughing, too. She said, "Let's just eat the bread and wine."

"Sounds like a plan."

Taylor and I tossed our plates. I was just happy she was confident enough to admit the food was horrible. I didn't rub it in. Instead, we ate the whole loaf of garlic bread and drank wine. After we were done, I suggested we go relax. She pulled a box of strawberries from the refrigerator and picked up the wine bottle, and we headed up to our bedroom.

She sat on the bed and began to take off her clothes, and I stared at her. She smiled at me and she took the bottle of wine and poured some in between her breasts. I walked over to her and began licking her and massaging her breasts. She rubbed my head seductively. I grabbed the bottle from her and lay her down. Then I poured more on her and grabbed a strawberry. As I tickled one nipple with the top of the strawberry, I swallowed a mouthful of the other. Taylor squirmed and tried to take my sweater off. I stood at the edge of the bed, quickly stepped out of my pants, and pulled my sweater over my head. I grabbed another strawberry and traced up and down the middle of her stomach with it. I carefully grazed her vagina with the strawberry and put her juices in my mouth, while she stroked my dick vigorously. I wanted to put it in her so bad, but I wanted to make her feel good. I spread her legs apart and plunged my tongue into her entrance. She clamped on to my shoulders and made sweet sounds. My hands pressed into her flat stomach, so that I could taste all of her. She was so wet. I had to feel her, and she summoned me to put it in. I climbed on the bed and entered her. She stared at me intensely as I went deep inside. She moaned and rubbed my back passionately as I stroked her. She sucked on my neck and I turned her face to kiss me. She told me how good I made her feel and I stroked harder. She yelled my name and I held her tightly, pumping faster until I came all in her. She sighed, "I love you, Devin."

I rolled over beside her and said, "I love you, too, TJ."

My eyes felt heavy and my body was sedated. She began to talk, but I floated in and out of consciousness, so I really wasn't listening. As I lay there feeling high from her love-making, I relished in that although she wasn't the greatest in the kitchen, she had mastered the bedroom. The trade-off was worth it.

4

◆

CLARK

My period always arrived approximately four days before the doctor's appointment. When it hadn't, I was partially excited, but I didn't want to start rejoicing and be disappointed. I kept it under wraps until we went to the hospital. Kenneth and I sat hand in hand in doctor's office. Our nurse came in and told me to climb on the table and take my clothes off. I was nervous because I couldn't lie there and stomach hearing bad news. My heart was racing by the time the doctor entered and greeted us with his signature greeting: "Hey, kids. How's it going?"

He told me what he was going to do and inserted the probe in me. The nurse pursed her pale pink lips, flicked her midlength blond hair behind her ear, and smiled as she hovered over me. When her bubbly grin finally broke through, it was confirmed. She nodded. "It took; you're pregnant."

I looked at Kenneth and covered my face. "Oh my God! Finally."

Dr. Battle took off his rubber gloves and told me he'd come back after I dressed to answer questions. This was our first positive in five years of trying. I wanted to jump up and down and shout for joy, but I lay there stunned. As I tossed and turned in bed the night before, I concluded that there were other ways to enjoy life aside from raising kids. Thirty-four is the age when your chances decrease, but obviously for me it was the age of fertility.

I noticed a tear in Kenneth's eye, which brought me to tears. He lifted his black frame glasses and rubbed his eye. He licked his dehydrated lips and smiled. "See, baby, I told you when it was our time."

"Your first pregnancy, right?" the nurse asked, bobbing her head side to side while she cleaned up behind the doctor.

My eyes shifted and I sat up on the table as I nervously said, "Yes."

She flipped through the charts. A dingy frown appeared on her face. "So why does it say here, one prior pregnancy?"

Her blue eyes circled as I tried to explain to her with my eyes that the pregnancy she was referring to was a secret. My doctor knew about it, but I'd never told Kenneth. He was against abortions and he'd probably preach to me the whole concept of the universe's laws of karma. I'd already beaten myself up about it in the privacy of my own mind, damn if I needed someone else's conviction. I had enough to cope with—the strains on my marriage, my pockets, and my body. I didn't need judgment, but this airhead had put me in a terrible situation. She was supposed to leave when the doctor left. Why was she still in the room, stirring up drama?

Kenneth glanced at my uncomfortable expression and his thick eyebrows gathered. My heart plunged and a lump sat in my throat. Finally, I said, "I don't know."

"Hmmm. Let me go talk to Dr. Battle."

He could read me, and when the nurse left the room, I didn't even want to look in his direction. I quickly jumped off the table and stepped into my jeans. From the corner of my eye, I noticed his thumbs twirling in his lap. He huffed uncomfortably as he adjusted his black pants. "That's strange."

"Yeah, I know," I said, still staring at the degrees on the opposite wall while buttoning my shirt.

I wanted Dr. Battle to hurry up and clean this up. He was aware of the pregnancy and the fact that my husband knew nothing about it. It wasn't pertinent information as far as Dr. Battle was concerned, though. He'd explained to me early on that because of my condition, I probably wouldn't have even carried that baby to term. He'd lifted that burden from me a long time ago, and now some dumb-ass nurse had brought it back to surface.

I sat stiffly beside Kenneth, and it felt like an eternity before the doctor came in the room. The excitement we should have been feeling was clouded with confusion. Kenneth sat there wondering what the nurse was talking about, and I sat there thinking, *This is some bullshit.*

Finally, Dr. Battle bopped back in, his white coat swishing from side to side. He was clearly happy that he'd successfully impregnated me. "We did it!"

He stood there as if awaiting a high five, and Kenneth said, "Thanks. I'm very happy."

Dr. Battle ran his fingers through his thick, curly brunet hair and sat down. Looking at my chart, he fiddled with his wire-framed glasses. He began discussing what I should and shouldn't be doing. I nodded and began to feel slightly anxious. In my mind, I saw this going differently. I thought I'd be crying and snotting, yet all I could think of was that stupid nurse and prayed that Kenneth brushed it under the rug. We just had to get out of this office fast. I nodded a lot and didn't ask many questions. Kenneth touched my leg. "Baby, you sure you don't have any more questions?"

I folded my lips and forced a stiff smile and nodded. Dr. Battle raised his eyebrows. *Let's just go.* Kenneth said, "Well, actually, I do." He pointed to the folder on Dr. Battle's desk. "Your nurse claims there was a prior pregnancy. Is that correct? Is it possible we had an incident like you told us before where we miscarried and didn't know?"

Dr. Battle looked at me and quickly composed himself. "I doubt it. It's probably just a mistype."

Kenneth said, "Oh, okay. Just making sure."

"I understand."

When we left the office, I planned to write Dr. Battle a letter explaining that he needed to train his staff that everything is not an open topic when couples are in the room. That could have been disastrous. When we got to the front desk, the nurse gave me a prescription for prenatal vitamins and a bag of maternity magazines and samples. As she explained what everything was, I just wanted to run. I felt like a thief in a hurry to leave the crime scene. Kenneth stood there waiting for me, with his thick eyebrows gathered together. Finally, we left. Out in the hall, I excitedly grabbed his hand. "Kenneth, we did it! I'm so happy."

"It's funny. I couldn't tell."

"I just didn't want them to come in there and say, sike, we're joking."

He smiled and said, "And why would you think they would do something so cruel?"

"I don't know, maybe I was just surprised. I mean, pleasantly surprised. Stunned. I don't know, but it doesn't matter. All that matters now is that we're pregnant, finally," I said, leaning my head on his arm.

"Exactly."

We walked out of the building, and despite it being the

end of October, the sun was beaming on us, offering us its blessings. I wondered if we should wait until we were out of the danger zone, which is typically after fourteen weeks, to share the news, but I couldn't. After all these years, all the not-this-time phone calls, I would be cruel to keep my cheerleading squad in the dark. First, I called my mother.

"Ma, guess what!"

She gasped. "Clark, oh my God, what?"

"Why you say, 'Oh my God'?" I said, laughing, because she obviously knew what I was about to say but didn't want to hurt my feelings if it wasn't what she wanted it to be.

"Just tell me. I'm not good at guessing."

"It worked. I'm pregnant."

She squealed. "Oh baby, my baby."

I could hear her crying, and for the first time since the nurse said *positive*, I got overwhelmed.

"Nobody deserves this more than you. I have waited so long for this."

She cried in my ear, and tears streamed rapidly down my face. "Thank you, Ma. Thank you so much."

"You know everything has its season. It's your season."

"You're right, Ma."

My brother has three kids, two by Tanisha and one by his ex-wife. Despite all those grandkids to love, my mother still couldn't wait to see her own daughter give birth. It was like it was a rite of passage that somehow defined my womanhood. She sniffed on the other end, and I said, "A'ight, Ma. You're getting me all emotional. Let me go."

Then I called my second mother slash best friend slash assistant director for my group home, Ms. Teeny. When she picked up, she was blasting one of those teenage hip-hop songs in the background. She swears you have to listen to hip-hop to relate to the kids, but it seems like she gets more of an adrenaline rush than the kids.

"Ms. Teeny, turn that music down."

"Girl, that's my song. What's going on?" she asked, and finally there was silence in the background.

"Somebody's pregnant."

"Those fast-ass little girls, lawd, they gonna kill me."

"Ms. Teeny!" I snapped.

"What?" she asked, and I imagined she was rolling her eyes.

"I'm pregnant. We had the ultrasound today, and I'm going to have a baby."

"Aw!" she yelled, half-laughing. "Aw! Lawd, you have given this girl what she wanted. Oh my God, Kenneth is probably doing cartwheels."

I looked over at him as he drove with a pleasant expression and nodded. "He's very happy."

"Happy? He better be doing damn cartwheels."

Ms. Teeny knew Kenneth before she knew me. She worked for him for several years as the juvenile event coordinator, and they were really close. So she often talked to Kenneth like she was his mother, too. But clearly, over the years, her dedication had shifted more to me.

I looked at Kenneth. "Ms. Teeny said you need to be doing cartwheels."

"My heart is doing cartwheels. Is that good enough?"

I relayed the message, and she said, "He always has to be so damn serious. Tell him to loosen up his belt strap."

I looked over at him with his shirt tucked neatly in his pants and his black leather belt pulled tightly and laughed to myself. I dared not tell him what she said, or we'd receive a long lecture on why a man shouldn't get too chatty with his wife and friends. He claims women lose respect for you when you chitchat with them. *Whatever.* I wasn't in the mood for that. I just wanted to celebrate. Ms. Teeny and I talked a few minutes more before hanging up.

Kenneth and I headed to lunch at Baja Fresh. That had become one of our favorite cheap escapes. We both ordered steak quesadillas and sat at a bar top table. He said grace and when he finished, I looked up and he was staring at me strangely. I smiled. "What's up?"

He said, "I think you were pregnant before."

My eyes bugged out of my head and my sweat glands expanded. I felt moistness on my nose, my forehead, and under my arms.

"I think they made a mistake. Did you notice how strangely they acted? I feel like we need to get a copy of your medical records."

"Baby, it doesn't matter. We're expecting *now.*"

"It does matter when we're paying for this out of our pocket."

The reason we selected Dr. Battle was because he offers a 10 percent discount on the cost of the transfer following a miscarriage, I assume as a type of consolation. I shifted uncomfortably, because I'd always been the one to question whether they would let us know if we miscarried before the actual ultrasound testing, or even if they could. As I sat there wondering how I was going to flip this around, I huffed, "That's absurd. Every time, I came on my period before the doctor's visit. No cramps or anything. There is no way they could have made a mistake."

"We should at least be willing to make sure."

"Should we really? Let's just be thankful that I'm pregnant now."

"I think we should still look into it."

Kenneth had a keen sense of discernment. It came primarily from studying people, and it had its pros and cons. Times like this, I hated it and partially hated him for feeling the need to get to the bottom of everything. He couldn't quite put his finger on it, but he knew there was something fishy going on. Several times over the course of a few hours, he brought it up. The way the nurse looked. The way the doctor looked to the left when he spoke. He insisted, "Clark, they were lying."

If I didn't confront it now, this topic would plague me for the rest of my pregnancy. I wanted to be happy and thankful. I didn't want my pregnancy to be filled with guilt and suspicion. This was a secret that Tanisha and I shared. She took it to her grave, and now I carried the burden alone. I had never uttered a word to anyone else, except medical professionals. I looked him in the eye and unemotionally said, "Kenneth, I was pregnant almost eleven years ago and I got an abortion. Dr. Battle knows about that, so it's probably in my records."

He looked like I'd shot him with a cannonball as his chest slightly sank. He didn't know what to say. So I continued, "I got pregnant right before Devin went to law school and I didn't want him not to go because of the baby. So, I got an abortion. Tanisha went with me and she's the only person that knew. I never even told Devin."

"Why were you so pressed to hide it?

"I wasn't at peace with it when I did it. And I've never really come to peace with it, and it just got worse when we started trying and I couldn't get pregnant. All I could think was, I shoulda kept my baby."

"So how was that possible without any fertility drugs?"

I shrugged. "Dr. Battle claims that I probably would have had a miscarriage anyway."

"Yeah, probably."

"Yeah, and for some people, PCOS gets worse with age."

"Yeah, well. I guess if you were smart, you would have kept your baby and you and Devin would be in marital bliss right now," he said sarcastically.

I took a deep breath and rested my chin in the palm of my hand with my elbow on the table. I stared out the glass window into the woods. The leaves had completely fallen from the trees. The wind blew them around, causing them to make sweeping sounds on the ground. I thought it would make me feel better finally telling someone else, but I felt worse, like I wanted to be gone with the wind, too. For the first time in a long time, Kenneth's arrogance forced me to fantasize about marital bliss with Devin Patterson.

5

✦

DEVIN

Congressman Grayford announced he wouldn't be running for another term just two short weeks before the December application deadline. Thankfully, I had stayed in the mix, in the school system, developing my foreign-relations experience through Love My People. My name was relatively popular on the Maryland political scene. My parents had pledged up to a million dollars for the campaign, and Congressman Grayford had made it nearly impossible for anyone else to jump on this opportunity. In fact, he gave me a personal phone call after his announcement.

"Son," he said, "I've held this seat for a long time. I'm passing the torch."

"Thank you," I said.

Despite my gratitude, I struggled internally. Taylor was really against this so soon in our marriage. I now had two weeks to get my mind right. I started not to accept the challenge, but then who would represent my people? It was one of those things that I'd set up my entire life for, to run for Congress. Why did I suddenly have cold feet? Or was it Taylor's voice in my ear?

My head was spinning as I watched Taylor prepare for

work. I wanted to tell her my plans, but I had a meeting planned for noon in DC with Curtis Thorpe, the president of the Young Democrats of Maryland, Congressman Grayford, and a few other political move makers. They were expecting to strategize my campaign and I hadn't even gotten an okay from my wife. I left the house shortly after to escape to my bachelor pad so I could clear my head and think like a single man.

My condo was within walking distance of Capitol Hill. So I went to the Hill first and stood there looking at the tourists, being filled up the same way I was when I came here in high school with the Junior Black Caucus. The large white building, the long stairs, heading toward the large doors, still stirred up excitement in me. I remember standing in the exact place at fourteen, thinking that I would be Congressman Patterson one day. In fact, I knew I wanted to be a politician since I was a little kid.

My parents started their firm right after they graduated from Stanford Law, and one of their first cases was a case that major law firms stayed clear of; it was defending a community living near power lines, and many of the kids had terminal illnesses. After they won, they went on to earn millions trying more cases of injustice, malpractice, and equal opportunity. While I saw the benefit in what they did, I always felt my purpose was to make a difference before the injustice was done, and politics was the one way I felt I could do that. And how ironic that my opportunity had been served to me on a silver platter. This was my chance to be heard and I owed this to myself. The bitter cold wasn't even a factor as I stood and visualized myself running up those stairs as a Maryland congressman.

Finally, I snapped out of my trance and headed to my condo

for some heat. When I swung the door open and stepped in, the loud echo of my shoes clacking on the hardwood floors made me feel that a herd of people had entered with me. I'd moved most of the living room furniture out and into the basement of my house. I stood in the middle of the floor, in my four-thousand-dollar-a-month headache. The real estate market had practically crashed, and I couldn't sell this place even if I accepted a hundred-thousand-dollar loss. So it sits here pretty much empty, and I use it as a place to escape.

The dent in the wall remained from when Jason zapped out at the bachelor party. No matter how many times I've stepped in this place since that night, I question everything. I think about calling him and often I dial the number, but as always, I get the answering machine. Each time, I say, "Yeah, dawg. It's D. Hit me back. We need to talk."

Then I headed into my office, sat in my leather executive chair, and contemplated the pros and cons of this election. I'd worked my way deeply into the political scene in a Democratic state where Democratic congressional seats don't become available frequently. It was now or never.

By the time I rolled up to Sonoma for lunch, I had made up my mind. When I got there, Curtis was the only one there. If he didn't have a mild speech impediment, he would have been the prime candidate. He was a young, bright political consultant like myself, but he spoke extremely fast, almost incoherently. Ironically though, if you could catch on to what he was saying you could gain a wealth of knowledge.

He stood up as I approached the table half-smiling. He looked like a little lemon in a snug pinstriped suit. I shook his hand and patted his shoulder, which was about a foot below mine. He was a little guy with a big personality. The moment we sat, he started.

"Yeah, D, man. You the guy for the job. You got what it takes. You got flavor. You got compassion. You dress nice. You got it. It's up to you. So, what's it gonna be? Can I start getting the campaign in order or what?"

"Man, I just got settled. Just got married. You know?" I said, just to see if he could rationalize my earlier apprehension.

"Don't get used to normalcy, dawg. If you gonna do it, now is the time. You gotta do it now. They are loving strong black men with a message right now."

I laughed. "Yeah, that's true."

"You know your stuff. You're about the people. You're handsome, you're charming. Get in the game or quit."

I nodded.

"So, what's it gonna be?"

I laughed. My spirit was feeling good. I reached out and shook his hand. "Man, I've wanted to take this step my entire life. Just needed a slick talker like you to push me in the pool."

"It's time to swim, my brother. It's time to swim," he said, rubbing his hands together like he was prepared to start a fire.

Taylor and Courtney met at least two days a week for happy hour, and I felt that would be perfect timing to make my announcement. Considering she discussed everything with Courtney, I figured I'd save her the trouble of repeating the story. The good thing about it, Courtney didn't always agree with Taylor because they were friends. She stood for what was right, so it could possibly work in my favor with her around.

Around six, I sent Taylor a text asking where they planned

to meet. She responded quickly and said they were headed to the M Street Bar & Grill. I considered taking a quick drink to loosen up before I got there, but I went sober. It made better sense to tell her with a sound mind.

When I entered the lounge, Courtney noticed me first and waved. Taylor's back was to me, but I could see they were laughing at something. Courtney's nearly pale skin was flushed, and Taylor was shaking her head. My palms felt like I was carrying two handfuls of water. I rested my hands on Taylor's shoulders, hoping that her heather gray sweater would soak up the sweat. I leaned over her shoulder and kissed her cheek. "Hey, baby."

"Hey, honey," she said, kissing me on the mouth.

I stepped around the circular bar table and hugged Courtney. She was a five-footer, so her crinkly, dark brown hair rubbed against my chin. "What's up, Court?"

"Nothing, DP. What's up with you?"

I grabbed a stool from a nearby table and sat down close to Taylor. "Just the regular. Nothing new going on."

I rested my hand on Taylor's knee and she reached over to touch my face. "What made you decide to come out tonight, honey?" Taylor asked.

"I don't know. Maybe I missed you."

She laughed and curled her lips at Courtney. "He's lying."

I looked across at Courtney and she shrugged her shoulders. I glanced down at Courtney's ring finger and noticed her engagement ring was off. I said, "So I guess you're Courtney without the ring tonight. You trying to pick up something?"

That was a running joke between Courtney and me. She had been engaged nearly a year before I met Taylor, and she freely took her ring off and on, depending on the occasion.

After four years of engagement, I assumed Courtney really wasn't interested in getting married, and her ring was just a statement when she needed to make one.

"No, Devin. Why would I want to deal with another man's issues? Mark is enough by himself," Courtney said, laughing.

Taylor pushed me. "Baby, why you all up in Courtney's business?"

"You know we play like that."

I reached over and gave Courtney a high five. She smiled. "I'm not thinking about Devin."

We all laughed, and they went back to chatting about their weight. I never understood their preoccupation with their size. They both went to the gym at least three times a week. They both were technically slim with weight in the right places, but I learned long ago to just mind my business during these conversations.

I called the waiter over to the table and ordered a drink. We ordered a few appetizers and decided we'd figure out what we wanted for dinner a little later. The Let It Flow band began to play, and I was enjoying the music. Taylor and Courtney usually followed the band around to various happy-hour spots, but I'd probably heard them play once or twice. The band had a "neosoul mixed with R & B mixed with go-go" style.

We were all nodding our heads and feeling the music. As we discussed our days and work, I kept trying to find the right segue into my announcement. It just never seemed right. Finally, Taylor asked me to dance and we stepped onto the floor. Once she started doing that little DC go-go swish thing with her hips, I put my hands on her waist and we rocked to the beat. She looked into my eyes, and her white porcelain teeth beamed at me as she danced harder. Her movement let me know how happy she was and how much she trusted me, and I just wasn't prepared to let her down— not yet, anyway. I decided I would hold off another day or two. Maybe it would be best to tell her alone.

6

♦

CLARK

Boom! Boom! Boom! The sound of a gun unloading blasted in my ear and my head sprang from the pillow. I gasped. Then I began to take deep breaths to calm my racing heart. One hand covered my chest while the other reached out for balance. I was hot and cold and frightened as I searched for the remote. The television was the only thing to distract me from the effects of this reoccurring dream. There were never any visuals involved, just two or three shrill gunshots. But I'd awake to a silent house. The dream started happening nearly four years after Tanisha died. Clearly, it was some weird connection to her death, considering she was shot three times while in bed. Whenever I'd ask if anyone else heard them, no one ever did. I'd long since concluded this dream's purpose. It always happened when something demanded my attention. It was an internal alarm clock that went off when I was being oblivious to something, the way I was the entire time Tanisha was with Fred.

I wiped my forehead and looked over at Kenneth sleeping peacefully beside me. A Jay Leno rerun played on the television. Just as I began to feel better, laughing at the show, a sharp pain rippled through my pelvis. I could barely lay back down. It felt as if the bullet had struck me in the midsection. I winced and tried to stretch out, but settled for a fetal position. The pain forced tears to well in my eyes. Suddenly, I felt like I had to go to the bathroom, but I didn't want to get up. I wished I could summon the toilet to my bedside. Nearly rolling onto the floor, I stepped out of bed and staggered into the bathroom. When I pulled down my panties, I nearly fainted and my chest tightened. I panted as I stared at the clumps of blood pouring from me. It looked like a heavy period, and if that was the case, I was no longer pregnant. My heart shattered into tiny little pieces and the tears sat trapped in my eyes. I couldn't yell. I couldn't move. I just sat there, stunned, rocking back and forth, wondering: Why did it have to be me? Why would this be my Christmas present?

When I got myself together, I cleaned everything up and hopped in the shower. By this time it was close to five in the morning. Cramps still had me crippled over as I stumbled back into my room. I climbed in bed beside Kenneth and watched him sleep, waiting for the sunrise to tell him that we'd lost the baby at the near eight-week mark. Looking at him rest peacefully finally made me cry. He had no clue what he would awake to. The moment the sun peeked into our bedroom, I shook him.

He squirmed. "Yeah."

"We lost the baby last night."

"What do you mean?"

"I woke up with cramps and I came on my period."

"That's impossible," he said, sitting up.

"It's very possible."

"This is unreal."

"No, it's very real."

Finally, he said, "Are you okay?"

"I'm in a lot of pain."

"Should we go to the doctor's?"

"It's probably a good idea."

When we got up, we went straight to Dr. Battle's office. He confirmed what I'd already known and he performed a D & C, which felt like he was removing my insides. After the procedure, he spoke with us and told us that it would be best to try in about three months. Kenneth listened intently, while I stared out the window. *Try again* was no longer in my vocabulary.

On the ride home, I found the courage to say, "Kenneth, I'm done. I'm not going to try again."

He rested his hand on my knee. "You're just emotional right now. You don't know what you're saying."

"It has nothing to do with emotions. I don't want to put my mind or my body through this anymore."

"You'll feel different in a few months."

"I can promise you that I won't. I thought about this a million different times in a million different ways and I still feel the same. I'm done."

"Are you saying you're giving up? You don't want kids? You've always wanted kids."

"I don't have to give birth to be a mother. I've been a mother to Mia and Morgan, and I don't have to be anyone's biological mother."

He grimaced. "You saying you want to adopt?"

"Yes."

"Hell, no. I'm not having it."

"What do you mean?"

"What do I do for a living?" he shouted.

I frowned, because I didn't know where he was going. He

said, "Talk to a bunch of nutcases all day and half of them are adopted. Messed up. Confused. Lost to the point of no return."

The subject seemed to have opened up some sores that I didn't know were there. "Kenneth, get the hell out of here. All your clients weren't adopted."

"Adopted. Abandoned. Foster care. Their parents don't want them. It doesn't matter if they get substitute parents. They're still messed up. I'm not adopting. If you don't want to try again, we just won't have kids."

I was in complete shock. How could a man that is supposed to be helping people say this? He didn't know what the hell he was talking about. I always felt he cared about his clients, but I couldn't believe my ears. Maybe he was just angry and wanted to drive his point home about not adopting. If that was the case, that would make Mia a basket case. Her mother abandoned her. Could this have been buried animosity from that situation? I didn't know where it stemmed from, but I felt that he was a complete jerk.

I wondered how he could be so cold, especially hours after I lost our baby. I folded my arms and stared out the window. Why would I want to have a baby by this fool?

Ten minutes or so later, he said, "Maybe you should have had Devin's baby and we wouldn't be going through this."

I reached over and pushed the side of his head. His glasses popped off his nose and the car swerved while he adjusted them. I yelled, "I hate you! I can't believe you said that."

He shrugged as if my anger didn't faze him. He meant what he said; he blamed me for what we were going through. We rode in silence to our house.

7

DEVIN

My parents had already wired one million dollars into the campaign's account. I'd designated Curtis as my campaign manager. He'd run Congressman Grayford's campaign in 2004. He'd done a fairly good job, but Grayford was basically a household name. So Curtis would have to develop something new and fresh for me, and I trusted that he could. He was innovative and strategic and that was all I needed to make this thing happen. We were meeting nearly every day to discuss our plans. We had what it took; since we weren't tainted with the old way of doing things, we brought young blood up into the mix. We were planning self-esteem seminars for the young people, because although they couldn't vote we needed the ears of their caretakers, their teachers. We had bimonthly happy hours scheduled throughout the year at various venues. The happy hours would serve as a combination of town hall meetings, good times, and dancing, all while fund-raising for the campaign. Each one would have live entertainment targeting the twenty-five- to forty-year-old, up-and-coming African-American professional. We would call these happy hours The Vibe. There would be a light jazz set early in the evening, where people could discuss their issues, so we would be on the same wavelength. Which ultimately enhanced my campaign, *The Voice You Can Trust*. Everything was laid out; it was just a process of executing it. I rented a four-thousand-square-foot campaign office space in an office park in Greenbelt. We'd ordered the furniture and the phone lines were on. Curtis and I had pretty much settled in the place. We were ready to get this thing popping.

Despite all the plans, I had yet to mention to Taylor that I already submitted my application. She was going about her day completely unaware that shit was about to change, drastically. We rarely argued, if ever, and I just didn't want to confront the opposition until I completely had to.

When I pulled up to the house, I didn't press the garage door opener. Instead, I sat in the driveway with my car running, gathering my words, my thoughts. I needed her beside me, holding my hand, looking supportive when I made the announcement. Women handle all news better with dinner, flowers, and a gift. I bought her a new pair of diamond earrings, I had had three dozen flowers delivered to the house, and my personal chef was coming over to cook dinner. I'd gone over the speech twenty times in my head. After maybe five minutes, my cell phone rang.

"Yes, TJ," I said, assuming she was watching me from the window.

"Devin." Her voice quivered.

I frowned. "What's wrong?"

"It's my father. He's in Prince Georges Hospital."

I hung my head, not that I'm not concerned about my father-in-law. But more important, that's how life works. I get amped up to let her know that I have a press conference scheduled tomorrow and her father is in the hospital.

"What's wrong?"

"Toni said they think it's a stroke."

"Do you want me to meet you there?"

"Yes, Devin. Please hurry up," she said, and she abruptly hung up the phone.

"Damn!" I yelled, as if there were someone in my car who would hear me.

Banging my fist into my palm, I prayed that whatever was going on with Bishop Jabowski wasn't terminal, because I had less than twenty-four hours to announce to the public my intentions.

When I walked in the hospital, I frantically called Taylor on her phone and it jumped to voice mail. Finally, I went to the information desk. Wouldn't you know? He wasn't in any damn room. He was in intensive care. I rushed up to the ICU.

Mrs. Jabowski stood when she saw me step off the elevator. She looked as if she'd rushed out of the house. Her short hair was on top of her head, and she wore a sweater that appeared a size too small and her slacks looked like she was in the middle of preparing dinner. It was shocking to see her without a face full of makeup, but surprisingly her brown skin looked smooth and even. In fact, I could see how much Taylor resembled her at that moment. Even as a plus-sized woman, Mrs. Jabowski had an hourglass figure. I rushed over to them, gave Mrs. Jabowski a hug. "What are they saying?"

Tears filled her eyes. My heart dropped. It was selfish, but I was thinking: *Not now, Bishop. Not now.* She took a deep breath, and it seemed several minutes passed before she spoke. "He had a stroke and it appears that his voice is gone."

That news was like loud cymbals clapping in my ears. That was probably worse than death for him. Words evaded me as I looked for the right thing to say to console her. I hugged her again. Taylor looked at me as if she needed me to say something, to do something, but I felt weak at the moment.

I said, "Where's the doctor? Is that what the doctor's saying? Is it temporary?"

Taylor's oldest sister, Toni, looked at me and shrugged. Taylor hung her head, and Mrs. Jabowski said, "Why don't you talk to him, Devin? Please."

I looked at Toni's husband, Walter, who sat there useless and wondered why hadn't they designated *him* to do the talking. Rather than entertain that, I took on the challenge. My wife, her mother, and her sister needed me. I headed to the nurses' station to investigate. Just as I stepped up to the desk, one of the nurses looked up at me like she'd worked all day without a break and I was the last thing she needed to exert her energy on. Her face scrunched up, but I greeted her with a smile.

"I'm so sorry to bother you. I would like to know if I could speak to the doctor taking care of Jacob Jabowski."

She took a deep, irritated breath. I spoke before she could: "I know that my family has probably been worrying you, but have you ever heard of Zion Baptist Church?"

Her frown lifted slightly. "Why?"

"That's the pastor, Bishop Jacob Jabowski, in there, and we just want to know what's going on."

I smiled at her again. Somebody had to care about the man of God. She sighed and scooted back from the desk. "I'll have him come right out. You can stand here or have a seat and I'll tell him to come over."

Something told me my chances were greater if I simply

stood patiently in front of her, than if I went away. I nodded.
"I'll just wait here, sweetheart. Thank you so much."

She sucked her teeth, but said, "No problem."

After five minutes or so, a young doctor emerged and before he talked to the nurse, I reached my hand out and shook
his hand. "Good evening, Doctor . . ." I said, squinting as if
I was attempting to read his name tag.

He said, "Fisher. I'm Dr. Fisher."

"Dr. Fisher, I'm with the Jabowski family and we want to
know about Bishop Jabowski's prognosis."

He flipped through his clipboard and flicked his pen. "I've
spoken to the family several times. At this moment, everything is still the same. He suffered a chronic stroke, and right
now his speech is gone."

"I mean, do you foresee it returning anytime soon?"

"Maybe. Maybe not. You can never really tell with
strokes."

I shook my head. "Nah, this can't be."

"Sir, I wish I had better news, but right now that's the
way it is."

"Are you a specialist?"

"No, but I have in my chart for him to be seen by a specialist once he's on the floor."

"When will he get on the floor?"

"It looks like he's in stable condition right now. So they'll
be moving him shortly."

I hoped to be the hero returning with better news, but
I strolled back to the waiting area with the same prognosis. And it didn't look good. I almost wanted to lie as I approached the three helpless women. Each of them looked at
me as if I was the pillar of hope. I said, "He's pretty much

saying the same thing that he told you guys, but I believe that only a specialist can really give a clear prognosis."

"What kind of specialist?" Mrs. Jabowski asked.

"A neurologist can give a better opinion. I'm sure it's not as cut and dried as he's making it. He's just trying to move him onto the floor."

Mrs. Jabowski shook her head. "It just doesn't make any kind of sense how they treat us."

I looked at Taylor staring at the wall. It bothered me the way she was handling this challenge. I sat down on the arm of the chair beside her and stroked her back. "You okay, baby?"

She huffed. "My father almost died. What do you think?"

"Taylor, he's alive."

"But he can't talk."

I could see that making her feel better was not happening so I just stopped talking. Somehow, I needed to find a way to get her to open up to me. I continued to just rub her back. Finally, she rested her arm on my leg and began taking deep breaths. She looked up at me and said, "I'm hungry."

"Let's go to the cafeteria." She stood up, and I looked at everyone else and asked, "Does anyone else want anything?"

Mrs. Jabowski stood. "I'm going to go with you."

No, lady. I need to talk to my wife. Instead, I smiled and put my arm around her shoulder and grabbed Taylor's hand. With the ball of her thumb, she stroked our clasped hands. I felt her relaxing. Truth be told, I've never dealt with any major illness with my parents. So I really didn't know what she was going through. All I could do was be supportive, but it would be a lot easier if I didn't have something to tell her.

After going the wrong way, following bogus directions, we

arrived at the cafeteria several minutes later. Mrs. Jabowski was doing all the talking. Taylor seemed to be in a daze, and I was concocting a smooth way to transition into discussing my run for Congress. I asked them what they wanted and told them to have a seat.

While I was ordering the food, Curtis called. "You tell her yet, man?"

"Can you believe her father had a stroke today?"

"No," he said, almost as if he was humored.

"Nah, seriously. And it ain't looking good. They're saying he could possibly not speak again."

"Dawg, that's tragic."

"Exactly."

"Man, you just going to have to spring it on her. I got the press and everything lined up for tomorrow morning. She has to be there. *You* have to be there."

I sighed. "You think I don't know that?"

"Nah, I'm just making sure we're on track. We're depending on you."

"Yeah, I know."

As I walked over to the table carrying their food, I realized that it was now or never, do or die. I put the tray down and went back to get the drinks and condiments. I came back to them discussing plans to call the assistant pastors and deacons and the spokesperson at the church. I said, "Do you guys think it may be premature to put out there that his voice is gone?"

"Devin, it's Friday. What are we going to do about Sunday? Somebody else has to preach and we need to make sure they're prepared," Taylor snapped.

"I know, baby. I'm just saying that maybe we let them know he's been hospitalized and ask them to give the family space. We don't need the whole county talking about him losing his voice."

Mrs. Jabowski put her hand on top of my hand. "Devin, I think you're right. We don't want people trying to snatch Bishop's throne before he's ready."

Taylor huffed, "Ma, someone's going to have to take his throne if he can't speak."

Shaking her head and sighing as if the thought upset her, Mrs. Jabowski rested her hand on her chest and said, "Taylor, prayer changes things."

"Mrs. J, I agree."

Taylor's eyes darted in my direction, like she felt I was patronizing her mother in vain. She said, "Ma, you have to accept the fact that the church may have to make some major organizational changes."

"Not until I speak to my husband," Mrs. J said humbly, and folded her arms.

I smiled at her, because that was what made her special. She knew how to be the wife of a powerful man. In spite of her husband's condition, she still looked at him as the leader, voice or no voice. She wasn't moving until she received his nod of approval and she knew that didn't make her any less of a woman.

Taylor shook her head. "Ma, you can't wait until then to start making decisions. That could be next week."

I interjected, "I think it's best that you should announce that he's been hospitalized. Have Rev. Baker preach on Sunday and deal with this next week. Can you imagine the hysteria that would surround your father losing his voice?"

Taylor smirked and appeared more resistant. Mrs. J nodded. "You're right, Devin. You're so right." She sighed. "You know, I prayed for you."

Both Taylor and I frowned, confused by where she was going. She continued, "It's always been Bishop's hope that his son would take his place when he was no longer able to." She chuckled. "Being that we had all girls, we prayed so many nights that they would marry men with a calling."

I was silent, because I definitely had a calling, but it wasn't ministry. My calling was to help communities, all communities. My message was wider than what a church could hold.

She smiled. "Devin, you got ministry written all over you. You should stop fighting it."

"Nah, that's not me. I . . ." It felt like the opportune time to announce the election, but I changed my mind. "I have a lot of growing to do and . . ."

I looked at Taylor, thinking she'd co-sign. She shrugged. My neck snapped back, trying to interpret her response. We'd discussed this. In fact, she was the least religious person in her family. Certainly, she didn't want to be married to a preacher.

Taylor rolled her eyes. "Well, Devin. I'm not saying you've been called to preach, but I definitely think you have ministry on you."

What? I thought for sure that she knew I had no plans of preaching, but the look in her eyes said she'd been praying with her parents. Okay, I meet her dropping-it-like-it's-hot at a party, we have a hot-steamy romance, I marry her, and now she wants me to take over her father's church. I looked at her again. *Who is this girl?*

"Yeah, my ministry is to help people." I looked deep into Mrs. J's eyes and then into Taylor's eyes. "That's the ministry you guys see. In fact, I plan to announce tomorrow that I've filed to run for Congress, District Four."

Taylor snapped, "What the—" She stopped abruptly.

I shrugged, and Mrs. J looked at Taylor. "You didn't know."

Taylor's eyes burned through me like torches. "Devin, what are you talking about? I thought you said—"

I nodded. "I know what I said. Congressman Grayford decided to retire two weeks ago and he called me himself. It was perfect timing, and chances are it could be my only time." I shrugged. "What was I supposed to do?"

"Talk to me. That's what you were supposed to do." Her voice was loud, piercing, obviously shocked and hurt.

I reached across the table to touch her. She snatched her arm back and got up from the table. I stood to follow her and Mrs. J grabbed my arm. "Devin, have a seat. Let her calm down."

I took a deep breath and contemplated if I should chase her. Then I looked at Mrs. J and she appeared calm and open. She was what I needed at the moment. When I sat back down, she said, "Weren't you married before?" I nodded, baffled. She continued, "Where do you think you went wrong in that relationship?"

"Well, my ex-wife tricked me. She trapped me by getting pregnant, and when I found out—"

"You left her. Is that what you did?"

I took a deep breath. That sounded harsh, but I shrugged, because I guess technically that's what happened.

"Do you think there was any other alternative?"

"No, not really. After that, I resented her and I felt like she was a liar."

"Is there a difference between a liar and someone who just didn't tell the truth?"

I paused and reflected and wondered if, in fact, there was a difference. Instead of responding, I shrugged and nodded in her direction for her to continue.

"If you want your marriage to last, there is no difference. A lie is the same as withholding the truth, the same as not exposing your intentions, the same as blatantly not giving your business partner access to the company documents."

My head lowered. I felt embarrassed. She lifted my chin with her finger. "Don't feel bad. Feel informed. You guys rushed to the altar. Bishop didn't do your marriage counseling because you'd been married before and you know he doesn't condone second marriages. But the fact that you had been married before is all the more reason to counsel you, because you think quitting is an option. Devin, quitting, lying, withholding the truth, these are not options when you make a vow to another person." She cleared her throat and continued to strike. "Honest communication is the only way marriages last. You are not a single man anymore. You are a unit, and decisions are made as a unit—as a family. Here you are running for Congress, and Taylor is the last to know. That's not right."

"You're right, Mrs. J. I really never looked at it like that."

"Now you go out there and find your wife and let her know that this won't happen again."

I leaned over and kissed her cheek. "Thank you."

"Don't thank me. Thank God. He put all the rules in the Good Book."

I went searching for Taylor. I walked the same path we took to the cafeteria but couldn't find her anywhere. I called her cell phone and she answered. No greeting, she just started speaking. "I refuse to be a wife of a politician at this age!"

"Are you saying you want out of our marriage?"

"No, I'm saying I want you to pull out. We said three to four years from now. What is the urgency?" she shouted.

"First of all, calm down and tell me where you are so we can talk face-to-face."

"Devin, I really don't want to see you right now. I'm shocked. I'm hurt and I feel betrayed. I feel like you knew you planned to run and you cornered me into a position that I would have to agree." She sniffed. "We've been married for six months. We're still learning to cope with this marriage and you decided that now is a great time to run. Devin, you are self-absorbed."

She hung up, and I stood there shaking my head. I really had no intentions of hurting her. I was just a prepared man approached with an opportunity to follow my dream, awaiting the right opportunity to prepare my wife. And it just so happens, the perfect timing turned into the worst timing, and now I looked like an asshole. I wandered back to the ICU. Taylor sat there looking like a live volcano, as if sulfur were rising from her ears and hot lava pouring from her scalp. Clearly she was hot to the touch, so I stood steps away from her. Toni and Walter looked at me pitifully. Trying to maintain my composure, I nodded and asked, "So, what are they saying?"

Toni huffed, obviously feeding off of her sister's emotions. "They're moving him to a floor now. We're just waiting for Mom to come down. Where is she?"

I gasped. "Ah, man, she's still in the cafeteria. Let me go back up there and find her."

Taylor brushed past me. "Don't worry. I'll go."

Damn if I really wanted to deal with this in the hospital. I thought maybe I should follow her. Then opted not to. I slouched down in my chair and put my head in my hands and began to wonder if I was really cut out for all the "unit" shit that Mrs. J explained. Isn't flexibility a part of marriage, too? There should be no time constraint on wanting your partner to be all they can be.

8

CLARK

I blamed him and he blamed me and nobody was talking. Our house was so quiet, you could hear a pin drop. I was tired of living like this, because each day it felt like we'd grown more and more distant. He discovered something ugly about me and he showed me an ugly side of him, but was it worth the noncommunication? I felt lonely in my own home and I wanted to make it right.

The television in the sitting area in my bedroom woke me and I stretched out to find him missing for the twelfth straight night. I sat up and looked around the column separating the first portion of our bedroom, and Kenneth was stretched out on the couch. Our sexual encounters for so long had been orchestrated: *Have sex at 2 a.m. this night, that will make your chances better. Don't have sex while taking this medication. And,* etc., etc. I thought for sure he'd be anxious to make passionate love, with no worries of conceiving or not.

I looked down at myself in embarrassment. A black bustier, garter belt, stockings. Still, my husband preferred to look at news clips of sweaty men running up and down the court. Fighting the notion that he was no longer attracted to me, I called his name. Partially hoping this was unintentional behavior was something my insecurities were just reading more into, I prayed he didn't answer. Maybe he'd been so tired for the last couple of nights that he stumbled on the couch, planning to get in the bed after *SportsCenter* went off but falling asleep before he had the chance. My heart dropped when he said, "Yes."

He was wide awake. Had he been up all night or was he just waking, like me? Whatever the case, why was he over there and I over here, lonely? I said, "Come, get in the bed."

He drew in a long, deep breath that rattled me. What the hell was going on with this man? Finally, he answered, "You know the Mental Health Summit is today at the center. I need to get up and start getting things together."

"I know, but isn't the staff handling the setup and all? I mean—"

"Didn't they handle it the last time and there were missing mics and missing vendor tables?" he snapped.

"I mean, okay. But it's six o'clock. Are you leaving now?" He huffed, and suddenly I became irritated. "Kenneth, I'm just asking."

"Clark, you know I have a lot on my mind and I like to meditate before major events. So why are you asking a million questions?"

"Did I ask a million or did I ask two?"

"It doesn't matter. I just need you to be quiet. I mean, just be still for a moment while I rest my mind."

I bit my bottom lip, because I was seconds away from cursing him out. He had a lot on him and I knew it, so I didn't want to be so shallow to think that his lack of affection had all to do with me. Maybe it was just stress. Maybe the summit had been his primary focus.

I hopped out of bed to put on something less seductive, yet

hoping he'd make mention of my attire. When I walked past him, he didn't even look up. A piece of me wanted to throw a remote control at him. It wasn't even worth it, though. I doubt he'd feel it as he gazed into space in a comatose manner.

After slipping on some pajamas, I walked out of the bedroom en route to the kitchen. But I guess I was affection starved, because I stopped by Morgan's bedroom and climbed into her queen-sized bed. Her room was always a peaceful retreat, because it reminded me of Tanisha. Pictures of her were everywhere, and her angelic spirit lurked there. Whenever I needed a hug, I went there.

I lay there, trying to close my eyes, tracing every second since the ugly argument in the car. It just wasn't clear. I wanted to talk to Kenneth, but I wanted to make sure I wasn't being a burden for no reason. So I figured it was best if I hid out in Morgan's room until he left. He used to ask for my assistance during events, but I had become more and more private when people began to ask about our pregnancy progress. At one point, I was so involved in his business that I knew all the interworking, event plans, workshops, and summits. Now, I'm lucky if I know anything.

I drifted off to sleep and popped up around eight-thirty. Now in a mad rush to make it to my nine o'clock weekly staff meeting, I stormed out of Morgan's room and into mine. The bed was made and the television was off. The house was completely quiet. After turning on the shower, I couldn't resist the urge to call Kenneth.

"Why didn't you wake me up before you left?"

"I left at seven-thirty. I didn't expect you to oversleep."

"Okay, whatever. I'll call you later."

I thought my snapping would cause him to soften up,

to want to make me happy. He said, "Alright." Then he hung up.

The water tapping rapidly on the porcelain shower floor reflected my tingling nerves. When I stepped out of the steamy shower, I was determined to take back the power. Whatever was on Kenneth's mind, whatever was bothering him was not and could not be related to me. At least, I didn't plan to carry the burden for the rest of the day.

9

♦

DEVIN

The press conference was at twelve. It was now ten and Taylor had yet to understand my position. She was literally pouting like a damn baby. Our five-thousand-square-foot house made it easy for her to avoid me. I hoped when I walked downstairs I'd find her doing our regular Saturday ritual. Unfortunately, I didn't smell her burning turkey bacon. Something told me I'd be eating a bowl of GOLEAN cereal before the meeting.

After we came in from the hospital the previous night, she cried and repeatedly told me how selfish I was. I argued my point, but she was determined that I pull out. Needless to say, we were going to have to agree to disagree. Wasn't totally sure what the ramifications of her not being there this morning would be, but I was definitely convinced it was my time.

As I entered the kitchen, I heard the garage door and I looked out of the sunroom to see Taylor's white Mercedes CLS backing out of the garage. She had her cell phone up to her ear and I ran my hand down my face. She was bundled in her black bomber jacket with a yellow scarf and hat. I picked up the cordless phone in the kitchen and dialed her number.

She didn't pick up and that made me angry. It seemed like she wanted to make me sweat. I pulled out the champagne that I bought for us to share the night before and made a mimosa. As I sipped, I dialed my daughter. The phone half-rang before she picked up.

"Hey, Daddy."

Her voice alleviated all my stress. "Hey, sweetie."

"Daddy, guess what? I already wrote my Christmas list and all I want is a new laptop. I want a white one."

I chuckled. "Nicole, do you know you have a MacBook Pro? It's silver because it's more powerful than the white one."

"Well, I don't want it to be powerful, Daddy. I want it to be pretty."

"Nicole, you are a trip."

"Why didn't you call me last night? You said that you might come to see me last night."

I sighed. I'd completely forgot that it was my weekend to go to New York. "Baby, I had some things to take care of. I may come up for a couple of days next week."

"Well, I have a sleepover next week. So don't come then."

"Okay, I'll check your schedule before I come."

She giggled. It felt good that I could do no wrong in her eyes. Why can't grown women be the same? The line clicked as Nicole talked about her Friday in school. It was Taylor. I was on a much more important call, so she had to wait now.

After I chatted with Nicole my ex-wife, Jennifer, got on the phone. I said, "Guess what?" I waited for her response, but she waited for my story. I continued, "I'm running for Congress."

She screamed. "Really, Devin. Oh my God, that's so wonderful. I mean, when, how? I want all the details."

"Actually, in the upcoming election. It was really fate. A really good congressman has taken the seat for years and he decided to retire at the last minute. He actually handpicked me. I'd worked on some committees with him in the last couple of years. The Young Democrats are behind me. Money is pouring in. My parents put up the base capital. So it's on. I'll be announcing it today."

"Oh my goodness. Devin, I wish I could be there."

"Thanks, Jennifer."

"So, what do you think your chances are?"

"We think they're pretty good."

"Devin, you really deserve this. I know you'll be great."

I leaned on the granite countertop and appreciated her support. Jennifer and I hadn't always been so close. In fact, there were years when I hated her, but all in all, she'd always understood my professional aspirations. Jennifer is a New York state's attorney, and she ultimately plans to run for district judge. So she knew how important public office was for me. I reflected on my conversation with Mrs. Jabowski. What if I had stuck in there with Jennifer—how would my life be different? Just as the thought popped in, reality set in. Jennifer and I started out with a lie. She went as far as taking safety pins and poking holes in my condom packets, hoping to get pregnant when we'd been dating for only a month. I love my little Nicole, but I could never be with Jennifer like that. I guess everybody has a different issue. It's all about what you can live with. We chatted for a while longer, and she pledged to support my campaign in any way possible.

Finally, I dialed Taylor back. She picked up right away,

but her tone was cold. She said, "Yeah, I was just calling to give you a status on my father. That's if you care."

I took a deep breath. "How's he doing?"

"His speech will be fine. They want him to stay out of the pulpit for a few months, which will probably give him a heart attack. But aside from that, it looks like he'll have a complete recovery. So that's a blessing. And his spirits are good."

"Well, I'll come to the hospital after the press conference."

Seconds passed before she spoke. "Well, have a good day."

It was good that at least she didn't sound completely angry, but I couldn't understand why she refused to be beside her man. I looked up at the clock and contemplated if I should ask. Even if she rushed home and changed her clothes, she wouldn't make it.

We decided to break in the conference room at the campaign office. Several volunteers were there to set up the office with snacks and drinks for our open house and candidacy announcement. When I pulled up, Curtis sat in his car talking on the phone. I hopped out of my car and Curtis followed suit. He nodded.

"Man, you clean! See, you look like you belong on the Hill. That's a nice cashmere coat you wearing."

"Get out of here."

We headed into the office and I put my coat on the rack. Curtis continued, "You got the Italian suit. A nice ten-thousand-dollar watch. Cuff links. Monogrammed shirt."

I laughed. "Man, get out of here."

Then he frowned. "Where's your wife?"

"Look, man. She's not here."

"Wait. She knows you filed, doesn't she?"

"Yeah."

"Man, she let you come out of the house looking and smelling like money, to announce to all of Prince George's County that you running for a major election, and she's not here? Either she don't love you or you pissed her off." He laughed.

"Nah, man. You know her father is in the hospital."

"Is he okay?"

"Yeah, he'll be okay."

"Yeah, 'cause we're betting on his congregation for support." He continued, "The other members of the Young Democrats should be here soon. That is if some of them aren't already here."

We walked into the conference room. People began to pour in as my conscience began to mess with me. It didn't feel right not to have her approval. Before the media arrived, I stepped out to call Taylor. When she picked up, I said, "I searched a long time for you and I don't want to lose you because of this. So I'm begging for your support and I'm asking you to forgive me. And if you can't do it, I will pull out of the race. We have until Monday morning to find another candidate."

I crossed my fingers, because I really didn't mean it. She sighed, "Devin, I'm very mad at you because we talked about this, but I know this is something you really want and I don't want to hold you back, because I don't want you to resent me. I'll try to support you."

I wiped the sweat from my forehead and headed back into the room. Seconds later, I looked up to find Taylor walking into the conference room. She wore a black Gucci pant-suit I had bought her with a zebra print collar shirt. I stood in shock as she removed her sunglasses from the top of her head and ran a finger over the longer side of her hair. Curtis yanked me in the opposite direction. I told him to hold up and walked over to Taylor. She smiled tightly.

"Thank you, baby. Thank you."

"Yeah, yeah, yeah. I think they want you over there."

I grabbed her hand and pulled her over to the podium with me. It meant everything to me to have her there. I wanted to be the politician with the humble but powerful wife by his side. The lights came on, and I held Taylor's hand and took questions. It now felt right. When the press conference was over, I hugged her. When she showed up, it made me feel better about marrying her. I'd begun to wonder if I got it wrong again, and I hadn't been prepared to deal with the ramifications of another bad marriage.

10

CLARK

When the girls came home for Christmas, they breathed life into the house for those four short weeks. I literally wished I could interrupt their education and force both of them to come home. Kenneth even seemed relaxed when they were here. But when they left in the middle of January, things returned to normal. As of late, normal for us was each calling to see when the other would be home, finding out what we were eating, and sleeping with our backs to each other. We had problems, but neither of us wanted to confront them. As long as he wanted to be stubborn, I was committed to being more stubborn. He was there physically, but his mind and heart were somewhere else. Consequently, the hostility grew like weeds between us. We were tangled up and couldn't find our way out. So he worked late and I worked as much as possible. Otherwise, I would have lost my mind.

My girls at the group home had done more activities than our budget provided for. So I sat at my desk going over grant proposals and planning fund-raising activities. I heard Ms. Teeny outside my office talking to one of the girls. I was certain she was on her way to my office to get me offtrack. I loved having Ms. Teeny working with me. She was the comic relief that I needed. She was all of four foot eleven, 110 pounds, and brown skin with small Asian eyes, and she was so animated that everything she said made me crack up laughing. When I complained about Kenneth, she'd say cheat on him and that would make things better in time. I wasn't sure how much time I had. I'd rather be alone than in a home with someone who won't talk. That life is for the birds. She walked into my office, carrying a stack of mail. So I'm not totally sure how many times she called my name, but when I looked up, she had a confused expression. I smiled. "What's up?"

Ms. Teeny said, "You know after the beginning of the year they start posting a lot of free teen seminars, and we have to register for them now."

"Yeah, I know."

"So if you have time, look through some of these pamphlets we just got today. Or if you need me to, I'll look through them."

I blushed. "Thanks, I think I got it. It's so good to have great employees."

"Oh, whatever, Clark. Don't try to get me all hyped. You wouldn't have it any other way."

She was right, because I'd had my share of losers, people who could care less about the girls. These girls were definitely my calling. After Tanisha was killed, it was revealed to me what my life was really about. It means nothing if you aren't helping anyone. So I'll be damned if I'll have people in my own camp speaking to or treating these girls like they're nothing. I try to hire mainly young people straight from college so that they care, and I can pay them a much higher rate than most sociology, psychology, and social work majors earn straight out of college. While we were doing the ground research, it appeared that pay correlates to the way the children are treated. I take cuts on what I earn to ensure I pay my employees at a competitive rate. That's why it hurt me so bad when Kenneth showed his true colors. It partially dehumanized him. Why do I even want to make it right with him? Each time I got amped up and angry, I would remember that he'd been doing this a lot longer than me. Maybe he should have the privilege of being fed up, too.

"Ms. Teeny, what's up for the day?"

"Your husband still ain't giving you any."

"Nope," I said, laughing.

"That fool is crazy. He just as mean as he wants to be. Why he so mad?"

"You tell me."

"If I was you I would just walk around the house naked."

I laughed. "Tried that."

"Well, hell. Maybe his ass is gay or he's sleeping with somebody else."

"Who knows?"

"Just plain ol' crazy," she said, standing up. "I'm going to lunch. You going to stay here working or you going to lunch?"

"I'ma stay here."

After she walked out, I began flipping through some of the pamphlets. There were several nature retreats that I thought were good, but I would have to check the budget. I entered the registration deadline into my calendar, so I wouldn't forget. My intent is always to get donations to take the girls on trips, but if I don't get what I expect, I usually just go into my own purse. It's worth it to me, though, when I see the looks on their faces when they are out of Baltimore, getting new experiences and meeting new people.

Just as I reflected on why I do what I do, my eyes bulged out of my head. I flipped an envelope over: *Girl Power, a girls' empowerment conference, brought to you by Love My People.* I slowly slid the envelope back over. *Devin Patterson, Democratic Candidate, U.S. Congress, Maryland, District 4—2008.* I swallowed, but a lump got stuck in my throat. Ripping the envelope apart, I tried to calm my excitement. When the pamphlet fell out, it confirmed the pounding in my chest. The head shot of my first love stared at me. I folded my lips in to constrain the emotions. My eyes watered, but not from sadness. I was overjoyed. Devin was everything he said he would be. We used to talk about life and our expectations out of life for hours at a time. It felt like he was smiling at me. I had sudden amnesia about all he'd done to hurt me—or maybe after so many years, after getting married, after suppressing all memory of him, I was finally at peace with our past. Even well into my marriage, the thought of Devin Patterson invoked so much anger in me that I had to pray every night to erase that part of my life from my mind.

I flipped through the pamphlet. Love My People, a nonprofit organization run by Devin Patterson, was funding a free one-day girls' empowerment seminar. There was no way that my girls could miss this. More important, there was no way I could miss the opportunity to see Devin. Everything else was on hold while I reminisced. While I daydreamed about the what-ifs, the office door opened and I nearly leaped from my chair. I giggled slightly when I looked up to see one of my workers. "Girl, you scared me."

She squinted and pulled her neck back, questioning my peculiar behavior. I laughed a little harder, because I felt suspicious, but I didn't know why.

"Oh, Dr. Winston is on the phone."

"Why didn't he call my cell phone?"

She shrugged and handed the phone to me. I answered, "Hey, babe."

"Hey. Why didn't you answer your cell phone?"

My eyes shifted to my cell phone and I noticed two missed calls. I shrugged as I looked at the log. "I don't know. I didn't hear it ring."

"Well, I was calling to see what we're eating this evening."

"I'm thinking leftovers."

"Leftovers?"

"Yeah, I have a lot of work to do."

"Okay, well, I'll see you when you get home."

Hanging up from the obligated but empty phone call made me pick up the pamphlet again. Before I slipped too deep into the fantasy, I pulled up Google and plugged in *Devin Patterson*. He was newly remarried to a chick named Taylor, daughter of Bishop Jacob Jabowski. She was also an attorney. *Just like Devin*. He married image again. My pressure rose as I tried to convince myself that I was happy for him and was hoping she was really the one.

His skin was so smooth, caramel and yummy. My mouth watered as I gazed at him on the screen. He still had a nice, even haircut with a meticulous shapeup, and his face was clean-shaven. It was like he had matured without aging. I stared into his chestnut eyes and it felt so familiar, so recent. Momentarily, I wished I'd found him eight months ago, when he was still single.

I snickered to myself. Like what would I have done with him? Eight months ago, I was adamant about starting a family with my husband and in what I thought was marital bliss. Since Kenneth and I hadn't really communicated over the past couple of months, I began to wonder what we ever had in common.

The number to Devin's campaign office beamed from the screen. I minimized the window and thought about the consequences. Then I opened it again. I looked at the cordless phone and dialed the number. It was nothing more than getting in touch with an old friend. I took a few quick, deep breaths, not sure where all the emotion was stemming from. Finally, a young lady answered, "Devin Patterson 2008. May I help you?"

My mouth stretched wide, but nothing came out. *What if this is his wife?* I cleared my throat. "Good afternoon. My name is Clark Winston. I am the owner of an all-girl group home in Baltimore, and I just registered eight girls online for the Girl Power conference."

"Yes," she said slowly, as if she was trying to understand why the hell I was calling.

I hesitated. "Well, I'm really impressed how the organization was able to pull this off for no fee and that's something that I've considered doing in Baltimore, but . . ."

I took a deep breath, because I didn't know what the hell to say next. She said, "Well, I don't know who's here that can help you, but I can have the event coordinator give you a call back."

I hesitated because I wanted to speak to Devin, not some event planner. "Uh, is it possible for me to speak with Mr. Patterson?"

"Well, he's really busy, and you may make out better speaking with his campaign manager or the event coordinator to get your questions answered."

"Is it possible that you can just give Mr. Patterson my

message and if I don't hear from him, I'll call back and speak with the event coordinator?"

She huffed like my request was senseless and didn't make sense to her, but I didn't care. I left my name and number despite her irritation and hoped she really gave it to him. I wanted my number in Devin's hands and I prayed that he would use it. If not, maybe that was good, too. Maybe that meant that I didn't need to talk to him. My hands covered my face. I couldn't believe what I'd just done. Did I open up a great big can of worms? My heart raced and I couldn't think of anything but how happy I used to be when I was young, problem free, financially free, and in love with Devin Patterson.

11

DEVIN

There was just me and a no-name on the Democratic ballot for the primary election. So I clinched the nomination hands down. As of February 6, 2008, I was the nominee and the campaign was on. Most experts suggest closer to Labor Day is the time to heavily campaign for a congressional run, but Curtis and I had new ideas, and we wanted to put them in motion ASAP. We held our first The Vibe Happy Hour last night, two weeks after the primary, and it was a major success. Raheem DeVaughn performed, and he donated his fee to the campaign. We promoted through the typical party promoter channels and mass mailings, and tickets sold like hotcakes. Since many of the targeted voters living in the Maryland district worked in DC, we held the event at the Posh Supper Club. People came mainly to party and unwind after a rough day's work, but I made sure they knew the purpose of the night. We worked with the restaurant to have a signature drink of the evening, the DP Congressional Cosmo, and it seemed to be a big hit, especially for the ladies. We had a voter's registration station at the front door and pamphlets for each person who entered.

But instead of celebrating the success of the Vibe event, I

was sending Taylor text messages, wondering what was tak-ing her so long. When she and Courtney finally arrived, they were dolled up in cocktail dresses as if they were coming to cop men. I was pissed when she finally walked through the door. Meanwhile, Curtis's wife and other female supporters were there from the time we opened the door, handing out pamphlets and pens and soliciting e-mail addresses for our database.

Taylor tried to offer help, but I was irritated and basically didn't acknowledge her existence. If she really wanted to be there, she would have come at an appropriate time. After I practically ignored her, she and Courtney rolled out close to the end of the event. When I got home, I decided to rest in the family room on the couch. I wasn't in the mood to deal with her.

I woke up the next morning and went into the bedroom and said, "Taylor, things have to change."

She pulled the covers over her head. "Tell me about it, Devin."

I stood over her. "We need to talk."

"You want to talk to me?" She sat up. "Really, I didn't know. You make all other decisions on your own—what do you have to talk to me about?"

I went into the bathroom to take a shower and think about what I wanted to say to her. I didn't know how to approach it, but I wanted her to play more of an active role. But on the other hand, I knew she didn't ask for this. So, I decided the more considerate route would probably be more effective than the angry approach. I came out of the bathroom and asked her if I could meet her for lunch. She sucked her teeth. "Text me and tell me where."

*   *   *

I sat at BLT Steak, waiting for Taylor to arrive, going over ways to get her on my side. She walked in bundled in a green wool coat and her shades on top of her head. She removed her black leather gloves and stuck them in her purse. She offered me a half-smirk as she took off her coat. "Hey, Devin."

"Hey, you. What's up?"

She adjusted the large belt wrapped around her tight-fit-ting black sweater dress before she sat down. Just then, my BlackBerry buzzed three times in a row. She huffed and her forehead wrinkled; clearly she was annoyed. I pulled it out of my pocket and cut it off.

She turned her lips up and I kidded, "Fix your face. You have my undivided attention."

"Oh, thank you. I'm so honored," she said sarcastically.

"So how's your father's rehab coming along?"

She shifted in her seat. "Do you really care?"

"Taylor? You know I care."

"He's doing fine. You know he's a fighter. He says he's going to preach this week."

"Didn't they say three months?"

"It has been almost three months, or haven't you noticed," she said defensively.

I could tell this conversation was getting nowhere fast. I'd hoped talking about her father would be an icebreaker, but clearly I was still out in the cold.

The waiter came over and took our drink order. I asked for a bottle of Shiraz, her favorite red wine. She ordered a royal red martini. I decided not to say anything. All I wanted was to have a glass of wine, toast, discuss my marriage. If she'd rather have a different drink, what could I do?

When the waiter brought our drinks, he opened the wine

and poured some for me to taste. I nodded and he looked at Taylor and she raised her hand. "No, thanks."

I lifted my glass and assumed she'd follow. My head tilted slightly. Finally, she lifted her glass, rested her elbow on the table. "Okay, you do the toast," I said.

Her neck rolled. "Oh, you don't want me to do the toast."

"Whatchu mean by that?"

"Well, I'm wishing for things that you're not wishing for."

"What?"

She said, "Devin, I want peace. I want the phones to stop ringing. I want to go out and have a drink and not worry about how I'm sitting. I want to hang out with my friends and travel and have fun and not worry about my image or about being by my husband's side for promotional pictures, attending fund-raisers, community events, school board meetings, or"—she used her fingers as quotation marks— "the damn campaign."

I laughed. "So I have a question. Do you think you'd feel this way if I ran in four years or if I did it now?"

"I really don't know."

"Did you marry me in hopes that this day would never come?"

"I married you hoping that we'd enjoy our life together for a moment and *then* the whirlwind would come. I never thought this whirlwind would come so early."

I nodded and thought about what I should say next. I wanted to be sure I was being fair. This was a selfish quest, but I searched long and hard to find a woman I thought could handle it.

"Well, Taylor, if you don't change your attitude we're going to have a long road ahead of us."

She shifted a little in her seat. I was tired of the bratty behavior. I thought I married a soldier, but obviously I didn't. We ate in silence. I wished I could tell her about all the exciting new things and upcoming events that Curtis had planned, but all she could see was how everything was inconvenient to her. Shit, the last time I checked, *marriage* is inconvenient.

As we were wrapping up lunch, I said, "Taylor, why are you so against this? I feel like you're losing sight of why you married me."

She looked down at the napkin on the table, then back up at me. She fidgeted a little. After taking a sequence of deep breaths, she said, "My mother." She closed her eyes. Finally, she continued. "She spent her whole life being supportive. I'm sure she had things she enjoyed doing and things that mattered to her, but I never knew what they were. She had to conform to the image. She was and still is nothing more than Bishop Jabowski's wife. When we were kids, we had to worry about how we dressed, what we said, how people saw us. Sometimes I felt so trapped, so restrained, that I could scream. When I finally got out of that house, it was like releasing a wild tiger. I wanted to be everything but a good girl. And for so long, they couldn't accept me for me. Finally, now that I'm married, I am back in the family and no one judges me." She looked at me. "And the second that I can be free without judgment, you decide that you want me to go back to being judged, to worrying about my image. I just don't want to."

I didn't know what to say. I couldn't say what I knew she wanted me to say. So I looked away and shook my head. She had her reasons. I had mine, but someone had to surrender.

She shrugged. "But like I said, I'll be there to do everything you need me to do, but that doesn't mean I'm happy about it."

It wasn't her job to be ecstatic about my dream, but some understanding was better than none. I reached out to shake her hand.

"Okay, Taylor. I promise I won't stress you about being excited and I'll make sure your schedule is as light as possible. Deal?"

She smiled. "Deal."

I stood up and pulled her chair out. I wrapped my arm around her shoulders. "I love you, Taylor J."

She swung around and pecked me. "I love you, too."

I grabbed her hand and was glad that we had that heart-to-heart. But at the end of the day, we both were still selfish. We held hands as we walked to her car. I gave her a hug and kissed her forehead. "I want to make love to you tonight."

"Well, don't stay out too long," she joked, and began singing, "Tapping my shoulder, thinking you gon' get you some."

Her silliness made me smile, because I missed that. I didn't really like the serious Taylor. As I closed her car door, all I could think about was getting everything done and rushing home to hold her. I drifted to my car and cruised down the road. There was no music playing, no thoughts roaming in my mind as I took in the momentary solace. Out of nowhere, it hit me. Shit, I'd had my cell phone off. I yanked it from my coat pocket and turned it on.

New messages filled the screen and I shifted my eyes on and off the road as I weighed the importance of each. I flipped through the phone message texts from my secretary. *Clark Winston.* I read on. She was a group home director in Baltimore, interested in organizing a free girls' seminar. I'd never met another female with the name Clark. For a moment, I hoped it was *my* Clark, but I knew it wasn't. *My* Clark was an engineer and had no interest in public service, nor could I imagine my feisty little ex-girlfriend not to hyphenate her last name. Yet I was anxious to dial the number.

The moment she answered, it felt like a missing piece of me had returned. I wanted to see her. She sounded exactly the same. Her smoky, soothing voice sent a chill through me. I let it seep through my veins like a drug. My temporary intoxication made me speechless. She repeated, "Good afternoon. Clark Winston speaking."

"Is this Clark Anderson?"

12

---◆---

CLARK

The blood circulating through my body stopped in its tracks. My jaws locked with anticipation and fear. I'd awaited this call all afternoon, so why wasn't I prepared? "Yes," I said finally, contemplating if I should acknowledge that I knew who he was, too.

He sighed. "Clark. Wow. This is quite a surprise."

"Yes, it is. I received a pamphlet today and I couldn't believe it when I saw your face. How long have you been in Maryland?"

"I've been living here for nearly two years, but I've had an office in DC for almost three years now."

Nervously, I chuckled. "Right in my backyard, huh?"

"Yeah, basically. Where are you? What are you doing?"

"Uh, I'm working. I'm in Baltimore. What about you?"

"I guess you know that I'm running for Congress."

"Yes, I know. I got your brochure for the girls' conference. You know I run a girls' group home now."

"Are you serious?"

"Yes, I'm serious. I've been doing this for five years."

"Clark, that's wonderful. I'm proud of you."

"I'm proud of *you*. Do you know that you told me that you

would run for Congress in the 2012 election when we were in college?"

He laughed. "I'm sure I did. That was always my plan. It just came a little sooner than I expected."

"I'm sure you were prepared, though. I'm really happy for you."

"Are you serious? I thought you still hated me."

I laughed. "No, I don't hate you anymore, Devin. I've been married for a long time."

"Any kids?"

My heart skipped a beat. "Nah, no kids yet."

"What are you waiting for?"

That question always hurt, no matter where it came from or how many times I heard it. "Just enjoying life. You know?"

"I feel you. I just have the one daughter and she's definitely a handful."

"I can only imagine." Though, inside, I didn't want to imagine the little girl that tore us apart.

"I would love to grab lunch and catch up one day soon, if that's okay with you."

"Uh."

"If I recall correctly, your *uh* means 'maybe,' and *maybe* means 'no.'"

I laughed, because Morgan and Mia say the same thing about me. "No, it doesn't. It just means 'uh.'"

"Uh, when would you be available for lunch?"

I wasn't ready for this. Not yet, anyway. I didn't even know why I called. The long pause forced him to rethink his comment. "Clark, just as friends. It's been a long time."

"Why don't you let me know when you're available?"

"I mean, my schedule is tight, with the campaign and visiting Nicole in New York."

"Well, just let me know," I said, trying to sound nonchalant.

"I have some free time this afternoon."

My neck snapped back. "This afternoon?"

"Yes. Does that work for you?"

"Uh." I contemplated. "That's tight. I mean, it just seems too soon."

"It *is* soon. But I just looked at my calendar and it's tight and now that I've talked to you, I'm dying to just catch up. It doesn't have to be a real lunch, maybe just coffee. What do you think?"

"You know what? Why not? Where do you want to meet?" I said, snapping to my senses. I quickly opened my makeup compact to check myself. I was fine, but was I fine enough to see him? I wasn't sure if it was appropriate to go home and change. Why did I need him to still find me attractive? I was confused, wavering between excitement and fear. There was no way a phone call should have made me feel this way.

"Are you near Columbia?"

"Yeah, I'm in Ellicott City. Actually I'm too close to Columbia."

He laughed. "Well, what about Route 29 and 216? Do you feel comfortable there?"

"Devin." I sucked my teeth. "It's not that I feel uncomfortable anywhere. I'm not exactly putting this meeting on my public calendar."

"Me either. There's a coffee shop, the Daily Grind, it's partially in the cut. If you could meet me there around four, that would be ideal."

I took a deep breath and held the phone closely. "I can

do that." Suddenly all the bad memories disappeared and my mind flooded with how wonderful our love used to be. The anxiety increased with each thought, and I couldn't wait to see him. I never knew or never wanted to accept that I missed him this much.

He paused, then said, "Please do."

He was always so eloquent with words. When I hung up, my body trembled and my mind did convulsions, but my heart was still. Still, mesmerized by him. By the time I could move, I was literally running to the bathroom. My stomach was upset and my breathing was rapid. I felt I should cancel this meeting. No other man should have this type of effect on me, but I knew even if I didn't go, it didn't mean the feelings would go away. It just meant I was suppressing them again. The way I'd been doing for the past nine years. It was time to be honest with myself.

I rushed home, hoping to get there before Kenneth. I rushed into my room to change my clothes. I put on jeans and took them off. I put on slacks and took them off. I changed my clothes nearly five times before settling on a nice sweater and jeans. Then I plowed through my shoe zoo to find the perfect pair. I slipped on a pair of sexy flats. Heels just made me look like I was trying too hard. Despite the commotion occurring inside, I needed the exterior to be effortless, composed, and serene.

13

DEVIN

Curtis had set up a few appearances for the evening, but they weren't anything major, small local events that were expecting twenty to thirty people. I wanted to see Clark and I was willing to sacrifice these events. When I called to let him know that there were some personal things I needed to handle, he didn't take the news well, but in so many words I used my father-in-law as the excuse.

I pulled up in the parking lot and considered shutting off my cell phone at that moment. Then it dawned on me: This would be the only way she could get in contact with me if she needed me. I was fifteen minutes early, and every second seemed like infinity. I'd waited a long time for the chance to apologize. What if that wasn't her? My mind played tricks on me all the way until I saw her in a white Toyota Camry pulling into a parking spot a few spaces away. She adjusted her orange plaid scarf, tucking it in her black leather jacket. Her gloves and hat matched her scarf. She pulled down her rearview mirror and checked her makeup. She glided her lip-gloss wand back and forth on her lips. After flinging her long, brown hair behind her shoulders, she took another glance.

When she stepped out of her car, I was smiling so hard and getting so much out of watching her I almost forgot to get out, too. Her skinny jeans hugged her grownwoman shape perfectly. Clark had finally got some weight on her five-foot frame. She was no longer the slim, petite chick I remembered. She was thicker and finer than I ever imagined, weight in all the right places. Her face was fuller and her high cheekbones were more distinct. I carved an image of her in my mind from years ago, but the real image was more satisfying.

She looked around the parking lot, her hair sweeping back and forth, and checked her watch. The crisp air made her round nose slightly red. And I just sat there watching, tripping that we had this chance.

She entered the café and I finally opened my car door. By the time I got in, she was standing in line to order. I walked up behind her, "Clark Anderson," I said, almost as if I still didn't believe it.

She spun around in what seemed like slow motion. Her expression was welcoming. She was peaceful, pleasant. Her smile was the same, but she seemed much calmer than I recalled. Almost like she was singing, her head tilted as she said, "Hey, Devin."

Her greeting gave me the okay to wrap her in my arms. We held each other, more like we both reached out for something and I apologized for everything. She was next up in line, but the cashier didn't interrupt us. Maybe she felt the energy. Finally, we pulled apart and looked at each other. After I fell in love with Taylor, I didn't expect my reunion with Clark to be so emotional. Her eyes watered and I hoped mine didn't. I smiled at the cashier and pointed. "I think she's waiting for you."

She turned around and pulled her Chanel wallet from her purse. After she ordered her drink, she looked at me. "Do you want anything?"

"Yeah." She raised her eyebrow. I said, "I want you to put your wallet away and find a table."

"Not a problem," she said, and walked away. I ordered a small coffee just for the hell of it. I stood at the counter and waited for the drinks. I needed to gather my thoughts. What did I really want to say? It had been so long. Was there really anything appropriate to say? The last time we were eye to eye, I was moments away from making the mistake of my life: marrying Jennifer.

Just before I'd walked into the chapel, Clark had confronted me. She'd stared into my eyes and demanded that I tell her I didn't love her anymore, and like a fool, I did.

When our drinks were up, I walked over to where she sat. Her deep beige skin and golden highlights complemented the cozy chocolate leather booth. It was almost unreal, like I was looking at a picture. I set her drink on the table and pulled off my black coat, hanging it on the brass hook on the pole next to the booth. It was obvious that she didn't know why she'd come or what she expected from this or what to say. And because I was the coward nine years ago and I was the man now, it was up to me to begin this uncomfortable meeting.

"Clark." Her name rolled off my tongue like I never stopped saying it. "Over the last nine years, I have wanted to tell you how much I regretted hurting you."

"Devin, you were young. I was young. You did what you thought you had to do." She chuckled. "Don't get me wrong—it took me a long time to get over it. I cried about you. I couldn't get past it. Even when I met my husband, I spent the first several months talking about you, trying to understand where we went wrong. But he was patient, and eventually I let it go."

"Everything was so abrupt, so immature, but if it helps, it haunted me for a long time, too."

"It doesn't help." She laughed. "Maybe some years ago, it would have made me feel better, but not now. I know you didn't know what you were doing. I know there were so many other things influencing your decision. I made mistakes, too. It wasn't just you."

As much as I wanted her to share the blame, I couldn't. I nodded. "I'm sure, but I walked away without giving you closure, and I hurt myself just as much."

"Devin, it's fine. I forgive. I do."

I reached across the table and touched her hand. She didn't tense up. Instead, she looked into my eyes and I said, "I'm glad you forgive me."

She took a deep breath. "I have something to tell you."

I wasn't sure I wanted to know. My eyes widened. "You have something you want to tell me?"

She nodded and hung her head. I thought this was my meeting. I thought I was the only one that needed to say something, but the long delay before she spoke disturbed me. Her long eyelashes blinked rapidly and my chest tightened. Finally, she said, "I've held on to something, too. Something I thought was best not to tell you." She inhaled all the air between us and exhaled dramatically. "My husband and I have been trying to have a baby and it seems like God doesn't want me to."

I was confused. Did she want me to help her get pregnant? My forehead wrinkled. "I'm sorry to hear that."

"I was pregnant before and I chose not to keep the baby. I . . ."

She paused and the look in her eyes struck me. A weird discomfort shot through me. We were eye to eye and I knew what she was about to say. My fingers choked the coffee cup, because I didn't want to believe it. My breathing increased and finally I said, "Clark, was it my baby?"

Her eyelids lowered, and when she looked up her eyes were full. She nodded. "I was pregnant when you went to law school."

She had accepted my apology so easily. How could I feel so much contempt toward her at that moment? My mouth hung open. I wanted to say I understood, but I didn't.

"I just didn't want to hinder you. So, I decided not to tell you. I just got an abortion."

"You didn't think I deserved to know."

"I wanted the best for you, and I believed with all my heart it was the right decision." She sniffed. "That is until it became clear to me that I will probably never have kids. God gave me that chance and I abused it." She spoke slower and slower. Her expression became perplexed. Water flooded her intense eyes. "I abused it because I didn't want you to stop loving me and you did anyway."

She placed her hand over her face. I stood up and scooted in the booth beside her, wrapping my arms around her shoulders.

"God isn't holding that against you."

"But He has to be. My husband, he doesn't understand. He wants us to have our own kids and I can't give that to him. I feel so inadequate."

I wiped her face and kissed her cheek, then held her

head to my chest, because I wanted to take all her pain away. I wanted to rewind time back to when she made that decision. Her life, our lives could have been different if she had just told me.

14

CLARK

A piece of me was embarrassed, but Devin was the only person I could break down with. He'd always been that person. He stroked my hair. "Clark, I'm sorry you made that decision, but don't blame yourself. If I'd been a better man, you probably wouldn't have felt the need to make that decision alone."

He held me so tight it felt like he was choking me. I felt safe and forgiven. It was as if God presented me with the opportunity to get this secret off my chest. I wiped my tears and tried to gain my composure. I took a deep breath, forcing a smile.

"There, now we put it all on the table."

He offered a sympathetic look. "You feel better?"

"I feel free."

"I wish this conversation could have happened several years ago."

"I wasn't ready then, Devin. I was still in a lot of pain and I was bitter, and I hated that you hurt me."

He pulled me to him. "Everything happens when it's supposed to happen, huh?" I nodded. He paused, gazed away for a minute. "I just wish time would have been on our side." I shrugged. He continued, "Clark, I missed you so much over the years. I compared every woman I met to you."

I wanted nothing more than to run away with him and forget about all the stress I was going through at home. It didn't feel like we'd been apart for nine years; it felt more like nine days. All my buried emotions surfaced as I stared deeply in his eyes.

"Devin, why did you marry Jennifer? Why did you hurt me like that?"

"I don't know, but I never got over you. I never got over us. I grew bitter with myself for being so stupid."

"Why did you two break up?"

He shook his head and smiled uncomfortably. "You know she actually *tried* to get pregnant. She pretty much trapped me—and you couldn't have paid me to believe it, but I heard it with my own ears."

"How?"

"She called into a radio station admitting she'd poked holes in my condoms when we first met. I knew her voice. I knew it was her."

My mouth hung open, partially because I couldn't believe it, but more so, because I envied her. How could she just plan to trap someone and be successful—and here I was standing on my head, injecting fertility drugs into my system, and I *couldn't* get pregnant? I didn't even want to discuss her anymore.

"That's sad. I wish I could say I'm sorry that happened to you, but—"

"I know. You don't have to say anything. I live with the pain every day. You can't imagine how many times I wonder how different my life would be if we stayed together."

"So when did you get over it?"

"I guess I never got over it. I just coped."

"But you just got married again."

"Men never really stop loving their first choice. You know?" He hung his head. "My wife, Taylor, she is a helluva second choice, but she's not you."

I cringed when he said her name. It came out so endearingly it made me slightly sad. There was a time when I felt like I couldn't ask for a better second choice than Kenneth, but he had grown into an all-out asshole and I wasn't sure if he should even be a choice at all. I nodded. "I do understand."

Minutes passed before either of us spoke. It was too late to do anything about our revelations. All we could do was accept the notion you don't always get to spend forever with your soul mate.

Finally, Devin spoke. "Clark, what are you thinking?"

"I don't know."

"I wish I could tell you that I got what I came for. I wish I could say you'll never hear from me again, but honestly, Clark . . ." He shook his head, almost as if he was ashamed for feeling what he felt. "I just want to go somewhere with you and spend the day and talk, like we used to do."

"We both have so much to lose."

"We do. I know we do, but we both have so much that we've carried over the years that I think we need to get off of our chests."

"Devin?" I knew what he felt, but it bothered me. It was as if he still let his emotions make decisions for him. "Your spontaneity scares me, always has. I mean, people don't change, but you've hurt a lot of people just doing what you felt at the moment."

"I'm not spontaneous. I'm passionate. But that's what makes me who I am."

I knew I needed to leave. One more second there, I would have agreed to meet him again. But I wasn't young and dumb anymore. People depended on me, and I couldn't just do what felt good. I had to be rational.

I grabbed my scarf and began slowly wrapping it around my neck. He reluctantly stood. Loneliness filled his eyes. Something was absent in him and I wondered why. He leaned in to hug me and the embraced lingered, and lingered. We peeled apart. I looked in his eyes. "It's too late."

He nodded cautiously and watched me leave. Through the window, I saw him sink back into the booth. As I headed to my car, I debated the purpose of the emotionally charged meeting. I don't know what I expected to feel, but I didn't feel better. The mere fact that I wanted more from him made me feel unfaithful. I drove home and couldn't take my mind off of him, off of us.

15

♦

DEVIN

Once I got in my car, I sat there for moments before driving off the lot. I ran into traffic on the ride home, but I wasn't even bothered by it. I kept replaying our relationship in my mind. I thought about our reunion and wondered if I said everything I could have said or if she'd felt any closure, because it still felt like an open sore for me. Finally, I pulled into my garage and snapped out of the trance.

I fumbled around before getting out of my car, because I didn't want to carry my thoughts into the house with me. After five minutes or so, I decided to creep into the house. I kicked off my shoes before entering the kitchen. My socks glided on the engineered wood floors, and the smell of spaghetti surprised me. It was Taylor's one other dish, and she only cooked when it was time to celebrate. Smooth music played through the home intercom system. Damn, I almost forgot Taylor and I had come to some sort of agreement hours earlier. She waltzed down the back stairwell leading to the kitchen, wearing Victoria's Secret PINK gray sweats and a pink camisole. The longer side of her hair was swooped behind her ear and her face looked fresh and clear, like she'd just had a facial.

"Hey, Devin," she said, reaching out for a hug.

"What's going on, Bae?"

I held her extra long, allotting myself more time to get my head together. When we pulled apart, it could have been my imagination, but she pierced through me like she knew I'd done something. She frowned. "What's wrong with you?"

I laughed off the guilt and jokingly said, "Nothing. What's wrong with you?"

She looked at the watch. "Uh. Kind of surprised you're home so early. I'm happy to see you, though."

"Is that right?"

"Yes, that's right, Mr. Patterson."

I smiled at her, but my mind was on the other side of town, and I definitely couldn't explain to her that I had a meeting with my girl that got away. I headed down to the basement and Taylor called from the top of the stairs. "Devin, are you going to eat?"

"In a minute."

I stood in my home theater, gazing at all the movie posters in the light boxes hanging around the midnight walls. Every heroine in the pictures momentarily resembled Clark. I put my hands over my face and shook my head. The disappointment and hurt in her eyes just wouldn't leave my mind. I wished I could give her a baby. I wish she had mine.

"Devin!" Taylor yelled, as she entered the room. She paced slowly around me, her face balled in confusion. I jumped, hoping she couldn't telepathically hear my thoughts. She tilted her head. "Are you okay, Devin?"

I took a deep breath and slouched into the red velvet love seat in the last of the three rows of seating. Before sitting beside me, she pushed the door shut, making the room pitch-black. I could talk without her really being able to see my expressions.

"You know, I really want to win this election. And I . . ." I paused and wrapped my arm around her. "I know this is hard for you and I know you said you'll support me, but there are going to be days that I need complete solitude. Sometimes I have so much on my mind that I just want to explode, and like, today, I canceled everything and came home just to think."

"Devin, I understand. I knew it would be this way. That's why I didn't want you to do this, because I wanted to at least have you for the first year of our marriage. I just thought we'd be having fun, traveling, celebrating."

"Taylor, there's more to life."

"Really?" she responded sarcastically, and shook her head. And there was an uncomfortable silence in the room. Finally, she stood up. "Well, Devin, I'll give you solitude."

She walked out and headed upstairs. Moments later, I heard her walking overhead, on the phone with Courtney. They took cackling hens to the extreme, laughing loud, talking about nothing, but I appreciated it. Their relationship allowed me the moments I needed to steal away. I reclined in the chair and stared at the ceiling, watching the reel of my life. After nearly an hour, I walked upstairs. The house was dim, and soft R & B played through the upstairs speakers.

When I entered the bedroom, the lights were still on and Taylor was sitting with her back against the headboard, wearing a sexy pink bra-and-panty set. She flipped through the pages of one of her little relationship books, which obviously made her horny. She looked up at me and reached down to play with herself. Usually, that would get me rock hard, but I was hardly aroused. I stood on the side of the bed and watched, coaxing my dick to get with the program. It just wasn't interested. She turned her body to face me and positioned me between her legs. I wrapped my arms around her and prayed that she would kiss it. She unbuckled my pants and finally I felt the blood rushing to join the party. She yanked it out my pants and I throbbed in her hands. She wrapped her soft lips around me like she loved to taste me. Finally, I was spiritually home with my wife. Some things are better left in the past. The worry and stress in my head disappeared as she soaked up my frustration. My hands clamped on to her hair and my breathing increased. Seconds away from my damn climax, she abruptly stopped. I looked at her and frowned. She yanked on my shirt. "Devin, where the fuck have you been?"

My penis hadn't completely gone down; instead, it, too, formed a question mark. My face twisted. "What the fuck?"

"You got makeup on your damn shirt!" She pushed me and stood up. My pants dangling around my ankles forced me to stumble backward. She grabbed the right side of my electric blue shirt in her fist. Shaking it up and down with every syllable, she said, "Whose makeup is this, Devin? Why do you have smeared makeup on your shirt?" Her voice quivered and the hurt lingered long after the last word.

My mouth was open, but I was like a retard. Incoherent sounds escaped and my tongue slightly dangled. Suddenly, her hand struck me across my face and I snapped out of it. I grabbed her arm and looked sternly into her eyes. "Taylor, calm down."

She yanked away from me. "Calm down? Tell me where the hell you've been to get makeup on your shirt first."

I reached down to pull my pants up, because this wasn't going so well and I didn't need her having the advantage over me. As I buckled my pants, I tried to appear calm. "Look, I'm running for office and—"

"Devin, don't talk to me like I'm crazy." Her eyes shot at me. "I'm not crazy. Where did you go from the time I had lunch with you until you came home?"

Damn, this shit was really blowing me. Maybe this is why I was never the cheating type. This was too stressful. It was like she knew from the moment I stepped in the door. She just needed proof, and here I was with the evidence smeared all over me.

"Taylor, baby?"

Tears filled her eyes. *You gotta be fucking kidding me!* I thought. This was too much emotion for one man in one day. I smirked and looked at her. "I went to the teachers union meeting at four, and those ladies were in there talking about their salaries and how the kids are delinquents." I took a deep breath. "Things got emotional. I hugged a lot of women. Honestly, I don't know whose makeup this is."

I dropped my head and huffed like I was frustrated. When I looked up, she looked embarrassed, confused, and convinced. It was bunch of emotions, with the cloud of woman's intuition provoking her actions. She felt vulnerable, so I reached out and pulled her to me. She lay on my chest and I stroked her hair.

She asked, "Are you sure that's what happened?"

"Yes, I'm sure."

Her reluctance lingered for a several minutes longer, but finally, she said, "I'm sorry. I don't know what came over me when I looked up and saw that makeup."

"Shh. Don't worry, baby. We all make mistakes." I repeated, "We all make mistakes."

She nodded on my chest, and I hoped she couldn't feel my heart beating. I said, "Taylor J."

"What?"

"I love you. I didn't get married to cheat. I got married to have a partner through thick and thin. Right?"

"I guess." She laughed a little. "I guess, Devin."

I held her shoulders and pulled back to see her face. "You know I'm right. I'm not stupid enough to come home with makeup on my shirt. Don't compare me to losers. I'm not a loser."

She pushed me and climbed back into the bed. I sat on the side of the bed and massaged her back. For the first time, I looked down at the makeup. Clark was still a part of me.

16

CLARK

I begged my mother for years to move in with Kenneth and me in hopes that she could help me out with Morgan and Mia, especially when we initially started trying to have a baby. It seemed she gave me every excuse in the book why she couldn't do it. But when my brother, Reggie, divorced his wife and moved back to Maryland from New York, she immediately put a FOR SALE sign on her lawn with no reservations. She claimed he needed her help more than me, because it's not intuitive for men to raise kids. Little Reggie was doing fine with his father the entire time they were in New York. I concluded that mothers have a different type of connection with sons than they do with daughters.

I called Kenneth to see what time he planned to come home. Of course, he was working late. So I headed downtown to Reggie's townhome on the pier of the Baltimore Inner Harbor to see my mother.

When I pulled up, I parked on the street. For a two-million-dollar home there should be more parking. Reggie lived in New York for eleven years, and when he moved back he wanted that same metropolitan type of lifestyle. He could have had a sprawling estate for the price. Instead, he had a four-story brick townhome and a two-car garage, with minimum street parking.

I rang the doorbell and looked through the keys as if I'd be able to find the right one. Finally, my mother opened the door. I barely saw her face. The back of her flowered housecoat swished from side to side and her slippers slid on the ebony hardwood floors as she rushed back upstairs.

The charcoal leather couch and large artwork that hung behind it was the first thing I saw when I walked up the short flight of steps leading to the grand living room. Cream pillows accented the neutral decor. The wall in between the living room and the family room had various-sized cutouts with glass sculptures in each. Reggie hired an interior designer to do it all, and it was obvious. The floors glowed, the white speckled granite countertops sparkled, and the glass accent tables were dust free and squeegee-clean. Reggie believed in doing it big, and each time I came here I was reminded of how little I could do. I needed a decorator and a housekeeper, too. Instead, all my money went to something that should cost nothing.

My mother had propped herself back on the long olive couch in the family room and pulled her many remotes from her pocket. She was hypnotized by whatever was playing on the fifty-inch flat screen. I stood at the edge of the room for a moment and delighted in her lax, lush lifestyle. Reggie had come back to Baltimore and lifted every burden she had. And she loved helping him raise Little Reggie and simply enjoying her retirement. Her hairdo was even worry free since she'd recently got all of her hair cut off, exposing her natural salt-and-pepper curls. She didn't have to do anything but wet it and go. It worked well with her naturally sun-kissed bronze complexion. She giggled at the show and finally turned to acknowledge me.

I smiled. "Ma, is this all you do?"

As I leaned in to give her a hug, she replied, "No, I cook dinner."

"Wow."

"Wow, nothing."

Little Reggie walked into the room, slugging down a Monster Energy drink. I gave him a hug. "How's my superstar nephew doing?"

He was a sophomore at the Gilman School, and he excelled in everything—sports, academics, and anything else. His average height and caramel brown skin reminded me so much of Reggie when he was fifteen. Although Little Reggie was quite a bit more muscular than Reggie had ever been. In between running with women, Reggie had done an outstanding job with him. I always prayed that Little Reggie never inherits that womanizer trait. Trying to take the Monster from his hand, I said, "You know you don't need to be drinking that."

"Why, Aunt C?"

My mother frowned at me, and I explained the problem: "Because some kids are drinking these and claiming it makes them feel drunk."

"Clark, you've been so uptight lately."

Little Reggie smiled, exposing his cosmetically engineered teeth. "That's the same thing Morgan said."

I opted not to debate with them. After all I'd been going through, they're lucky that I'd only been uptight. My mother asked, "What made you come over here?"

"Just felt like I wanted to see you and Reggie. Where is he?"

"Probably out to dinner." She used her fingers as quotes. I wasn't sure if she was trying to infer that he was on a date or out drinking. Fact was, he wasn't here and I needed his energy at that moment. My brother was the life of the party, the funny man who managed a bunch of money. He was always out wining and dining rich clients. So there is no wonder he was always in a great mood.

"So, whatchu cook, Ma?"

My stomach growled, but I didn't want to swallow. I just wanted to think about Devin and imagine my life if we were together.

"We had leftover fish." I frowned and she scrunched her eyebrows. "Well, that's what we had."

"I'll pass."

"Clark, you crazy, girl. So what brought you down here?"

I asked Little Reggie to go upstairs, and he bopped away in his baggy sweats and large T-shirt. I needed to speak to my mother alone. By the time he hit the stairs, my mother sat up and lowered the volume on the television. "What's wrong? Is Kenny okay?"

I chuckled a little. "Why you ask that?"

"I mean, Morgan said that when she calls home, he's been working late and acting strange."

"I mean, yeah, he's been acting that way since I told him that I refused to keep putting my body through this. That was like two and a half months ago, and—"

"Clark, that's not a decision you can make by yourself. Did you ask him?"

I sighed, "Ma, it's my body. He doesn't understand, but honestly, that's not what I came here to talk about."

She made a face as if she couldn't imagine what could be

so serious. I smiled to lighten the mood some. "I saw Devin today."

She nearly popped up off the couch. "Devin? Your college boyfriend, Devin?"

My college boyfriend. That seemed to belittle his significance, but I nodded in agreement. She shook her head as if my seeing him was bad news.

"Ma, don't worry. It was innocent."

"Innocent. Clark, who do you think you're fooling? That boy hurt you so bad, I never thought you'd be with anyone else. So, where did you see him? What's he doing?"

"Running for Congress."

Her mouth dropped open. "United States Congress?"

I nodded.

"Clark, that's good. He's not married anymore, is he?"

"Not to the same girl, but he's remarried." I noticed disappointment in her face. "He's having an event for at-risk girls, and I'm going to take my girls and—"

"I don't think you should."

"That's what I came to ask you. I mean, the visit was innocent, but I still felt butterflies when I saw him. Is that normal? After so many years, does that ever go away?"

"Not when you really love somebody. And it's just playing with fire to hang around someone like that."

The sound of the garage door opening alarmed us. She said, "That's Reggie, and Lord knows we can't talk when he gets in here."

"Yeah, I know. So, you think I should just stay away from him?"

"Kenny is a good man who loves you and wants nothing more than to have another group of kids and a happy, long marriage with you. You'd be a fool to go out here and sneak around on him for someone who proved a long time ago that they didn't give a damn about you."

Her words hurt, and if Reggie hadn't bounced through the side door, I may have started crying.

"If I would have known you were coming downtown, I would have taken you to dinner with me," Reggie said, smiling.

"If you call me sometimes, then you can find out."

I stood to give him a hug, wrapping my arms around his expensive black suit. His clean-shaven face felt like sandpaper when I kissed his cheek. He couldn't resist the urge to mess in my hair. I returned the gesture and rubbed my hand in his black, curly, low-cut hair. He kissed my forehead and I sat back down. Then he went over to the couch and leaned down to give my mother a kiss. "Hey, baby girl."

"Hey, Reg. How was your day?"

Reggie said, "The regular. Fantastic. Where's Little Reggie?" Before we could answer, he scoped the room and squinted. "Why y'all in here looking suspect?"

My mother said, "Boy, go somewhere. I'm talking to my daughter."

He loosened his tie and headed out of the room. "As long as y'all not talking about me."

"We should be," I said jokingly.

My mother curled her lips. "Now that one right there, any woman he meets ought to strap on her running shoes." She shook her head. "I'm just glad that Little Reggie's car comes so early, 'cause God knows it's a different woman every night. I mean, he shows me enough respect to creep them out of here. But he ain't serious about nothing and nobody."

I nodded. Reggie got married to Sheena almost six months after Tanisha died, but their marriage began with drama.

They got married, primarily because they had spent nearly fifty thousand dollars by the time Sheena realized Tanisha's boyfriend killed her because she and Reggie were still sleeping together. Initially, she called the wedding off, but, just like Reggie, she's a stockbroker, too. When she started calculating the investment, she was going to get a return. God only knows why it made sense to her to just do it, but she did. It was over almost as it began. They fought it out for nearly four years, but one day they were both adult enough to walk into their million-dollar condo in New York and admit they were together for the possessions and the possibility of earning millions together, but the love was never there. They were still good friends, but unlike Tanisha, Sheena was not letting Reggie sneak into her bedroom when he felt inspired. And I wasn't even certain he was interested.

It was as if my mother was warning me of the ways of men and reminding me that of everything my husband was and wasn't, he was never a pussy hound—and that's more than I can say for most men. I debated in my mind, but neither was Devin. He was a one-woman man, a consummate monogamist, that was his biggest problem.

Reggie came back downstairs, and I stood up and walked into the kitchen. He began to brag about a deal that he just closed. "Yeah, man. I just closed with the CEO of an ad agency downtown. I mean, their profits are over five million a year. Man, Clark, your brother is the man."

"I know."

He opened his wine cooler. "C'mon, celebrate with me. Whatchu want, red . . . white?" He stopped abruptly. "I'm sorry. I forgot."

"No, it's okay. Let's have Chardonnay."

I hadn't even been able to drink in a while because we

were trying and I didn't want to make a mistake. But I was ready to live again. He tilted his head and smiled. "Word?"

"Word."

"Yo, that's what's up."

"Just pour the wine."

He put the wine under his fancy electronic bottle opener and grabbed two wineglasses from the see-through charcoal cabinets. As he spun around and placed a glass in front of me, he asked, "You sure?"

"Sure what?"

"You can drink, punk. That's what."

I laughed, because I was acting like *he* was crazy for asking, but *I'd* been the one normally acting strange, checking my calendar to see if I could or not.

"Yes, Reggie. Just pour the damn wine."

As he poured, he went on about this being a nearly one-hundred-dollar bottle of wine. I rolled my eyes. He held his glass up to mine. "You toast, 'cause I'll be talking forever."

"Exactly." I cleared my throat and thought about what I wanted to toast to. "Well, I would like to toast to . . ."

Just as I started, it seemed like my mother turned the volume on the TV up to the limit. I turned to see what the hell her problem was. Then I realized she wasn't paying us any attention. *American Idol* had just come on. So I continued. "To being true to yourself, against all odds."

"Yo, what's up with you?"

"Just drink, damn it."

He threw back a gulp and I followed suit, cracking up inside. This expensive wine tasted just as good as my cheap wine. It seemed like after two good swallows I began to feel a buzz, and suddenly I got the giggles about everything that came out of his mouth.

He joked, "Yo, Clark. I miss you, man."

"What!"

"This Clark disappeared a long-ass time ago."

It was strange that I was here covering my pain and hurt, and he thought I was happy. Finally, I said, "I saw Devin. You remember him?"

He said, "Yeah!"

From his expression, it seemed as if he was more excited to hear about him. Which was a surprise, because he hated him when we were together. He continued, "I saw him a few years back on the train when I was moving back down here."

"Why didn't you tell me?"

"I mean, I didn't think you needed to know. He's doing alright for himself. He was a cool cat."

"A *cool cat*? Reggie, you beat him up in the club."

"Yeah, man. That wasn't cool. We actually had a real good talk on the train. I never really gave him a chance."

"Why?"

"I don't know. You know, I was always the man around here, and maybe I just wasn't ready to share my shine."

I wanted to jump across the bar and knee him in his balls. For years, I questioned what he saw in Devin that I didn't see. "Reggie, are you serious?"

"Yeah, I guess. I don't even know."

How could he be so selfish? It was personal. It was never about me. I was pissed. Why was I feeling these strong emotions about a situation that could not be changed? I took a deep breath and convinced myself that the outcome would have been the same whether Reggie liked him or not.

I lifted my glass. "You're an asshole. Pour me another one."

"I used to be an asshole."

We laughed as we sipped our third glass of wine. My mother stood up and came in the kitchen with us. "I'm going to sleep. Clark, I hope you don't plan on driving home in that condition."

By the time I had my fourth glass of wine, I didn't even want to go home. Although my evening had been slightly emotional, as I drank and giggled with my brother, I felt happy. I didn't need to go home and ruin my mood. I checked my cell phone, assuming Kenneth had called several times. No missed calls. I contemplated what I wanted to say, and finally I dialed.

He picked up and I said, "Hey."

"Hey."

"I'm at Reggie's."

"I know. You sent me a text."

I'd literally been in the daze after I left Devin, I didn't remember. "Well, we had too much to drink and I think I'm going to stay here."

"Okay."

"Not unless you want to come get me."

"It seems like you should be more responsible than to drink so much that you can't drive."

"Well, I did, so—"

"I hope that's not what you're using as a coping mechanism."

I frowned at the phone and wanted to burst out laughing, but I knew that would infuriate him more. He clearly needed to find a coping mechanism, because it felt like a stranger was in my house and he was getting on my damn nerves. He needed an outlet so he could stop taking his frustration out on me. I decided to kill him with kindness. I said, "I know, baby. You're right. I love you."

"Thank you."

My eyes shifted. I stuttered momentarily. Then I recalled the advice he always shared with others. That you won't always feel love for your partner, and for the sake of not lying to them, don't say *I love you, too* if that's not what you feel at the moment. I mouthed, "Thank you."

Maybe the expensive wine I was drinking had some miracle ingredients, because it just rolled off me. Or was it the thought of Devin's strong arm around my shoulder that made his silent treatment not so effective?

"Kenneth, you're welcome. See you tomorrow."

I held my cell phone in my hand, still feeling the sting of his words or lack thereof. My recent calls lit up the screen after the call ended. DP was in the list and I wished I could call him. I checked the time and was certain that he was home relaxing with his wife. I couldn't resist the urge, so I sent him a text message: IT WAS SO GOOD TO SEE YOU TODAY.

17

DEVIN

Taylor and I rested in bed, watching *Law & Order: SVU*, when my cell phone buzzed on the nightstand. She sucked her teeth and I knew it was Curtis, reminding me of the nine o'clock meeting with the executive board for the Girl Power seminar. Finally, Taylor said, "Go ahead and get it. I know you want to."

"Nah, I'm cool."

"No, go ahead. I'm used to it. My new husband is now married to his campaign manager."

Every muscle in her body tightened as I stroked her shoulders. I knew she had an attitude and I thought we'd gotten past this, but obviously not. I huffed, "Taylor, look, I really don't need your sarcasm."

She turned her back to me. "And I really don't need your phone blowing up all evening long."

"So, why don't you get involved in the campaign? That way we'll be in this together."

She sat up. "Devin, I told you that I'll support you, but this is not my dream. It's yours. I don't feel like running around doing a bunch of damn community service and just being plain old phony."

She spoke with emphasis, like she wholeheartedly was against my mission and against me. I said, "Damn."

There was nothing left for me to say. I leaned over to grab my phone and damn near dropped it when I saw C WINSTON. I got out of bed and headed for the guest room. When I lay down on the bed, I stared at her message, trying to read between the lines. I wondered where she was and if she was somewhere in her house or her husband was somewhere around. After turning the television on, I texted her back: I WOULD LOVE TO SEE YOU AGAIN.

I sat there for nearly ten minutes, hoping for a response, and nothing. Just as I dozed off, the phone buzzed again. She responded: WHEN.

I thought before responding. Then I wrote what I felt: TOMORROW.

HIT ME TOMORROW AND LET ME KNOW.

I was glad that Taylor had left me alone, because I dozed off with a smile on my face. Although I wasn't totally sure where we were headed, all I knew was that I wanted more of whatever time she had.

The iHome speaker in my bedroom went off around seven-thirty as usual. Taylor let the music play for a while before getting out of bed. I lay still, staring out the window and planning a date with Clark in my mind, when Taylor swung the guest door open.

"Devin, I'm sorry."

With my back to her I said, "Taylor, *sorry* is an action word."

She climbed in the bed and scooted her naked body close to me. "I know."

I turned to face her and she wrapped her leg around mine.

Her soft hands stroked my face. "Baby, I know that I can be spoiled sometimes, but I don't mean to upset you."

I leaned in and stuck my tongue down her throat, cupping the back of her head and pushing my body against hers. I reached down to touch her and she drenched my fingers. My penis stiffened. It turned me on that she was always ready. I plunged my fingers in and out of her. "Get on top," I whispered in her ear.

She didn't hesitate to climb on me and lower her vagina onto my pole. Slushy sounds came from her as she bounced on me. I pulled her close to me. Her breasts rested on me as she whispered in my ear, "I love the way you fuck me, Devin."

I held her hips and thrust myself deep inside of her. She moaned louder and louder with every stroke. "You like that."

She bit on my neck. "Yeah, baby. I like that."

I flipped her over. As she lay on her back, I pushed her legs over my shoulders to get a better angle. Deep and strong, I made love to my wife and released everything inside of her. Sweat poured from me and she wiped my face gently. My muscles relaxed and I lay on her. We held each other, and she stroked my back.

"Devin, I'll try to be more understanding."

I didn't respond, because she'd tricked me with that already. She knew it sounded good, but I wasn't convinced that Taylor wanted to be understanding. So to avoid ruining the moment, I stroked her face. We lay silently for seconds before my phone buzzed. She glanced over at it, and I prayed she didn't check it. Things were good this morning. The last thing she needed to see was an inappropriate message from C Winston.

I said, "Are you going to work, baby?"

"Yes, Devin. I go to work *every* day."

I rolled off of her and prayed she'd get up before me. Instead, she folded a pillow behind her head, and looked at me. "Did you hear what I said?"

"About what."

"I'm going to try to be more understanding."

I looked at the clock and realized I needed to be out of the house in thirty minutes. I wasn't ready to get into it with her. So I sat up on the side of the bed. "Okay, baby. I appreciate that."

I grabbed my phone and walked out of the room. When I touched the screen, I was slightly disappointed to discover that the new text message was from Curtis, not Clark. After I showered, I cleared the log of previous messages and texted her: WHAT TIME ARE YOU AVAILABLE TO MEET?

When I came out of the bathroom, I put my phone on the charger, since it hadn't charged all night. Just as I walked into my closet, Taylor entered the room. She was bubbly and excited. "Guess what?"

"What?"

"I think I'm going to stay home today."

"I thought you went to work every day."

I put on a crisp white shirt and pulled a black cardigan sweater over my head. I wasn't going to come home twice with makeup on my shirt. As I stepped into my jeans, I heard my cell phone buzz. My heart dropped to my feet when I walked out of the closet and Taylor had my phone in her hand. She was still smiling, so she couldn't be mad. She said, "Here. Curtis said, 'Same time, same place.'"

There was no way Curtis could have responded like that. It was Clark, and she probably wasn't sure if C Winston was

Curtis. I almost didn't want to take the phone from her when she handed it to me. It bothered me that I was being sneaky and she didn't have a clue, but right there in front of her I responded: OK.

18

CLARK

Kenneth and I had probably spent no more than two nights apart my entire marriage, but when I woke up in the frilly teenager room decorated for Morgan, I felt young and happy. I headed into the Jack 'n' Jill bathroom that connected Morgan's room to Little Reggie's room. I grabbed a washcloth from the freshly folded towels in the linen closet. Standing in front of the mirror, I washed my face, but the smile just wouldn't go away. When I walked down the stairs, my mother, wearing a peach and black housecoat, was preparing a pot of oatmeal. She was the only person I knew that didn't put it in the microwave. I grabbed a couple of bowls from the cabinet. We chatted and ate breakfast. Then I reluctantly headed home.

I decided to stop at the group home first. I wanted to take care of business in the morning and have the entire afternoon at home to primp and get prepared to see Devin again. I hadn't had the chance to speak to Ms. Teeny since I left Devin. I knew she was dying to know. I called her on her cell phone before I just popped up, since it was relatively early for me to be coming in. When I walked into the house, some of the girls in the GED program were there, lounging on the couch.

"Hey, Ms. Clark," one of the girls said.

Tiffany, another girl, said, "Ms. Clark, why your hair all over your head? I'ain never seen you look like that."

"Mind your business, Ms. Tiffany."

Ms. Teeny walked out of her office. "Girl," she sang.

I hugged her. "Hey, Ms. Teeny."

"You look real happy this morning. Let's get some coffee."

As we walked in the kitchen, she said, "And I know you ain't go lurking after just seeing him once."

I pushed her and she laughed. "Was it good?"

"Ms. Teeny, I didn't have sex with him."

"You look real loose like you had sex. I know you didn't get none from Kenny." She rolled her little slanted eyes. "Plus, you look like you stayed out all night. What's up with that?"

"I stayed over at Reggie's house."

"Tell Reggie he and I can have a one-night stand any day."

"Ms. Teeny, you can't do anything with Reggie."

"You must not know 'bout me," she huffed. "So what about you? What happened?"

"When I saw him, it was like . . ."

She pumped her arms in the air and yanked my arm. "It was like *whoa*."

"No, Teeny. It was more like we were still connected. Real connected."

"That big-head nigga better stop acting crazy before you be hangin' out with Davon."

I smiled. "*Devin*, Ms. Teeny. His name is Devin."

"That's what I said. So what did y'all talk about?"

"We talked about where we went wrong. And I told him about the abortion. He was kind of upset. I broke down and started crying." I laughed. "I don't know what got into me."

"Girl. You so damn emotional lately."

"I know. What's up with that?"

"So are you going to see him again or what?"

"I wasn't at first, but last night I was at Reggie's and I called Kenneth to tell him that I might stay the night. He was so nonchalant. It just feels like he doesn't even like me right now for something I have no control over."

She twirled her neck and let her head dangle a little. "Girl, I keep telling you. Gon' and get your freak on. He'll come around. And see the fling came to you. You didn't even have to go looking for it."

"Ms. Teeny, you ain't right."

"Sometimes men ain't right, either. So you got to step out, and when you do, they step up. It's a proven fact. The key is not to get caught."

"I don't know, Teeny. I still have feelings for him and I'm not sure it would be as simple as stepping out."

"He's married. All y'all can do is step out and at least you don't have to get to know a stranger. Girl, you just got ding-ding served to you on a platter. You better hop on it."

I laughed. "You are so crazy."

"No, you're going to be crazy if you stay in that house with a man who won't talk. He ain't having sex. He's so positive and holier-than-thou, with his nose up in the air. You're going to be the crazy one. But if you go get your freak on, trust me, it will make your home so peaceful."

"How do you know?"

"Look, this experiment is tried and true."

We laughed like teenagers until one of the girls came into

the kitchen. She looked at us suspiciously, and we returned her look and started laughing again. Teeny grabbed my hand. "Clark, baby girl, you need this."

She couldn't possibly fully understand what I felt for Devin. There was no way she would believe that as good a man as Kenneth was, I never loved him the way I loved Devin. That was validated in the way Devin captivated me when I saw him. He was even finer and smoother and everything he told me he would be. I could imagine us together. He was never a fling to me. All I knew was that I couldn't wait to see him today, and it was the only thing on my mind. Teeny's advice was dangerous, because she was encouraging me to do something that could turn my world upside down.

19

DEVIN

I rolled up beside Curtis, as he sat in his BMW 540 in the parking lot of the high school where we were hosting the mentoring conference. He was studiously going over his notes, and I beeped the horn. He looked up and smiled, and offered me his corny salute. I shook my head.

When I opened the car door, he put his finger up. I raised my hands, telling him to take his time. I pulled my black knitted hat down on my ears and blew warm air into my fists. After a few more seconds of freezing my ass off, I walked into the supersized school. This was the newest school in the county and cost nearly five million dollars to build. I looked around in awe. It was what politics was all about for me. Change. Progression. Innovation. As I stood in the school's atrium, spinning in a slow circle, I smiled. Curtis rushed in during my daydream. And the moment he said, "Hey, man . . . ," a security guard popped up.

"Can I help you gentlemen?"

"We're here to meet Dr. Woods and Mrs. Dillon about the Girl Power conference we're having here. This is Devin Patterson. Democratic candidate. District Four. U.S. Congress," Curtis rambled.

He fumbled through his laptop bag, while I reached out to shake the young man's hand. Curtis clutched his bag and clumsily handed him a trifold brochure about me and my campaign. His neck snapped back, somewhat like he could give a damn. He nodded. "A'ight then. Let me guide you down to the office."

We'd obviously walked into the wrong side of the building, because it felt like we walked nearly a mile before we saw the large, glass-enclosed front office. A couple of committee members sat patiently in the waiting area. I entered and put my hand on my chest apologetically. "It's not my fault. I was waiting for Mr. Perfection," I said, referring to Curtis.

He snickered and reached out to shake the hand of a young lady as Mrs. Shawna Dillon introduced her. Then Mrs. Dillon reached for a hug from me. She always embraced me endearingly, like she wanted me to make a move on her. She always leaned her soft mocha cheek into mine and puckered up her thick lips to kiss the air. When I backed away from her, she gave me that same seductive wink. I smiled and reached out to shake the other young lady's hand. "I'm sorry, I didn't get your name."

"Michelle. Michelle Mason," she said stiffly, smiling tightly with her thin lips.

"Okay, M & M."

She chuckled some, and Mrs. Dillon shook her head. "Didn't I tell you? He's a trip."

Dr. Woods came out of the office with a loud, infectious laughter, "Hey, gentlemen. Ladies. Missssussss Dillon."

It was funny that he always accentuated Mrs. Dillon's marital status. Maybe she gave him that flirtatious vibe, too. It may have been his way to remind himself that she belonged to someone else. The fact that she was shaped like a damn plump pear didn't help her case. Even as grown-ass, happily married men, when Mrs. Dillon sashayed ahead of us in the direction of the conference room, all eyes shifted to her tight-fitting black skirt. But, of course, we all quickly regained our composure.

We sat around a conference table, and Mrs. Dillon handed out the meeting agendas. "I e-mailed you guys minutes from the last meeting," she said, as she rested her hand on my shoulder.

Doing business with this chick was risky business. It was clear that I needed to handle this firecracker with care. She had the potential to blow my fingers off. The fire inside her radiated from the palms of her hands. Shortly after the meeting commenced, she made a major announcement. DC's own Amerie would be the keynote speaker for the event. We needed to re-print flyers and change some of the promotional material. All the workshops were outlined and the speakers were booked. There would be a hair and fashion show. I felt like I was just the face of this mentoring extravaganza, because Mrs. Dillon had it all together.

It was more than either me or Curtis originally imagined when he came up with the idea. Dr. Woods took us on the tour of the section of the school where we'd have the conference. We had room for over a thousand girls to attend. Multiple rooms for the workshops. All Mrs. Dillon needed was the room numbers and a map of the area. She'd already come up with the workshop schedule and had partitioned the girls off by age and registration date. We were basically spectators in the whole event, because she'd tied up every loose string. Curtis and I were pretty much handling the funding. I did have one request. There was a workshop titled The Battle: Beauty vs. Brains. It was a subject I thought Taylor could help the girls with, considering she had both, and the girls could probably connect with her personality. I asked Mrs. Dillon if she could pencil my wife in as one of the panelist. She frowned unconsciously, but agreed. Her reaction didn't give me a comfortable feeling, but I shrugged it off.

Finally, when we wrapped up, Mrs. Dillon gave her affectionate embraces before putting on her long beige trench coat. She and Michelle left, leaving the men to discuss how well everything was panning out. Dr. Woods gave us a head nod. "Man, the conference is going to be big. We'll have to do this every year. Win or lose."

Curtis's swagger surfaced as he grinned. "Man, we don't even discuss defeat. Got it?"

I gave him serious dap. "Exactly."

"No, I believe in you. I'm just saying I believe in this conference, too," Dr. Woods said.

"Well, say that then, man," I said, laughing.

"Gotchu, man."

Dr. Woods walked us to the door. Curtis suggested that he and I get together a little later. He had some things he needed to take care of first. I looked at my watch and it was a little after twelve. I had a two o'clock meeting and that undisclosed four o'clock. Curtis said, "Four works."

I said, "What about seven?"

"Seven?"

"Yeah, gotta fit the wife in at some point," I said, lying. I knew Curtis would fall for that excuse, being that his wife ran their relationship.

"Yeah, I feel you, man. That will give me some time to go home, too."

We laughed and headed out of the building to tend to our personal business. Momentarily, I thought about canceling my meeting with Clark. But I quickly reverted back to my original plan of action.

20

CLARK

I was plagued with so much fear as I turned into the same parking lot I left just twenty-four hours earlier. Yet now I was anxious to just be near him. To share some time with my old boyfriend, my first real boyfriend. When I pulled into my parking space, I recognized Devin's sporty, black Benz SL500, parked two spots over. He was already in there, and I didn't hesitate jumping from my car and waltzing into the café to explore the possibilities or nonpossibilities.

When I entered, I noticed him sitting on the couch in the back with two cups of coffee on the table. I walked over to him. He stood and hugged me closely, kissing my cheek. Chills ran up my spine as I quickly sat on the couch. He sat closely beside. "I got you a café mocha. Right?"

"Yes, Devin. The same thing I drank yesterday."

He laughed. "The same thing you've been drinking for about ten years."

I blushed. It was strange that he remembered so many things about us. So many things I'd forgotten, but the butterflies in my stomach remembered it all. The feeling hadn't changed. In fact, they were heightened. Even as I sat there, nine years more mature, nine years past the situation, seven years into my marriage, still I was drawn to him like the young college senior I was when we first met.

As my mind wandered, he said, "What made you change your mind?"

"Huh?"

"Yesterday, you told me that I couldn't have what I wanted. That I couldn't see you again because somehow it was wrong and I was too spontaneous," he said, smiling.

I took a deep breath. "Devin, I don't know what to tell you. I don't know why I agreed to see you again. I love my husband."

"I love my wife."

My heart plunged. It took me seconds to recover, but I wasn't sure if I concealed the hurt. Why did it not feel so good to hear him say that, after I'd just said it? My mouth hung open midthought and he said, "Time has gone by and we've made commitments to other people and—"

"You're right. We're wasting our time."

He laughed. "That's not what I was going to say. Just because we've been forced to move on and to love new people doesn't change the way we feel about each other. I mean, I could be just speaking for myself, but it's like when I saw you yesterday, that empty feeling. It was like it disappeared. You know what I mean?"

"Yes, I know what you mean."

It seemed like we both reflected on what we felt when we first saw each other again. I sipped my coffee and he sipped his. "Are you hungry?" he asked.

"A little."

"Can you still eat a lot?"

I pushed him. "No, my metabolism isn't what it used to be."

"You still look good, though. You want to get out of here and grab a bite to eat?"

My eyes shifted. "Where?"

"I'm sure there's somewhere we can go in Silver Spring."

"It doesn't matter."

He searched for a place to eat on his cell phone, while I searched my soul to define what I was feeling. Then, we left the coffee shop and headed to Nicaro Restaurant Lounge in Silver Spring. When we got there, we discovered they didn't open until five-thirty. Devin wavered. Maybe we should wait? Wouldn't all the good restaurants be open then, too? Finally, we agreed to wait in the car.

His plush leather seats hugged my hips, and the cushion felt like it was molding to my body, as the heat warmed my bottom. It felt good to relax in luxury. I took my gloves off and unbuttoned my wool jacket. Devin looked at me and we both smiled. Then we began to walk down memory lane. We were so made for each other back then. Time was erased as we talked about everything, and before long the restaurant opened.

By the time we sat down, I was starving. Devin told me to order whatever I wanted. The waiter came over and we ordered appetizers and drinks. It felt good to go out to dinner and not be on a budget.

The dim lighting and soft music inspired a romantic mood. We stared at each other while we indulged in the half-shell oysters and grilled calamari, and sipped our two-for-one drinks. Though we weren't doing anything major, I was having the time of my life. When our dinner came, I was full, but I still took a few bites. We both talked more than we ate. My hand rested on the table and Devin reached over to touch me. I looked at him as our fingers intertwined.

My heart felt like it was sinking. Devin smiled, breaking the intensity. He said, "Clark."

"Yes."

"Nothing. I'm just trippin'. I can't believe I'm sitting here with you," he said, shaking his head.

Then he checked his watch and gasped. I wasn't sure what was going on, because he checked it again shortly after. I hoped he didn't have to leave, because I didn't want our time to end. He excused himself from the table and I saw him near the bar making a call. I wondered if it was his wife. I didn't like the way the speculation made me feel.

When he returned, he explained that he had a meeting with his campaign manager and he was trying to cancel, but the manager wasn't picking up his phone. Did that mean our date was over? Obviously my eyes asked the question, because he smiled. "I'm enjoying myself. He's going to have to wait."

Ten minutes later, he tried again. I noticed his irritation. "Devin, why don't you just go? It's okay."

He reached out for my hand. "I don't want this to end."

Neither did I, but it had to. My head hung. "What do you want, Devin?"

"I want to spend a little more time with you. I feel teased by these brief hookups. You know what I mean?"

I nodded. He huffed and shook his head. "I visit my daughter in New York at least once a week. Would you be willing to come hang out with me there?"

"I don't know. I'm not sure if I can get away."

"Can you at least try?"

"Why would we do that and risk everything we have?" I asked, looking for an explanation to why I was actually willing.

"Don't you feel like this is an unfinished story? Don't you need to know how it really ends, too?" The intensity in his voice demanded my honesty.

I nodded, but my mind flooded with emotions. I didn't know what I wanted, but we definitely needed to close this open book. It had been way too long.

21

✦

DEVIN

I beat frantically on the steering wheel, willing the traffic to move faster. I continued calling Curtis to let him know I was running late, and his voice mail kept picking up on the first ring. I figured I'd push my way through and get to him when I got there. The Beltway traffic had me trapped. My hand ran down my face impatiently.

I decided to turn my music up and stop stressing. My phone rang, and when I noticed it was Taylor, I decided not to answer. I quickly pressed IGNORE. I really didn't have any reason to be on this side of the Beltway, and I wasn't in the mood for explaining anything. I was organizing in my mind how Clark and I were going to get to know each other and stitch up this hole. The thought made me laugh. We both were crazy, but no more crazy than we'd be if we had suppressed these feelings for another ten years. Taylor called right back. That was strange, because Taylor was usually respectful of my time, and she usually knew that if I pressed IGNORE I was in a meeting. I continued to press IGNORE nearly five consecutive times before I answered. She calmly said, "Devin, are you doing something you have no business doing?"

I laughed to give myself a minute to think. "Taylor, I thought we had this conversation last night."

"We did, but I'm wondering why Curtis just called here to speak to you and you told me you'd be with him and he told me you told him you'd be with me? So, you're not with him. You damn sure aren't here with me. Where the hell are you?"

"How many times do I have to tell you my plans can change at the drop of a dime? Curtis doesn't know every move I make. I'm still a consultant. Do you know that?"

She took a deep breath. "It's almost eight o'clock. Your campaign has no record of any meetings and most of your clients meet you during working hours. Whatever you're doing, Devin, I suggest you stop, because I will not tolerate it. I will not sit around wondering where my husband is. That is an absolute no-no. I'm not having it."

"Look, I had a meeting and I've been trying to call Curtis, but his voice mail picks up on the first ring. Of course he doesn't know where I am."

She huffed. "His battery died and he only knew the house number by heart."

I wanted to choke the shit out of Curtis. He didn't know that men don't say shit like this to another man's wife. I was infuriated. This asshole's battery died, so he wants to disrupt my life. I huffed, "Did he leave a number?"

She didn't respond and I heard three consecutive beeps, signaling that she had hung up. I considered calling her back, but I didn't. It was weird how she knew something wasn't right, but it wasn't like I could tell her what I was going through. I felt bad lying. But what was I supposed to do?

A few minutes later, an unfamiliar number popped up

on my phone. I quickly answered, assuming it was Curtis. "Yeah, man."

"Devin," she said so sweetly.

"Hey, Clark. I guess you're in traffic, too. I'm sorry. We should have probably just parted after we left the Daily Grind."

"No, actually I just had to drive down Twenty-nine. There's no traffic going my way." She snickered. "I actually stopped at Columbia Mall and I'm on my way home now."

"What did you buy?"

"I splurged a little on the purse."

"Oh yeah, you still love to shop."

"Not as often as I used to, you know. We've been on a budget for so long, I'm literally in a purse depression."

"You've always been a purse fiend."

"Yeah, but I've been forced to go cold turkey. In fact, I'll probably get in trouble when I get in the house, because this thing isn't in the budget."

I felt sorry for her. "Look at it as a present from me. I'll give you the money back when I see you again."

She sighed. "Devin."

"No, don't worry about it. How much was it?"

"Don't worry about it. I'm not a charity case, Devin."

"Look, you know me. I got it."

She sucked her teeth. "Okay, Devin. Whatever you say. Anyway, I just wanted to call you and give you my new number. I bought a Go Phone so that we can communicate. My phone is on my husband's account. So if you could, replace that number with this one."

It never even crossed my mind that I should just pick up a phone specifically to communicate with Clark, but then again so many people call me during the course of a day, it would take Taylor years to track down Clark's number. "Okay, I'll be sure to do that."

"Okay," she said in a lingering tone, as if she wanted to keep talking. I wanted to keep talking, too, but I had to call Taylor back.

"A'ight, baby. I'll call you tomorrow with all the details for New York."

I didn't know what New York meant for Clark and me. It was possible we could just hang out and have a good time. I wasn't sure, but I knew for sure that I had to make Taylor secure again. I'd messed up two days in a row and I couldn't go down like that.

When I walked in the house, all the lights were off. I headed upstairs to the bedroom. I tried the door and it was locked. So, I tapped on the door.

"Yo, TJ. Open up the damn door."

"Devin, go back to wherever you been."

"Taylor, look, let's handle this like adults. Open up the door."

I heard her get out of bed and stomp to the door. It swung open and she posed with her hands on her hips. "Okay, you want me to open the door and look at you while you lie to me."

"Really, Taylor. I have nothing to lie to you about. I don't have any excuses. I was out handling business."

Still standing in the door, she huffed, "Well, why would Curtis say you were supposed to be here?"

"I was. My intention was to come home and spend time with you, but I got sidetracked. So forgive me for not being able to do what I planned to do. Something came up."

She left the door open and walked back to the bed. I followed and decided to give her a moment. I didn't want to say too much and incriminate myself. I walked into my closet and pulled my sweater off and stepped out of my pants. On my way to the bathroom, Taylor looked at me and said, "Look me in the eye and tell me you're not lying."

"Taylor, I'm not lying to you." I said, leaning in to kiss her.

She turned her head and shrugged. "Devin, I don't want to be that girl."

"What girl?"

"The one that's the last to know that her man is cheating."

I touched her face, "TJ, don't start being insecure now. That's not the person I fell in love with."

"I don't know where this is coming from."

"Me either," I said, kissing her again. But I knew why she was insecure. She wasn't doing her job, but I wasn't in the mood to drill that in. I wanted peace. There was too much on my mind, and I had to get my house in order.

I went into the bathroom and turned the shower on. She came in behind me and took her pajamas off. We stepped into the shower together and as the water poured on us, I wondered why I was struggling emotionally. I'd thought Taylor was everything I needed, but I wasn't so sure anymore. When we stepped out of the shower, I could tell that she wanted to make love, but I told her I just wanted to hold her and make sure she was secure.

22

CLARK

Almost a week later, Ms. Teeny drove me to the train station so that I could sneak off to New York with Devin. When we pulled up, she laughed. "You make sure you turn him out like I taught you, girl."

I laughed and reached over to give her a hug. "Teeny, you ain't right."

"Whatever. You need to get you your freak on with *somebody*. So call me when you get there."

"Okay." She kissed my cheek and ran her finger through my freshly roller-brushed and blow-dried hair. My stylist brightened my highlights. It felt good to do something spontaneous. Devin always had a way of bringing that out of me. After I grabbed my backpack from the trunk, I peeked back in and said, "Thanks, Teeny."

"I love you, girl." I nodded. Not sure if she could read my mind or not, but she said, "Don't feel guilty. You're only doing it to make your marriage better."

I nodded as I closed the car door. My hair bounced on my cream wool coat and I adjusted my shades. A young college boy held the door open for me. I smiled and thanked him, while adjusting my black and gold purse on my shoulder. He smiled back. "My pleasure."

I blushed a little longer than necessary as I headed over to the kiosk to get my tickets. As far as Kenneth knew, I was going up to New York to visit Reggie's ex-wife, Sheena, and my youngest niece, Sage. I explained to Kenneth that I needed a break, but I was on my way to be unfaithful and I was excited as hell. I'd locked my wedding band away in my office at the group home. Over the last few months, I wondered what it all meant. Do all marriages literally become institutions? I hated the stringency the word implied. Why can't we love and be together and enjoy those moments without rules and regulations? When the love is gone, we can just pack up and go. Love shouldn't be legally binding; it should be voluntary.

Four hours later, I sat in Nobu, pouring wine and reminiscing about old times. It was funny to see how we'd both graduated from beer to wine, from irrational kids to successful adults. Yet, we were still in touch with the purest parts of each other. The connection was still there, and I wondered if we would have been the same if we stayed together. Would we have grown together at the same pace?

Every specialty roll I inquired about, Devin ordered. When the sushi came out, our table was packed as if we were a party of ten. I sampled one or two of each roll and began to feel stuffed. Devin asked the waiter to warm up some sake. He swore it would settle my stomach. I was already feeling the buzz. I definitely didn't need anything else, but when the waiter returned with the little porcelain sake cups, we toasted and swallowed. It was warm and bitter.

Devin reached across the table and held my hand. "I never forgot about you. You know that?"

"I tried so hard to forget about you that I didn't even realize it, but I guess a part of you has always been with me, too."

"Damn, Clark. Why couldn't we have found each other a year ago?"

"Why? So this would only be hard for me? Not you?"

"I'm sorry. You're right. There I go being selfish again."

"Yes, Devin, you're a self-serving bastard, aren't you?" I said, laughing.

I expected him to laugh, too. Instead, he looked crushed and confused. His eyes looked lost as if he'd began to feel the guilt of what we were doing. I intertwined my fingers with his, "I'm sorry, Devin. I was just joking."

He nodded and said, "You know Jason and I aren't friends anymore."

"Jason. Your best friend, Jason."

He cracked a smile. "Yeah, my best friend, Jason."

I didn't really want to know what had happened. It obviously had something to do with Devin's selfishness, because his confession came from left field. I wanted to suppress the realization that Devin was self-centered, but if I was considering risking my marriage for these deep feelings for him, I thought I should know.

"What did you do to him?"

23

DEVIN

I gulped down the remainder of my sake and proceeded to tell Clark how I met and married Taylor. I wanted her to react, but she literally sat across from me, stunned. Her mouth hung open and she shook her head slowly.

"Oh my goodness, Devin. That was just mean. How could you do that? That was so inconsiderate."

"You think so."

"Hell yeah. I would be sick if one of my close friends ended up with you. Relationships aren't forever, friendships are."

"I wish I never lost your friendship. You were always the one that told me the truth, not just what I wanted to hear."

"Where is Jason?"

"I believe he's still in Connecticut."

"You should find him. You can't keep leaving loose ends all over the place."

I nodded and felt slightly bad that I'd even brought the situation up. I grabbed the wine bottle and put it up to my lips and swallowed. Clark laughed.

"Devin, you're crazy. Stop!" she said, as she reached across the table to grab the wine bottle from me. "People are looking at you."

"Man, you just made me feel worse about it. I need something to make me feel better."

She grabbed my hand again. "You are selfish and I don't know how you sleep at night. But I guess what most people are too scared to do, you're just willing to take the risk. The same thing that I hate about you is probably the same thing that still makes you so exciting."

"I thought you were going to say it's the same thing that you love about me." I reached over and held her other hand. "I never thought I was being selfish. I was just anxious to feel that feeling again that I had with you. I missed it. Didn't you?"

She sucked in her bottom lip and brushed her brown hair from her face. I didn't know much about her marriage or why she was here, but obviously she missed it, too. I wanted to lighten the mood some, so I settled the check and asked Clark if she still liked to smoke cigars.

"I haven't smoked since we were together."

"Let's make up for lost time."

We left the restaurant and headed over to my late-night cigar spot. I ordered the best cigars in the place. We sat in a cozy little corner to ourselves, drinking Crown Royal Reserve straight and puffing on our cigars. I played in her long, bronzed curls and looked into her eyes. This was supposed to resemble getting to know each other again, but this night confirmed that nothing had changed.

I leaned over and kissed her passionately. Her arms wrapped around my neck and I stroked her back. She was warm and soft just as I recalled. She even tasted the same. We couldn't keep our hands off of each other. So we split the joint and headed back to my place.

Clark pinned me to the back of the elevator when we

stepped in and pushed her hand down my pants. She moaned, "Ooh, it feels just like I remember."

When the elevator doors opened, we fell into my apartment and began ripping each other's clothes off. I picked her up and she wrapped her legs around my waist. I sat her on my pool table and kissed her breasts, while my fingers made love to her. I rushed to my bedroom to grab a condom from the nightstand, only to discover that I didn't have any. I was sure that I had some left over from my single days, because I had tons when I met Taylor. Obviously, Taylor and I had more sex than I realized. Shit. I paced back and forth. I didn't know what to do. I slouched back out of the room. She sat patiently, seductively, on my pool table prepared to get the game on.

She said, "What's up?"

"I don't have any condoms."

"I have some in my purse."

I looked at her suspiciously. She smiled. "I have a group home with fast-ass teenage girls."

I rushed over and grabbed her purse and handed it to her. While she fumbled, I proceed to taste her. My tongue traveled down and dipped in and out of her entrance. She whined for more. I pushed my thumb inside of her and cupped her crotch as I tantalized her clitoris. She clamped my shoulders. I stood up and she dangled the condom in front of me.

"Here, hurry up. I need to feel you inside of me."

Her request sounded sincere but desperate, and I was anxious to make her feel better. Once I rolled on the condom, I lifted her up on me and submerged myself in her. Her vagina opened more and more with each stroke. We kissed passionately and moved slowly. While still inside of her, we waddled over to the bar stools. I fell onto the stool, with Clark straddling me. I pulled her hair back so I could see her face. I needed to stare into her eyes. This wasn't a dream. I was with my baby again. We transitioned from the stool to the bed and I was afraid to ejaculate. I needed to be one with her for as long as possible. I didn't want anything to break us up again. As I tried to control the biologically impossible, I exploded inside of her. The side of my face touched the side of her moist face when I dropped my head on the pillow beside her. I touched her face to see if it was sweat or tears. It felt like a little bit of both. I said, "Are you okay?"

"Yes, Devin. Just a little afraid."

"Don't be scared. I promise I won't hurt you again."

"Devin, don't lie to yourself. You really can't make that promise."

I wasn't sure *I* even knew how I could uphold that promise, but I knew I wanted to. "Look, I promise that I'll do my best to never hurt you again. You like that better?"

She touched my face. "I like you, Devin."

"I like you, too."

It's funny that as strong as the love was between us, we would only allow ourselves to verbally proclaim strong *like*. *Love* was too big of a cross to bear. I rolled over on my side and propped my head up on my elbow and admired her silhouette beside me, staring at the ceiling.

24

✦

CLARK

I began to squirm around six in the morning. Guilt consumed me in the form of nausea. I was sick. I needed to speak to Kenneth. I wanted him to say something in the form of *We can get through this.* My hands stroked Devin's shoulders as I questioned the spontaneity that was supposed to make me feel better. It was supposed to make me more desirable to my husband. So why did I feel like a lost slut?

Finally, I slid from the bed and tiptoed into the living room, searching for my purse and my clothes that were scattered around the floor. I pulled my phone out and sat Indian style on Devin's soft leather sectional. I stretched Devin's T-shirt over my knees. His scent lingered on me as I touched the screen to see if my husband still cared. Ms. Teeny called three times. Kenneth called twice. Sheena called shortly after Kenneth's last call.

I dialed Sheena first, and the phone rang a few times before her voice mail picked up: "You've reached Sheena. Leave a message."

I mouthed *shit*, because I needed to speak to her first, but I wanted to talk to Kenneth. As good as I felt with Devin, I still couldn't suppress my obligation to my marriage, to the life we'd built. Though we were at a communication dead end, I wanted to say something, anything. I dialed home.

He answered on the first ring, but his voice was groggy. "Hello."

"Baby."

"Yeah, how's it going up there? Sheena told me you went to sleep early."

I looked up, thankful that He'd provided me with an alibi and that Sheena had stuck to the plan. "Yeah, I was so sleepy."

"Why?" he snapped.

My heart plunged. I wasn't sure if it was his normal arrogance or if he was insinuating something. "Mental fatigue, probably."

"Did you get an estimate for the new beds in the group home?"

"No. Why?"

"Just asking. Did Teeny meet the new girl you hired?"

My eyes filled. I found the courage to say what I'd wanted to say for weeks. "Baby, talk to me. I'm tired of you talking around me and about everything except us."

"Clark. Don't start with all the emotion. While you're there for your little mental break, there are things that need to be taken care of."

Here I was, in another man's house, emotionally pleading with him. Still, Kenneth acted as if I was irritating him. A tear rolled down my cheek. I tried to hold back the sniffing, because I didn't want him complaining about that. I wiped my face and walked into the kitchen. When I opened the refrigerator door, I was happy to find several bottles of Corona lined on the side of the door. I looked up at the clock on the stainless steel microwave. Six-twenty a.m. Somehow, all I could rationalize drinking was an ice-cold beer.

"Kenneth, I just woke up and wanted to hear your voice. I didn't call to talk about what I need to do. Teeny is taking care of it."

"I know."

Kenneth often made me feel that I could do nothing without Teeny. That was the sacrifice I made working with him. Somehow, he'd forgotten that I was a successful engineer before I followed my man. It always ate at me, but when he was emotionally available, it didn't hurt as bad. With the absence of his affection, it felt demeaning and downright disrespectful. I rummaged through Devin's utensil drawer for a bottle opener. Finally, I found it and quickly cracked the bottle open. I took a quick gulp.

"Okay, I'll call you a little later this evening."

"Aren't you coming home later?"

It was funny how this conversation could have gone in an entirely different direction. My plan was to leave, but Devin begged me to stay another day. Kenneth's attitude told me that it didn't matter if I stayed a month. As long as the business was taken care of, it made no difference in the world where I was. Why not stay with a man that wants to be in my company?

"Nah, Sheena has this event she wants me to go to this evening. So I'll be home tomorrow or Saturday."

"A'ight. I have to get ready to get to the center."

"Okay."

Neither of us said good-bye. Instead, the call ended with no hope. I walked over to the huge window with a fabulous view of Manhattan. As I stood there numb, staring at the city, I wondered when or if we'd get it together. Certainly, my being here, with nothing under my T-shirt, feeling love for Devin, couldn't be a remedy for a crumbling marriage.

I called Ms. Teeny for some encouragement. She always knew how to make sense of Kenneth's mood changes.

"Did you screw his brains out dot com?"

I laughed. "First of all, I'm mad that you said *screw*. But to answer your question, I think I did a pretty good job."

"I hope you did better than just a good job."

"Ms. Teeny, stop!"

"Girl, I hope you used those tricks I taught you."

She had me cracking up, loud with no consideration that it wasn't even seven o'clock in the morning.

"Yes, I did all of them."

"He was screaming for more. Haaaaaaaa!" she screamed. "Clark got herself another piece of ass, finally." She spoke as if being faithful to your husband was a crime.

"Ms. Teeny, you are crazy."

"No, girl, just crazy about new sex."

It was no wonder Teeny was on her third marriage, but Bernard loved her to death. So she was obviously doing something right. As I fathomed that cheating could help my bad marriage, Devin walked out of his room, wearing nothing but his boxers. My bottom lip hung, and I was mesmerized. He smiled and mouthed, "Your husband?"

I shook my head and rushed Teeny off the phone. "Alright. I'll call you later."

Devin walked over and hugged me. He greeted me graciously without mumbling a word. We stood in the window, exposed, clinging to each other, wishing we could be this free anywhere. Moments later, he kissed my forehead. "You're up early."

"Yeah, I wake up early. You know?"

"You want to order breakfast?"

"Ah, I guess."

"Remember those banana pancakes you used to love?"

"Yeah." I said, flattered that he remembered such intricate details. Then again, he always loved to make me feel good, to comfort me, to spoil me. My head tilted slowly from side to side, wondering how he could still be so sensitive and considerate.

He stroked my hair and proceeded to roll off my order. "Banana pancakes, eggs over hard with cheese, and turkey sausage."

"Exactly."

He grabbed my hand and guided me to walk with him. We walked into the kitchen, and he picked up the phone and called the restaurant. He put his arm around me. Just then, he noticed the beer in my hand. As he placed our order, he pointed and mouthed, "What's up with that?"

I pursed my lips and shrugged. He shook his head as if he wasn't judging, just curious. I rubbed his face and each moment with him made me recall why I thought he was so perfect. It seemed he was just like wine, even better than before. He made me feel like a natural woman. Yet at home I was begging for R.E.S.P.E.C.T.

When our breakfast arrived, he said, "I was going to ask if you wanted to have mimosas, but since you've started off with beer . . ."

"We can put orange juice in beer."

He laughed. "I haven't done that crazy shit since—"

"—we were together."

"Exactly."

I hadn't done so many things since I'd been with him. My life had been filled with service and structure. There was a time when that worked for me, but I was in desperate need of something more, especially since it seemed that I wouldn't be having kids. As I walked into the kitchen to make our beer-mosas, I found myself blushing. Devin directed me to the black see-through cabinets. I poured equal portions of beer and orange juice into the flutes, while Devin set the dining room table.

I returned to the table and Devin sipped his drink. "It still tastes the same."

"Really," I said, tasting mine. "It is good."

"Some things are just as good as the first time."

I sank into my seat and my heart did the same. A piece of me wanted his statement to be true, but the reality that this would be as good as before could only be trouble. He looked into my eyes and said, "Some shit never changes."

"I know, Devin. What is that?"

He shrugged. "It could be love. It could be chemistry."

My mind had escaped from my marital drama and moved on to what I wanted from Devin and how I could achieve some sort of compromise. I picked up my fork, and the pancakes melted in my mouth. Nothing like the senses to rewind you back to a place in time. I was in Devin's first apartment, eating breakfast with my man. We had no worries, no obligations, and we were each other's significant other. Why didn't we get it right the first time?

He interrupted my reminiscent mood by shaking my forearm, "So what are you going to do?"

"About what?"

"About staying an extra night. If you leave, that means this is it?"

"*It*, meaning?"

He smiled. "Meaning until you and I can get together

again. I need to spend some time with Nicole and take care of some business. When I leave, I won't be back until around nine. If you leave, I will be missing you and not enjoying time with my baby. If you stay, I'll just be anticipating coming home to be with you."

"Devin, I'm—"

He rested his hand on top of mine. "I know. It's probably selfish of me, but it seemed like you were having a good time, too, last night. I mean, you're not the same woman I met a week ago. You seemed like my Clark."

It was flattering the way he took ownership of me. He was pleading a noncase. I was convinced that I needed this for me. If you don't make yourself happy, you sure can't make anyone else happy. Maybe this affair would save my marriage.

"I'll stay."

"Good," he said, standing from the table and grabbing our plates. "Every little bit helps."

He walked in the kitchen and threw the plates in the sink. When he turned on the faucet, I said, "I'll wash them."

"When I'm here, my housekeeper comes every day."

I stopped in my tracks and did a slow U-turn. "Oh."

"All I want you to do is have a good time." He stood in front of me and brushed my hair back. My neck tilted, as I looked up at him. He planted a gentle kiss on my forehead. "A good, relaxing time."

We went to his bedroom. He proceeded to run bathwater in the tub, while I tried Sheena again.

"Clark, why in the world were you calling me at six o'clock this morning?"

"Because I knew Kenneth probably called you."

"He did and I told him you were asleep."

"I just wanted to make sure."

"Where are you, anyway?"

"I told you I got a hotel. I just needed a break."

I heard Devin talking on the phone and completely blocked out Sheena's voice. I stepped closer to the bathroom. "Taylor J," he said. "I miss you."

My heart sank. How could he be claiming to be having the time of his life with me, but missing her? I told Sheena I'd be to her house shortly and hung up. Posing in the doorway of the bathroom, I watched him quietly. When he noticed my presence, he wrapped his conversation up.

"Yeah, baby. . . . No, no. She's out of school today. . . . Yeah. . . . No. . . . A'ight. Have a good day. I'll talk to you later."

I shifted my weight onto the opposite foot, wondering if he'd have the audacity to pledge his love while I stood there. He pressed END, and it seemed like a feeling of relief came over me. I felt bad, because I didn't want him to be in marital bliss when I wasn't.

"You ready to get in the tub?" He reached out for my hand. "Take a bath with me."

I wanted to be resistant, but how could I be mad at him? We were both being unfaithful to other people. Devin lifted my T-shirt over my head and admired my body. I shifted uncomfortably and he wrapped his arms around me. He stepped from his pants and helped me into the tub first. The water was warm and inviting, and the sea salt opened up my sinuses. My pores felt free and clear, as Devin stepped in behind me. My back rested on his chest and my arms rested on his knees. We relaxed and reminisced and forgot about the other side of our lives. He reached down in front of me, rubbing me in between my legs. I turned to kiss him. It felt right. It was passionate. He dipped the sponge in the water and drained it on different parts of my body. Then on my hair, drenching my one-hundred-dollar hairdo. Yet my heart pounded with excitement, anxious to feel him in me again.

Devin sat on the side of the tub, water dripping from his sculpted body, and all my intelligence evaporated. I straddled him and sucked on his glistening neck. He took mouthfuls of my breast, as I grinded on him. We moaned and groaned. He held my legs, and my arms clamped around his neck as he stood to his feet. Nearly slipping in the tub, we staggered backward to the other side. He pushed me up to the window for the whole of Manhattan to see my ass. I gripped the windowsill as our bodies crashed repeatedly together. It was enthralling, invigorating, and everything I needed. Devin had always been a marathon lover, and nothing had changed. Finally, he released inside of me.

We moved from the tub to the shower. Inside the shower, we held each other as the water rolled down our skin. When we got out, Devin scurried around his room getting dressed and gathering his things. Before he left the apartment, he gave me four American Express gift cards, totaling two thousand dollars.

"Is this enough?" he asked.

"For what?"

"For whatever."

I handed them back. "Devin, I don't need anything."

"No, I want you to buy whatever you want. You're in New York. Buy yourself a purse or something."

He sure knew what to say to tempt a girl. After he refused to take them back, I relented. He leaned in to kiss my cheek, gave me the elevator code to get back into the building, and told me he'd see me around nine. We planned to have another night on the town. I saw him to the elevator door and we kissed. I felt high as I floated back to the kitchen to make some coffee, but I stopped short of my quest when I noticed the music speaker system on the wall. I flipped through the music selections and found Brandy. She took me back to when Devin first moved to New York, as her *Never Say Never* album blasted through all the speakers in the condo. *Never Say Never.* It was the perfect sentiment. I never thought I could ever feel this way for Devin again. I never thought I would cheat on Kenneth. I never imagined adultery would feel so good.

The elevator bell rang and interrupted my mood. As I walked over to check who it was, an older lady entered. I assumed she was the housekeeper. She smiled and said, "Mrs. Patterson?" with a West Indian accent.

I considered explaining to her that I should have been Mrs. Patterson, but unfortunately, I wasn't. I was just Mr. Patterson's mistress, but I smiled and said, "Yes."

"Nice to meet you."

My eyes rolled as we embraced. This didn't feel right. I suddenly felt slimy. Now, I was standing here pretending I was the wife. My heart began to race because I'd momentarily lost control. Then, I reverted to the conversation he had with his wife. Though he claimed he had a lot to lose, I had more to lose. Kenneth and I had a business together. We were going through a rough time, and an affair would only ensure the demise of our marriage. I had to get out of his space and think about what I was doing.

25

✦

DEVIN

Devin, I'm not ready for this. You have a greater potential to hurt me than I have to hurt you. I think it would be best if we end this now. Every moment we shared was special. I hope it was enough to help you close this chapter of your life. I wish you much success.

Love, Clark

I reread her short note that lay beneath the gift cards I'd given her to shop. It was around twelve when her GoPhone just stopped working. I thought there was some mistake, and I'd erased her other number from my phone as she'd recommended. I called the number back over and over, hoping there'd been a mistake. Finally, when I stepped in the house it all made sense. Or better yet, it made no sense. She'd disconnected it.

If she felt the way I thought she felt, there was no way she could have left this message without speaking to me first. Suddenly, memories of our first breakup flooded my head. That same get-you-before-you-get-me attitude was why we weren't together. My confusion turned into frustration.

I looked up at the ceiling, questioning God for his place-
ment strategies. Why her? Why now? Why not? I stood up
and paced the floor. Then I walked into the kitchen to pour a
glass of wine. I had to let go of this dumb-ass fantasy. Clark
and I would never be together, and maybe we'd never meant
to be. Suddenly, I realized I hadn't called Taylor to check in.
She picked up.

"Hey, Devin."

"Hey, TJ. What's happening?"

"Watching *CSI: Miami*."

"I don't know how you sleep watching that mess."

"Whatever, Devin. You should be asking how I can sleep
when my husband is never home."

I hissed. It bothered me that she expected that I should
just visit my baby for one day and come back home. I ignored
it and jumped to another topic. "So, whatchu do today?"

"Courtney came over earlier. We had happy hour, of
course."

"Of course."

"Why you say it like that?"

"How else should I say it?"

"You make me sick. Don't hate because you missed happy
hour," she said, laughing. "Sike, baby. I'm just playing."

"Nah, I'm cool. So, what else you do?"

"We went shopping for our vacation."

I ran my hand down my face. I couldn't describe what I
was feeling. Taylor having her own life and doing her own
thing was the one thing that I loved about her. So why was
I feeling like she could totally live this life without me? She
and Courtney made each other happier than any man could
ever make either of them.

"You know Courtney and I are going to the Bahamas for a few days, right?"

"Yeah, that's cool."

I needed something from her at the moment. I needed something to confirm she was the one for me. I wasn't feeling it. Taylor had a way of living in bliss and ignoring my emotions. I used to think that it was cute, because no matter what, at least she was happy. But as I sat there, needing her sensitivity, I finally realized that was what my marriage lacked.

"So, what did you do today?" she asked.

"Just hung out with Nicole." I yawned. "Yeah, and I got a lot of campaign stuff on my mind, and a bunch of briefings to read. I'ma talk to you in the morning, a'ight, baby?"

"I love you, baby. Have a good night. Don't work too hard."

"I won't. I love you, too."

I placed the phone on the coffee table and strolled back into the kitchen to get my glass of wine. After I few swallows, I was convinced this was all a big prank, and I dialed Clark's number one more time.

"This number is not in service."

26

CLARK

When I walked into Sheena's apartment, she looked at me suspiciously and asked, "Clark, where did you stay last night?"

I'd told her several times that I wanted to stay in a hotel and clear my mind. I needed some space. Yet she asked the question with such conviction, so she obviously suspected something.

"Where did I tell you I was staying?" I said.

"You told me you'd be downtown in the Hyatt. I mean, Times Square is not peaceful at all."

My eyes rolled. "Okay."

"And I called there after I called you and you didn't stay there."

"Okay, so arrest me." I walked toward the bedrooms. "Where's Sage?"

"She's in the shower. Your mom called last night."

I walked back into the living room. "You got any coffee?"

"She told me that you went to see your ol' college boy a few weeks ago."

I sucked my teeth. "Why did she tell you that?"

We walked into the kitchen. Sheena pulled a bag of coffee from the cabinet and handed it to me. "Well, I think she thought you may be here seeing him."

"Y'all are funny. I decide to get away and clear my head. Now, I'm here seeing Devin." I shook my head and scooped the coffee. "Not to mention, he lives in Maryland."

She raised one eyebrow. "Yeah, and she said he's married."

"He is," I snapped. "So why are you questioning me?"

"Clark, girl. You know me; I'm not going to accuse you. I'm just warning you, because your mother is really concerned. She doesn't want you to start fooling around with that loser again and lose the good man you have."

Once Sheena set her mind to believing something, that's what it was. I decided it might make better sense to just leave it alone. Not to mention, I was technically *fooling around* with Devin. It rattled me that they thought he was a loser. Married, but not a loser. They didn't see what I saw. What made Kenneth a good man? He'd said less than twenty words to me in about three months. That didn't seem good to me. As I set up the Devin vs. Kenneth battle in my brain, I concluded at the end of the day that Devin belonged to someone else and, if nothing more, Kenneth belonged to me.

I hung my head, and finally looked back up at Sheena. Before speaking, I took a long breath to gather my thoughts. Finally, I said, "I can't explain why I came here to see Devin. But—"

"Clark, no! Are you really seeing him?" she asked as if she were stunned.

A part of me wanted to laugh, because I thought she was already convinced. Hence that is why I'd confessed.

"Sheena, Kenneth has been so cold, and when I got in contact with Devin, it seemed like the right thing to do."

"What? Go sleep with your old boyfriend because your husband was tripping?"

I sucked my teeth. "No. It wasn't about sleeping with him. I just felt loved again when I was with him and I haven't felt that in my home in a long time."

"You're not playing house. This is the real world. You're not always going to feel loved at home."

"Maybe I just needed some affection."

She huffed. "Clark, affection? Are you serious? You're going to throw your marriage away for some temporary affection? You're going to fuck up people's lives for some temporary affection?"

For some strange reason, I couldn't fully explain what I was feeling. It seemed that no matter what I said, it sounded stupid. Maybe this whole thing was stupid. Maybe only Devin and I could understand why we needed to see each other despite our commitments to other people. I looked at her with no answers.

"Your brother," she said with conviction. "He probably hooked up with Tanisha for affection and look what happened. She's gone. Two kids without a mother, all for temporary affection. Is that what you want to do? Follow in their footsteps?"

That realization stung as it dawned on me how cheating drove Tanisha's boyfriend to that point. And based on the way Kenneth had been acting of late, I wasn't certain what he was capable of. As I watched Sheena, her veins popped from her temples, like she and Reggie broke up yesterday, when nearly four years had passed. I didn't want to inflict this kind of pain on Kenneth or anyone else. I shook my head, feeling slimy for what I'd done so far and vowed to

myself that I would end it now. It was too late to turn back
and we had to accept that our time had passed.

"Too many other people are involved now, huh?"

"Basically. Let bygones be bygones."

She pleaded with me for just seconds more before I rushed
out of there and back to Devin's house to drop off the gift
cards, and to the AT&T store to disconnect my secret cell
phone. I didn't want to lose it all for something that probably
wasn't worth it.

After I went to lunch with Sheena and Sage, I headed
for the train station. I had to accept the cards I was dealt.
I vowed to love Kenneth in sickness and in health. Maybe
he'd eventually get over the ills plaguing our relationship,
because there was a time when we used to be happy. I just
wanted to go back there.

When Ms. Teeny picked me up from the train station,
I threw my luggage in the backseat and climbed in. She
smiled from ear to ear, waiting to hear about my sexual escape. First I told her about that, and she squirmed in the
driver's seat like she was getting it.

"Dag, Ms. Teeny. Calm down," I said smiling.

"So, when y'all getting together again?"

"We're not."

"If it's that good, why not?"

"My best friend died cheating on her boyfriend. It ain't
worth it."

"What did he say when you told him it was over?"

"I just left a letter, because if I talked to him, I'm not sure
I'd be so strong. You know."

She reached over and popped me in the back of my head.
"You are just as silly."

"I know. This relationship can hurt too many people. It's just not worth it. Mia is coming home from school for the summer. Morgan would be devastated. I mean, it's just not fair."

"Being neglected in your own home ain't fair, but it don't stop that ol' rockhead husband of yours from doing it, does it?"

"He's just bitter that I won't try again and he thinks I'm quitting for wanting to adopt. He just wants us to have a family and he's angry with me, angry with God. He doesn't mean it. You know, Kenneth has never acted this ugly."

"I don't know, but he sure is acting ugly now. But I guess you can't make your body do something that your heart can't handle. Maybe all you needed was a one-time shot. Kenneth might shape up now. I'm telling you, it's like they can sniff you and know something changed, and they need to step up their game."

"I hope so."

"For your sake, I hope so, too," she said, shaking her head.

I hung my head, because I wondered if we'd ever get past this phase.

I walked in the house to the same cold husband I left the day before. He sat in the family room watching a basketball game. His stomach poking out of his wife beater greeted me.

"Hey, Bae."

"What's going on?"

He glanced at me and quickly switched back to the television. His jeans were unbuckled and he looked like a slob. After the last few years, he picked up at least ten pounds a year. After looking at Devin's physique, I was instantly repulsed looking at Kenneth. I pulled my roller backpack behind me, as I headed through the kitchen toward the stairs. "Did you eat yet?"

When I heard his footsteps behind me, I flinched. For a second I felt like he knew what I went to New York to do and he was coming to attack me. Surprisingly, he smiled. "When you said you were coming home, I ordered Famous Dave."

I smiled back, though my heart still pounded a mile a minute. I continued toward the stairs and he headed back to the kitchen. I paced the floor of my bedroom, wondering what I could say when he asked about my trip. When I got enough courage, I walked downstairs, grabbed a soda from the pantry, and plopped beside him on the couch.

"Who's playing?"

"The Celtics."

"Are you going to eat dinner with me?" I asked.

"I already ate. The food is in the refrigerator."

"Whatchu get?" I said, as I stood to head into the kitchen.

"The All-American Meal."

My neck snapped around and I frowned slightly. Why would he get such a large platter of food for the two of us? We used to order that when the girls were home.

After I warmed up my plate, I sat back beside him. He reached over to my plate and grabbed a buffalo wing. I tapped his hand and he smiled. I returned the smile. I'm not a complex person. All I need is a smile and something that resembled communication. I hoped we were at a better place and things could work out. As I sat there befriending my husband, I wondered how Devin was coping and when he'd be back in Maryland loving TJ.

27

DEVIN

By the time I left New York, I decided Clark's disappearance might be for the best. If I was going to make it work with Taylor, I didn't need distractions. They say the first year of marriage is the hardest and if you can get past that, things get better.

When I walked in the house, Taylor burst out of the laundry room full of energy and walked over to hug me. I arrived early on Saturday afternoon so that we could spend the day together. She was wearing a tank top and thin sweatpants. I wrapped my arms around her waist and lay my head on her shoulder. I just wanted to be quiet and hold her for a minute. She pulled away.

"I'm glad you made it home so soon."

I pulled out a chair at the kitchen table. "You happy to see me?"

She rested her weight on one leg, tossed her hair out of her eye, and said, "Devin."

"Taylor," I said in the same tone that she spoke.

She slouched toward me and stood in between my legs. I leaned my head into her stomach and ran my hands up and down her round butt. As she wiped my forehead, she asked, "So what are we doing today?"

"Whatever you want to do."

She pulled away and sat in the chair adjacent to mine. She smiled sneakily. I said, "What?"

"I want to go shopping and out to eat and to the spa and to the movies and dancing and—"

"Taylor, pick two things."

"You said 'whatever.' I was just giving you options," she said, laughing.

"Alright," I said, standing up to grab my bag. "Let me shower and get ready. Dinner and a movie good, maybe Zanzibar?"

She shrugged. "It doesn't matter, as long as we're together."

I tried to take a quick nap while Taylor got ready. As I lay there across our king-sized bed, I wondered how Clark was able to just cut off her feelings. I ran my hand down my face and kept telling myself I just wanted forgiveness from Clark. And she'd given me that. So why was I still tripping?

When Taylor came out of the bathroom wearing purple thong panties and bra, I watched her walk past the bed and head for her walk-in closet. She caught me peeking and said, "C'mon, Devin, get up and get ready."

I sat up reluctantly and said, "You want to just spend the day chilling? We can get a couple of movies, order in, and—"

"No, I want to do something."

"We always do something."

She stood in front of the bed. "Not lately."

To avoid the drama, I decided not argue and walked into the bathroom. I stood in the shower, but my eyes were heavy and I sat on the bench, trying to decide what we could do to make sure Taylor had a good time. After sitting there procrastinating, I got out and headed into the room. Taylor had on a pair of jeans and a tight-fitting long sweater that hugged her hips. She stood before the full-length mirror outside of the closet. I walked up behind her, wrapped my arms around her waist, and rested my chin on her shoulder. She raised her arms up and wrapped them around the back of my head.

"We look so good together, don't you think?" she asked.

"Yeah, picture-perfect."

She laughed and pulled away. "You're trying to be smart." She touched my chest and attempted to push me. Her eyes turned seductive, as she rubbed my muscles.

"You like those abs, huh?"

She looked down at my towel, still wrapped around my waist, and ran one finger up and down the middle of my stomach. "Actually, I like something else better."

I let my towel drop. "You want it?"

She walked away from me and headed into the bathroom to put on her makeup. "Devin, don't try to tempt me. You're just trying to stay in the house."

I stood naked at the bathroom door. "We can do that and go out."

"Devin, put some clothes on and we'll go out and *then* do that." She winked. "Deal?"

We headed out of the house shortly after, and we did almost everything she wanted to do. I guess a part of me felt guilty, and I wanted to make it up to her. If I was going to make this work, it was best that I stop complaining and start doing what I could do to make sure she was happy.

28

CLARK

Unlike what Ms. Teeny claimed, that one night with Devin didn't make my marriage stronger, it made it worse. I found myself thinking about him twenty-four-seven for the following two months, wishing the situation were different, wishing it were in my favor. Instead, all I had was Kenneth. My heart and my body wanted so much more, but he was mine and Devin was hers. So I resisted the desire to call him and tell him that I wanted to rethink my rash decision. Each morning, I had to make a conscious effort to reaffirm to myself that this marriage was for better or worse and eventually the tide would change.

As we rapidly approached the end of April, I was counting down the days until Morgan and Mia came home. At least then Kenneth and I would have to pretend we were a happy family. Something was better than nothing. The rainy days hadn't been helping either of our moods, but the sun came up one morning, and I decided to lean over and kiss his forehead. I rubbed my hand over his five o'clock shadow. He lay there like he was dead and I just stared at him, because I know he felt me. We hadn't made love in nearly a month. The little affection we'd begun to have ended abruptly when he rolled over one morning to ask me if I had changed my mind about IVF. I flipped out, because not only was he not listening, he was determined to change my mind. So, we reverted back to this, to the empty, noncommunicative thing we called a relationship.

I got up, showered and rushed to the group home extra early. I wanted to be anywhere, except in my house. When I arrived, most of the girls were still asleep. So it gave me time to organize things. Around eight, the house came alive as the staff worker cooked breakfast and the girls prepared to leave. Ms. Teeny arrived shortly after, and I opened my office door just to let everyone knew I was there. As soon as I did, Raven, aka Ms. Attitude, strutted into my office.

"Ms. Clark, you gonna let me cop this purse?"

I looked at her. "Why would I do that?"

" 'Cause you just should. You owe me."

I laughed. "Oh really, I owe you. What exactly do I owe you?"

"Just know that you owe me."

She put my colorful Dooney & Burke bag on her shoulder and pranced around my office. Raven had like a twenty-six-inch waist and a fifty-inch backside. She was sixteen but more developed than any woman I knew, and she was an average-height girl, so she could pass for at least twenty-two. Her facial features were even mature. She wore more makeup than necessary over her unblemished mocha skin. I shook my head at her as she pursed her lips and rolled her neck in the mirror. She was the unofficial resident hair stylist. There were times when I'd even allowed her to do my hair. I laughed while she posed in the mirror.

"Yo, I would be so tight if I wore this to school."

"School?" I laughed. "I get a phone call every day and they say you aren't even there."

"Whatever, Ms. Clark, if you let me rock this bag, I would go every day."

I shook my head. "Honey, you need to have more on your mind than carrying a nice bag."

"Do you?" she said, as she flung her hot pink, highlighted bob haircut around and strolled out my office.

"Raven, bring that purse back in here."

I could hear Teeny fussing at her in the hall, demanding that she bring my purse back. Teeny stormed in my office holding my purse.

"That girl is crazy. She was taking this purse."

"She's not crazy."

Teeny frowned at me, and we burst into laughter. She said, "Whatchu say?"

"Not like that." Teeny jerked her head back as if she thought I was crazy for defending her. "Yes, she does have a chemical imbalance, but she's not known to be a thief," I whispered.

"I been in this industry long enough to know, I don't put anything past any of these little girls. We trying to help them, but they're damaged goods."

It bothered me that the very people working in human services were the ones that gave up so easily on kids who had no control of their situations. Momentarily, I saw Kenneth all over her. Why did they do it if they didn't believe people could change?

I told Teeny to close the door and I said, "All of them aren't damaged goods."

"Okay, just like eighty percent," she said, laughing hysterically.

I took a deep breath. "It's not funny."

"It sure isn't. I been doing this for thirty years, and I'm sorry, I just call it like I see it. You still think you can save the world. You're still fresh and new."

"I just want to help them."

"That's nice," she said sarcastically, and plopped into a chair. "Ah, speaking of helping them, are we going to your baby daddy's conference this weekend?"

My heart sank, because I had completely forgotten about Devin's conference, considering my plan was to just stay as far away from him as possible. Anything within ten thousand feet wasn't good for my health. My eyes switched from side to side and I took a deep breath. "Maybe you should take them."

"You want me to take eight girls without you?"

"You can get another staff member to go with you."

She reached across my desk and grabbed my hand. "I don't like them. Why don't you go with me?"

I looked down at my wedding ring and then back up at her. My head tilted, hoping she understood. "I can't go, Teeny."

"Stop being a sissy. Why you scared to see Devin?" She shook her head. "Girl, you just as soft as cotton."

"Teeny, Devin is like kryptonite to me, and I think I just want to stay away."

"You can control it. He's nothing but another man. His drawers get dirty just like the next man's."

I blushed, and visions of our night in New York flashed in my gazing eyes. "Nah, Teeny, he's more than just a man."

She laughed. "You are certified crazy."

"Crazy for Devin Patterson."

"Look, you have a job to do. These girls are expecting you

to go with them, and you're acting like a teenager yourself. Get it together. You better learn how to get it and quit it and go home like nothing happened."

"Teeny, I'm not like you."

"I know, 'cause I would go to the conference and steal a piece in the bathroom and go home like nothing happened. You're making it too deep. That's what an affair is. It's an event that's not supposed to linger on forever. You leave your feelings at the door."

"It's not deep. It's just not right. You know?"

"C'mon, Clark. You can go. You can be a big girl for once." She pouted. "For me?"

I sighed. "A'ight, Teeny. I'll go."

"Yeah, just play cool. You can do it."

A part of me felt that I was making a big mistake, but the other side of me wanted her to coax me into going. I had thought about Devin every day. Why shouldn't I go and refresh my vision of him?

29

DEVIN

Having the perfect campaign manager and the right people in leadership is pertinent to success. The night before the Girl Power conference, I was briefed by Mrs. Dillon at the school. She flirted and talked at the same time. We walked through the schedule, the food stations, and the posted directions to make sure the conference flowed smoothly.

As we left the building, Mrs. Dillon grabbed my hand. My eyes quickly shifted to Curtis. He wasn't paying us any attention. She tickled my palm. I pulled my hand from her, and she smiled sneakily. I gave her a stern look, but she smirked as if to say at the right place and time, she could get me.

Out in the parking lot, everyone said their good-byes and got into their cars. I tried to keep Curtis out there for a minute, hoping Mrs. Dillon would keep it moving. Instead, she stood there beside me like it was cool. She let me wrap up my conversation and I opened the car. When the locks popped up, she put her hand on the car door. "Can I sit in the car with you?"

"What's up?"

"I just want to talk."

I didn't want to be too presumptive, so I shrugged. When

we sat in the car, I looked at her impatiently. She tucked one leg under her like she planned to be there for a minute. "What's going on?"

"Are you happy with how everything is working out?"

"Yeah, you did your thing."

She reached over and put her hand on my leg. I looked down at her ring. Still, it was hard to believe that someone actually made a commitment to this chick. She massaged my thigh and I instantly pushed her hand away. There was just something sneaky in her eyes.

"So, what's up with a permanent position with Love My People?" she said seductively, as she put her hand back on my thigh.

I grabbed her wrist. "You know you don't have to do this to get a permanent position with the foundation. You know that, right?"

She reached over with her other hand and cupped my dick. Chuckling, she said, "What, this?"

Looking down at her hand, I said, "Yeah, this."

"I'm doing this because I want to. Is that okay with you?"

I had to be careful how I handled this. I didn't want to brush her off too abruptly, but I knew I couldn't submit to my manhood rising in her soft hand. "Look, I'm a married man."

"And I'm a married woman. What does that mean?"

"It has to mean something at the end of the day."

"You ever see my husband?" I didn't respond. She proceeded: "Exactly, and I've never seen your wife. So she's obviously not concerned about what you're doing."

"Look, Mrs. Dillon."

"Call me Shawna," she said, as she massaged me vigorously.

Just as my penis began to respond, I grabbed her hand. "Look, Shawna, I don't do this. I don't cheat on my wife. I respect her and my marriage. So I'm sorry."

"Please. All men cheat," she said with an attitude. She took her hands off me and rolled her eyes. "If you're not attracted to me, just say so."

"It has nothing to do with my attraction to you, and all to do with my commitment to my wife."

"Is your wife so committed?" I shrugged my shoulders, and she asked, "You don't know what she's doing, and you've never cheated?"

"No, I've never cheated."

She laughed. "Oh, that's right, you're still a newlywed. I'll give you a few years and you'll be jumping all into this hot black pussy."

I frowned. I wasn't sure if she thought she was turning me on, but she made it sound like she was burning. All I could think of was how many men she had fucked this week. Suddenly, I was irritated with her and didn't really care about her feelings.

"Shawna. I'm not that dude." I reached out my hand to shake hers. "I'm going to see you tomorrow."

She sucked her teeth, didn't shake my hand, and stormed from the car. I felt sorry for the dude that married that freak. I sat in the parking lot for a moment and let her pull out. Finally, I headed home. When I opened the garage and noticed Taylor wasn't there, I called her.

"Hey, you," she said.

"Hey, you, where are you?"

"Courtney and I met for drinks."

"A'ight. Hurry home."

"Okay, baby."

It was two hours later when I heard the garage door open. She walked up the stairs with a cheesy-drunk smile. She was trying to unbutton her black fitted shirt. Her jeans were already unzipped. She sang my name, "De-vin."

Her eyes looked like little slits. It was clear she'd had too much to drink. "Did you drive home like this?" I asked.

"No, Courtney's home girl Rachel drove us home. You're going to have to take me to pick up my car in the morning," she said before collapsing on the bed.

I stroked her back. "Not tomorrow morning. We have the conference."

"Conference, bonference. It's always something."

I proceeded to help her out of her clothes. "You know you're scheduled to talk to the girls, right?"

She turned to look at me with a forced sober stare. "So what am I supposed to say to them?" She plopped back down on the bed.

I stood over her, wondering if she was serious. Trying to talk to her in this state was useless. Instead, I climbed on her and started kissing her breasts. She held my face between her hands. "I love you," she said.

I kissed her lips, wondering if she or I even knew what love was. I rolled her over on top of me. She twirled her hips. "You love me, too."

"Yeah, baby, I love you."

I yanked her panties to the side and began rubbing her butt and sliding my fingers up and down her crack. She moaned and I felt the moistness between her legs. She started sucking feverishly on my chest. Finally, I tickled her vagina with the tip of my penis. I wanted to be inside of her.

"Put it in, you."

"You like me, baby."

"Yeah, TJ. Put it in."

"How much do you like me?"

"Baby, I love you."

"Okay, now you can have me."

She slid down on me. I almost came instantly, as she smothered me with her warm, juicy vagina. I pushed deep into her, nearly ripping off her panties, which were still pushed to the side. She yelled loudly. Her screams made me want to love her longer, harder. Finally, after she came, I released in her. She rolled off of me and was snoring seconds later.

My alarm clock went off at six o'clock and I popped up. When I looked over at Taylor, she looked like a dead person. I shook her and she took the pillow and hugged it around her ears.

"Baby, we need to be at the school at seven-thirty."

"What time I gotta speak?" she groaned.

"The panels start at around nine, but the keynote speech is at eight-thirty, and we'd like all the panelists to be there for the speech. Isn't that what your invitation says?"

"I didn't read it. I don't have to be there at eight-thirty. My head hurts so bad. Let me sleep a little longer."

"It's all that wine you had last night." I said, as I climbed out of bed.

By the time I reached the bathroom, she was snoring again. I glanced back at her and shook my head. When I got out of the shower, she still lay there. I called her name multiple times. She tossed and turned, but didn't get up. I told her to drive the BMW and we'd get her car later. She nodded but was clearly incoherent. I figured she would figure it out when she woke up, because I had to run. So I set the alarm for eight, and prayed she'd wake up and be there by at least nine.

When I got to the school, the hospitality room was packed with people. There were tons of bagels, croissants, muffins, coffee, and fruit. Shawna was the first to greet me. "Good morning, Mr. Patterson."

"Good morning, Mrs. Dillon."

A bunch of volunteers were running around. I grabbed a cup of coffee before figuring out what I could do to help. As I stood in the hospitality room, sipping my coffee, Shawna walked in with a volunteer. She gave her instructions on which table each guest should be seated at when they signed in.

I said, "Shawna, everything is perfect."

She brushed me off as she headed for the door. "Yeah, thanks."

It was clear that she was offended, but what other choice did I have than to resist that burning booty? I stayed in the hospitality room, greeting the panelists and thanking them for taking the time to come out for the kids. The keynote speaker arrived around eight, and she was so excited to be giving back. Her excitement made me feel good, but it shifted my mind to Taylor. Where was she? Had she even gotten up yet? As I sat there, entertaining Amerie, Shawna stormed in and excused herself. It was partially rude, but she handed me a walkie-talkie. "Here, Mr. Patterson. The entire staff is connected. Just state who you are, where you are, and what you need. Okay?"

I nodded and continued chatting with the various panelists. Finally, my walkie-talkie beeped. "Mr. Patterson, we're about to get started. Can you come down to the gymnasium?"

I pulled out my cell phone as I headed downstairs. Taylor didn't answer the home phone or the cell phone. Shawna flipped through the pages in her clipboard, checking off the panelists that were already there. We decided to move the panelists from location to location, instead of moving the girls. That would cut down on a lot of the hysteria.

One of the volunteers ushered me to a seat onstage. Once I sat down, Shawna flipped through her pad, "Mr. Patterson, is your wife here?"

"No. She's not here, yet," I said, slightly embarrassed.

"Okay, well, I asked for the panelists to check in no later than eight. I'll have a backup take her place on that panel and if she shows up, she can participate in the afternoon."

I wished I could tell her that was wrong and that she should keep my wife's spot, but I couldn't. To be perfectly honest, there was no reason that Taylor wasn't there, except for a lack of consideration. Suddenly, I was mad as hell. I couldn't believe that she would just totally disregard this event.

The gym was packed with tons of young ladies there to learn from all the powerful women we'd invited. Looking out over the crowd made me proud. This had begun as an election strategy, but the deeper we got the more excited I'd become.

Another volunteer ushered in the rest of the panelists, and I hoped Taylor would surprise me and be there. Still, no Taylor. I flipped through my index cards, making sure my speech was airtight. Once all of the panelists were seated, Shawna stepped onstage and calmed the crowd. She talked about why we were here and gave me a serious introduction.

"He is a man for the people. The founder of the Love My People Foundation. This foundation helps people of color all over the world. He believes that love can save our communities, our children, and our people. Mr. Patterson is on a path to change the way things are done and he carries our people on his shoulders. The next United States congressman from Maryland District Four: Devin Patterson, Esquire."

30

CLARK

Ms. Teeny glared at me as I gawked at Devin. He stood up at the podium. He wasn't wearing a sharp suit as I expected, but an aqua Lacoste shirt and jeans. Even in his casual wear he looked like a leader. He was composed; his voice was clear and confident. Teeny mouthed, "He's fine." Then, she fanned herself. "Whew. Jesus, take the wheel!"

Her antics made me smile, but my stomach tumbled endlessly. I missed Devin. Our two-day reunion played frequently in my head. I felt so complete with him. And although Kenneth and I were talking, I still felt empty, and I wondered if I ever felt something real. How could two days with Devin force me to question seven years with Kenneth? As his voice, his hope, spread through the crowd, I looked onstage for Devin's wife. He was such a good man and he claimed to still be in love with me. What was I thinking to not at least see if he was telling the truth?

As I went back to gazing at him, I wondered why I listened to Sheena, why I listened to my insecurities. I wanted to just hold him one more time. His spirit was so positive, so influential. I needed to feel him again. Teeny snapped her fingers, sitting a few seats away from me. When I looked at her, she mouthed, "Snap out of it."

I smiled, then Raven's eyes caught mine. She turned her lips up suspiciously. I shifted my attention back to Devin. I wondered if he saw me, if he even wanted to see me. After he introduced the keynote speaker, he returned to his seat. He seemed to be preoccupied. His eyes were here, there, and everywhere. I wondered if he was searching for me. Did he remember I was coming?

The crowd began clapping. Amerie had finished her speech, but I was studying Devin. I hadn't heard a damn thing she'd said. The crowd began to shift around as the lady host instructed the groups to go to their designated rooms. She spoke loudly: "If you're between twelve and fourteen, you will remain here. And . . ."

Teeny looked at me and winked. "You want to stay with the twelve-through-fourteen crew?"

I looked back to the stage, wondering what my chances were to talk to Devin alone. I shrugged. "Yeah, I'll stay here."

It took about ten to fifteen minutes for everyone to move around. Finally when the dust settled, there was a panel on the stage and no Devin. I looked around and asked the girls to stay seated, while I went to the bathroom. After I found the bathroom, I walked aimlessly through the hallway, hoping to run into Devin. Back and forth and no Devin. I walked back toward the gym and there he was, standing at the entrance with another guy.

My pace slowed because I wasn't sure how I should act or how he'd react to me. He saw me before I was prepared. I thought he would smile, but instead he squinted like he wasn't sure it was me. I smiled, reaching out my hand to shake his. He looked stunned, confused. He reached out for a hug.

"Wow," he said.

The short, light-skinned, stubby guy he was speaking with reached out to shake my hand. "Hi, I'm Curtis Thorpe. I'm Devin's campaign manager."

"Nice to meet you."

"It's my pleasure." His eyes returned to Devin, questioning who I was.

Devin spoke, "Curtis, this is Clark. We went to Hampton together." Nodding, he continued, "She's a really good friend of mine."

Curtis smiled politely. Devin gave him a look that asked him to excuse us, and Curtis walked away. He ran his hand down my face. "You know you hurt me, right?"

"Devin, how did I hurt you?"

"Clark, I think you think I'm trying to be a player or something."

"I don't know what you're trying to be, but I heard you tell your wife you missed her and there was so much love in your voice. It just scared me, I guess."

"Do you love your husband?"

My eyes shifted to the floor as I nodded.

"But obviously something is missing, right? You say you have more to lose. Have you looked around here today? Look at all the people I would hurt, but it's worth it for me."

I looked up at him. I had to go with what I felt and ignore all the history that told me differently. "Devin, I—"

The young lady that introduced Devin walked toward us and grabbed Devin's arm. She looked me up and down. "We need you in here," she told him.

She nearly dragged him onto the floor. I couldn't remember her name. I wondered if she was his wife, because she looked as if she wanted to know why her man was hemmed up in the back of the gym, having an intimate conversation with me. He raised his finger. "Ms. Winston, we'll finish this conversation in a minute."

When I snuck back into the workshop, my girls were surprisingly well-mannered and even asking questions. It seemed like they never noticed I was gone. I shifted around, back and forth in my seat, wondering if Devin would walk in to get me or what.

I felt like I was twelve and had just gotten a new love note from a boy in my class: *Check yes or no.* At this moment, I wanted to check yes. The only problem I was having was what was our purpose, and where were we going, or how did we plan to keep this going.

Devin appeared in the door and gave me a nod. My heart sank, but I excused myself again and walked to the door. He started walking and asked me to follow. I felt the girls would be fine until I returned. We snuck off to a little room and Devin held me in his arms. I felt protected. He kissed my forehead.

"Clark, what made you come here today?"

"I don't know."

"I'm glad you came."

"Was that your wife that came to get you?"

"Not at all. My wife's not here." He let me go and laughed. "She's not here."

"Why?"

He hung his head. "Clark, I don't know. I wish I knew."

"Did you ask her to come?"

"She was supposed to be on one of the panels."

I didn't ask any more questions. Instead, I made assumptions. How could you let your husband put on an event of this magnitude and not be here? "Its okay, Devin."

"That's cool. You're here. That's all that matters."

He sat on one of the writing desks in the room and I leaned in between his legs. He wrapped his arms around my waist. "Clark, did you leave because you felt like I loved my wife, or did you leave for another reason?"

"I'm afraid that I'll be the one to get hurt."

He stared in my eyes. "I promised that I would never hurt you again. You are the best thing that ever happened to me. Before all of this, before anything, you loved me for me, and that's priceless. Especially for a man like me."

"So, would you leave your wife for me?"

"If we decide we want to be together, yes. I've cheated myself long enough."

It felt like he meant it. "Do you think we're being honest with ourselves by thinking we want to be together?"

"We've already loved each other before and we were happy at one time."

"But Devin, we were young."

"Did you feel the same in New York?" I nodded. "A'ight, then. Feelings aren't rocket science. You either have a connection or you don't. And we have it. Always have."

His walkie-talkie beeped. "This is Mrs. Dillon. I need everyone to the hospitality room now."

He jumped up from the desk. "I'll be back. Stay here."

"Devin, I have to go out there with my girls," I said, following him.

We walked out of the classroom and, of all people, I saw Raven out in the hall on her cell phone. I was shocked. She gasped and I wanted to run back into the room. There was no way I could explain creeping out of a deserted classroom with some man. I said, "Raven, why aren't you in your work-shop?"

She rolled her head. "Why aren't you in yours?"

"That's none of your business."

She sucked her teeth and walked in a different direction. "It's down this way. Ms. Teeny is in there. You don't have to hold my hand."

I didn't care to hold her hand, because my palms were sweaty. She was no fool. Clearly, she knew something was going on. I just hoped she kept her mouth shut. I headed back to the gym and my heart pounded in my chest. The fear rummaging in me suggested that I wasn't cut out for this, but, like Devin said, "We couldn't deny the feeling."

Devin rushed around, handling business for the remainder of the conference. We got another second to talk. He said, "I'm going out of the country on Monday and I'll be back in two weeks. I want you to think about everything we talked about while I'm gone. I don't want you to get cold feet again."

"Where you going?"

"I'm going to Nicaragua."

"With your wife?"

"No, I'm going alone. It's an outreach mission."

I didn't know what he meant by *outreach mission*, but I felt like I wanted to be a part of it, or a part of *him*. "Can I go?"

His eyes stretched open. "What are you going to tell your husband?"

"That I met some women from another group home going on an outreach mission to Nicaragua and I wanted to go."

The lie popped in my mind so quickly and effortlessly that I felt that it must have been meant for me to go.

31

◆

DEVIN

Taylor's blatant disrespect made me more interested to see where things would go with Clark. When I held her, all I could think was that if she were my wife, she would have been there. Instead, my wife had a hangover. It was clear: I had made another crucial mistake. While I was so focused on having a wife to show some stability, I didn't pick the right one once again. I needed a woman that was down for the ride and cared a little about the community. I couldn't blame anyone, because people let you know who they are when you meet them. Taylor never planned to be a politician's wife. She loved her social, carefree life. This was more than she bargained for, having to wake up on Saturday mornings to do a conference. Taylor would probably make out better with the average nine-to-five guy that makes a bunch of money for her to spend.

I sat there in the classroom with Clark and stared in her eyes, admitting that if she left her husband, I would leave Taylor. If that meant blowing this election, that's what it would be. The way I saw it, I was thirty-two and I had a bunch of years ahead of me. At least, neither of us would live a lie any longer.

Taylor sent me a text around two o'clock: BABY, I WAS SO
SICK. I WAS THROWING UP ALL MORNING. HOW DID EVERY-
THING GO?

I didn't even respond. She was technically still single in
her mind. The whole idea of this partnership was a joke to
her. I went into the computer resource room and printed out
my entire itinerary for Clark. I needed her with me and I
wanted to be sure that she had all the information.

When I walked into the gym for the wrap-up, I searched
for Clark. Before I got onstage, I walked through the crowd
until I spotted her. She sat there laughing and talking to her
girls. Several of the girls clung to her arms. I stood there and
absorbed it for a moment. She was beautiful, even more so
now than before.

Shawna stepped up behind me, startling me. "Mr. Patterson, we need you on the stage in five."

She kept moving. And I pulled out an envelope and folded
it, stooped down beside Clark. When I handed it to her, she
looked at me strangely, questioning my boldness. She quickly
slipped the envelope in her purse.

"Ms. Winston, this is the information about the trip, if
you're really interested."

"Thank you so much," she said passively.

When I stood up and walked away, I could hear her
girls saying *ooh* and *aah*. I kept my head up and headed to
the stage, and didn't look back. I jumped up onstage and
grabbed the mic.

"Did everyone have a good time?"

They cheered and clapped. I looked over at the panelists
and said, "Many thanks to my panelists for taking time out
of your busy schedules to come save the next generation."

The girls stood to their feet, giving the panelists a standing ovation. I allowed the whistling and clapping to go on for several minutes. "Okay, so how many people are going to use what they learned this week in school?"

They raised hands and called out. I laughed and continued to motivate them. Finally, I brought the conference to a close, but I was still excited and convinced we should do this every year. I was high from the conference, high on the possibility that Clark was going to Nicaragua with me.

32

CLARK

When I stepped in the house, Kenneth was nowhere to be found. I was glad that I didn't have to have a high-level conversation with him. After watching Devin speak on that stage and witnessing how people responded to him, I stopped questioning my feelings. He was a man with everything, with personality and sensitivity, and he claimed that all he ever wanted was a chance to make it right with me. I would be crazy to stay here and forgo the chance at true happiness again.

I sat at my home computer and pulled out Devin's envelope. He enclosed a short note with the credit card number and all of the instructions. I booked a round-trip ticket to Managua, Nicaragua. Once I arrived there, depending on what day, Devin would meet me there and we would fly to Corn Islands. I was simply down for the ride. As for the mission—the only mission *I* had was to see how serious Devin was about us.

Surprisingly, I found a flight for below four hundred dollars, and for some reason I felt it made sense to buy it on my card and not Devin's. I wasn't certain why he was so sloppy, but I had his back. So, there was no need for him to worry.

Devin's instructions told me to wear neutral colored clothing and no expensive jewelry, bring no expensive purses, and to pack lightweight hiking clothes as well as things for the beach. Plus, I needed to buy insect repellent with at least 30 percent DEET as the active ingredient to keep the mosquitoes away, since I wouldn't have a chance to take the necessary malaria medication. I was risking it all. Once I had my ticket, I sent Devin a text with the flight information and arrival time. He responded: FANTASTIC, I GET IN ABOUT TWO HOURS BEFORE YOU. MEET YOU IN MANAGUA. HASTA LUEGO, CHICA.

My adrenaline was racing, as I rushed from the house and to Target to buy some necessities for the trip. I had yet to discuss my trip with anyone, not even Teeny. I didn't want anyone talking sense into me. It felt good to lose my mind. Simply flying to a country that I knew absolutely nothing about was somehow thrilling. And going there to be with Devin was even better.

Before I got home, I called Teeny and told her the plans. If anyone would support this decision, I knew she would.

"You have lost your damn mind, Clark! You are not going to some third-world country for a piece of ding-ding!" she exclaimed.

"Teeny, it's not a piece of ding-ding. Devin and I are going there for a medical mission and to see what we want to do."

"Clark, where are you?"

"I'm in Columbia, on my way back home."

"Pull over. Right where you are. So, I can come out there and knock some sense into you. You just need a fling. You don't need to be flying to Nicaragua to see this man."

"Already got my ticket." I said.

She paused. She began to speak and paused again. Finally, she said, "Jesus, take the wheel!"

I laughed. "Ms. Teeny, I got this."

"How do you have this and you couldn't even handle a one-night stand with him? What has changed?"

"It's what hasn't changed. Some people just have a hold on you. Sometimes you can't fight the feeling any longer."

"I feel so bad."

"Why do you feel bad?"

"Because I should have known you weren't the type to get it a couple of times and quit it. I thought I taught you better than that. Uh, uh, uh." She gasped with frustration.

"Ms. Teeny, honey, this ain't your fault. This is a feeling that had been there long before I knew you or Kenneth."

"So, what you going to tell Kenneth?"

"That I'm going on a medical mission. We've discussed doing charity work around the world, but we couldn't afford it." I huffed. "Paying for fertility. You know?"

"I feel you, Clark, but I just don't want you going over to some war zone for a rendezvous. I told you that the key to cheating is not getting caught. Now, you trying to get caught."

"I'm not trying to get caught. I'm just trying to find my-self. And while I understand what you're trying to tell me, right now this is what I'm doing. So here's what I need you to do . . ."

I laid out the instructions of whom, where, and what I'd be doing in Nicaragua. Teeny agreed to support my scheme. I told her how much she meant to me and thanked her over and over again.

"You just make sure you get back here safely. 'Cause God knows I don't want this on my conscience."

I laughed. "Teeny, you don't have a conscience."

"Like I said, you better come home in one piece."

"Trust me, I will."

I called my mother shortly after and told her the same lie I planned on telling Kenneth. She didn't ask a bunch of questions, but I felt like she thought I was going crazy again, too. I was in my right mind, and I knew what I felt, and I had to respect my feelings for the first time in years.

Before I walked into the house, I prayed for forgiveness. I knew that I was about to sit in my husband's face and tell a big, fat lie. I looped the Target bags around my wrists and went into the house. After I dropped the bags on the floor, I said, "Hey, Kenneth."

"Hey."

He turned to face the television. I leaned on the half wall separating my kitchen from the family room. I stared at him before I spoke. His ashy size-thirteen feet were propped on the coffee table, as he scoffed down a big bowl of Kellogg's Honey Smacks. Milk dripped on his navy T-shirt. Clearly, he could feel my presence, but his eyes focused on the television and his food. Just as upbeat, I said, "Kenneth, you're not going to believe this."

"What?" he said without facing me.

"I met a few women at the conference today that have a nonprofit organization, and they travel to third-world countries providing aid and medical assistance to black people. I mean, they focus mainly on countries that a lot of people don't realize have black people, like, Belize, Nicaragua, and Honduras. You know, all through Central and South America."

I was spitting out the plan just as Devin had explained it to me. Technically, I wasn't lying; I was simply substituting.

"They had an upcoming mission scheduled and I asked if I could be a part of it."

He nodded. "That sounds good. When are they going? How long?"

"Monday. This Monday. They're going to Nicaragua for two weeks and I told them I'd go and I—"

"You didn't think you should speak to me first?"

"We don't have any kids around here. They aren't coming back until a week after I'm scheduled to return. Why shouldn't I be able to go away when I want to?"

"Clark, you're right. It might be good for you to get away."

He leaned back on the chair, folded his hands behind his head, and went back to watching television. That was usually my signal that the conversation was over. I picked up the bags and took them upstairs to my room. Then, I came back down to grab my luggage from the basement. I walked through the kitchen, feeling like I had one last thing to say to Kenneth, but I decided not to and headed back upstairs.

I turned up the Classic R & B music channel on the television. I sang and packed. Oddly enough, I felt no guilt.

33

DEVIN

When I was finished packing for Nicaragua, I told Taylor we needed to talk. She slouched beside me in the bed. I looked her in the eye and said, "I need more from you. I didn't get married to be single and it's obvious you did. And if things don't change, I can't say how long I'll be here."

Her mouth stretched open and she pushed me. I was unemotional. After yesterday, she needed to know what I was feeling. If I walked out on her, I didn't want it to be a shock. I wanted her to know it was about more than seeing someone else. It was about what I wasn't getting at home.

"How can you say that? You act like you're happy."

"I am happy and you are happy. So, we appear to be happy, but you do your thing and I do mine. I mean, at times that's cool. And it's just getting more evident to me now that we're in a single marriage."

"That's 'cause you're so busy all the time. We don't spend any quality time together."

"You know, you being on that panel was quality time for me."

"I was sick!"

I looked at her. "Really?"

"Yes, really."

"Look, I'm leaving in the morning. I'm going to take this time to really think about where we're going and what this marriage is all about."

"Are you trying to threaten me?"

"You don't get it, do you? Like I said, I'm going to do a lot of thinking and I suggest you do the same."

"I don't have a problem with you. You have a problem with me, so you need to think, obviously."

"Taylor, we have problems in our relationship. Fractures. And if we don't fix them, it will eventually end."

Taylor was furious, but I promised myself a long time ago not to hold back my feelings or my thoughts for the sake of protecting a woman's emotions. I knew I was suffocating her with my words, but she needed to know that we were losing the connection we once shared. And the saddest part about it: We were only ten months into the marriage. I was at the same checkpoint when I realized my first marriage wouldn't work. Was this my commitment threshold? A slight part of me was bothered by that possibility, but I knew it couldn't be true.

She got out of the bed and walked into the bathroom. I could hear her sniffle, but I had no sympathy for her. She was never around when I needed her. Mrs. Dillon clearly thought my wife was nonexistent, and often I thought she was, too. So it was time she knew what I was feeling. If, after the trip, Clark and I decided to take our relationship further, Taylor would not be blindsided.

It would be in my best interest to prolong my marriage until the election, but it made sense to start planting the seed now. She walked out of the bathroom and said, "Devin,

I wasn't the one that wanted to rush into this marriage. You were."

"We're here now. So, whatchu going to do about it?"

She got in the bed, tossed and turned irritably, covered her head, and went to sleep. I kept looking at TV. I didn't really expect her to willingly discuss our problems. She would have rather ignored them so they wouldn't interrupt her daily agenda.

At times like this, I wondered if this was my punishment for disrespecting my man's wishes. I stared at the basketball game and thought about my boy. Then I would glance at Taylor. Karma had a vendetta against me, and maybe if I made it right with Clark, my future would run smoother.

34

CLARK

Kenneth dropped me off at the airport at four-thirty in the morning. He seemed slightly excited that I was leaving, even leaning in for a kiss when he took my luggage from the trunk. I left my wedding band home because it would be safer there. I wasn't trying to get jacked for a ring that I wasn't sure I'd be wearing much longer. I'd washed my hair and pulled it back into one ponytail. I had on a pair of wide-leg khakis and a lightweight denim button-up, with a white tank top underneath. I swapped my designer shades for a pair of knockoffs. I got my boarding pass and headed to the departure gates. I had a four-hour layover in Miami, then on to my destination.

When the plane landed in Managua, I couldn't wait to see Devin. He told me he'd be standing right outside of customs. It had been a while since I'd been to a Spanish-speaking country and I didn't have the opportunity to brush up on the language.

Finally, after I went through customs and picked up my bags, I walked out of the airport. The heat was smoldering. Cabdrivers screamed "Taxi" from every direction. People asked me questions and I looked at them like I was an alien, completely from another universe and searching for something familiar. My body spun continuously, and I wondered where he was. I began to feel regretful, confused, afraid. I didn't go over the itinerary after Devin said he'd meet me here and I was afraid to pull it out in the crowd. What am I doing here?

Using my hand as a visor, I looked left and right impatiently. Everything was blurry, even my thoughts. My heartbeat thumped slowly and suspiciously. When I saw Devin appear clean and crisp from out of the mist, it felt almost magical. I blushed uncontrollably and all my questions vanished with his presence. So I stood there and Devin walked toward me. He wore a pair of long fatigue shorts, Pumas, a T-shirt, and a baseball cap. He wrapped his arms around me and held me tightly. I said, "I made it."

He grabbed my luggage and said, "I'm happy. I really am."

He started walking, and I followed him to a small airport that would take us to the Corn Islands. Devin explained that the flight didn't technically leave on a schedule. It would leave once they had enough passengers. We laughed about it, because it really didn't matter. It was whatever, and if we had to stay the night in Managua it didn't matter. I was with the person I wanted to see.

We walked into the airport and up to the counter holding hands. Devin was simply good at everything. I watched in awe as he fluently talked to the airline representative. He said something about me, assumingly positive, as the attendant pointed and nodded. I smiled back. Devin told me to get on the scale with my luggage. Suddenly, I began to question this connecting flight.

"This is one of those little tiny planes. Oh, God."

Devin wrapped one arm around me. "If you gotta die, you may as well go in style. On a plane in Nicaragua, headed to the Corn Islands on a mission."

He laughed, but I didn't like the sound of the headline. "Personally, I'd rather not die."

"It's inevitable, though. That's why you have to live for today. *Pura Vida.*" He explained, "Pure Life. It's a common slogan throughout Central America."

I guess that was what made Devin Patterson special. He was multidimensional, a master at most things. And of everything he was, he didn't have an inflated view of himself. He was still simplistic and easygoing. I smiled back. *"Pura Vida."*

"You might want to text someone to let them know you arrived. My cell phone doesn't work well in the islands."

I sent a safe-arrival message to Ms. Teeny and Kenneth. Kenneth responded: GOOD. Teeny responded: HAVE FUN.

When time came to board the plane, I held Devin's hand. He wrapped his arm around my shoulder. We climbed into the little ten-passenger plane. Devin sat by the window and I took the aisle seat. Within minutes we were on the runway. The plane rocked sloppily during takeoff. I crunched Devin's hand. The plane felt extremely unstable. Once up in the air, it fishtailed continuously. While Devin tried to show me sights from the sky, I started singing gospel songs. It got so bad at one point, I was singing, "Yes, Jesus loves me."

Devin looked at me and burst into laughter. "Clark, don't worry. We're going to get there safely. God promised me this election. I can't win if I'm dead."

"Devin, stop joking."

"People that are afraid of death aren't doing what they want to do. You know that. Right?"

"I'm not afraid of dying; I just want it to be an easy death. A plane crash seems like torture before death."

"I'll protect you. I promise. Just relax and enjoy the ride."

When I felt the plane finally descending, I covered my face. My palms were damp and I looked over at Devin and he said, "It wasn't that bad, huh?"

"I guess not."

The plane struggled to balance during landing and I felt like there was a baseball in my throat. I dropped my head in my hands and Devin massaged my neck. Finally, it touched down on the short, asphalt runway, and I kissed Devin. He looked at me. "You still with me, baby?"

I nodded and quickly climbed from the plane. We walked into the miniairport and waited for our bags.

Taxi drivers asked, "You need taxi?"

Devin negotiated a price with one and we headed to the hotel. While we rode, Devin explained that a lot of African settlers came to this part of Nicaragua to escape slavery. They speak a mixture of English Creole and Spanish, so he didn't expect too much of a language barrier.

Devin said, "You used to speak a little Spanish. What happened?"

"If you don't use it, you lose it."

"You haven't lost anything. Nothing."

His eyes scanned me from head to toe. The taxi driver asked, "Honeymoon?"

Devin said, "Yes." Then he looked at me. "A long overdue honeymoon."

I nodded in agreement. Our love was long overdue, and it was unfortunate there were so many obstacles in front of us preventing it. But I planned to live it up while we were thousands of miles away from all the obligations and false commitments.

The taxi pulled over to a small resort at the side of the road. Devin hopped out and I followed. I could see the beach through the walkway. The water crashing up on the shore made me feel good. Devin said, "Welcome to paradise."

"Thank you."

After we checked in, we headed to our cabin-style room. I walked in and the suite was surprisingly beautiful. Dark hardwood floors and furniture, a very large bathroom, a sitting room, and a high-post king-sized bed. Devin sat on the couch and asked me to sit beside him. He said, "We're going to have fun. We'll be at the clinic from nine to twelve each day. Mainly the students will be there. I just came to oversee things."

"The students?"

"Yeah, it's a program for law students interested in politics or community service. A different group each year, so don't worry."

"Devin, I don't know. That's not cool to flaunt me around these students."

"You could be my wife."

"I should be your wife."

He gave me a high five. "Absolutely."

We changed into something more comfortable and headed to the resort bar. Devin purchased a bottle of ron de caña and a bottle of Coke. The young lady at the bar flirted with him. She spoke English, but I could barely understand her. He grabbed my hand to guide me to the cabana on the beach deck.

"What about the drinks?"

"She's going to bring them to us."

"It's not like she has to make it."

"Yeah, I know."

We sat side by side in the brightly colored wooden beach chairs. The sun had just started to go down, and we watched in awe. The water washing up on the rocks beneath us gave the beautiful sunset a melody. The sea met the sky and it seemed like the perfect picture. The beach wasn't loaded with a bunch of people. Aside from one or two other people, it was just Devin and me. When I was done soaking up nature, I looked at Devin and he grabbed my hand.

I said, "Don't you wish life could be so simple?"

"It can be."

He grabbed the side of my chair and pulled me closer to him and began to stroke my hair. Finally, the waitress brought our drinks down, with two glasses of ice. Devin sat up to mix the drinks and handed me one. He'd boasted about how sweet this rum was and how it was like honey. I couldn't dispute his claim. It went down so smoothly you could drink it straight, which Devin did.

By the time the sun was gone, we were in one chair. My back rested on his chest and my hands stroked his legs, while he rubbed my shoulders. We talked about our relationships and how despite being apart, we'd grown together. We weighed the risks, and that night we agreed that we all have a short time on this earth and you may as well follow your heart.

DEVIN

When we arrived at the clinic the next morning, the students were having their introduction briefing. Some had their backpacks. Others appeared to be dressed for the beach. The AIDS Outreach Center was run by Señora Gonzales. She was a middle-aged nurse who decided she had to do something for new mothers living with HIV. And she took what little she had to open up the facility. They didn't have much and survived mainly on donations. She tried to take as many women and children as possible, and often they'd share beds. But she was more concerned with them having food, shelter, and medical care. Love My People volunteers came in to help cook food, wash clothes, and provide Señora Gonzales with any support she needed. Many of the volunteers in my foundation were first-year law students. I designed the program so that students could experience and identify with the people; that way they would be more compelled to fight for injustice around the world after graduation. Many other foundations also supported her with similar programs.

Señora Gonzales and I immediately developed a special bond the first time I came to Nicaragua. She was a petite, dark-skinned woman with steel caps on her teeth, but her motherly spirit was bigger than life. Not that she wasn't thankful for all the help she received, but she was ecstatic to see someone her color running this type of organization. She would encourage me: "Devin, bring more of my color to Nicaragua."

The home sat up on wooden stilts and was constructed of wood and cinder blocks. It was a large home and many of the women had small cots to sleep on. When we walked up the stairs, Clark looked at me with an uncomfortable expression. I put my hand on her back to let her know this was cool. When we walked in, Señora Gonzales said, "Devin, thank you so much. I am so happy to see you."

I gave her a hug, and she quickly turned to Clark. "Oh my, is this your wife, ay?"

"Yes."

"She is beautiful," she said, hugging Clark.

"I smell coco bread, Señora Gonzales."

She pushed me. "You know I made coco bread."

She led us through the open house and briefly introduced us to the women staying there. "These are my ladies. They are about to have a class."

She took the bread out and handed me a warm loaf. I began breaking pieces off and tearing it up. I pointed the loaf at Clark. Initially, she looked like she didn't want to snatch a piece. After she tasted it, she was nearly tackling me for the bread. Then we started talking to the women.

Clark smiled and greeted them. She even had the courtesy to ask them if they wanted to eat some of our bread. Each of them refused, as they were trying to be hospitable. Clark asked their names and held the babies, while Señora Gonzales and I talked about the goals and necessities of the week.

Clark's nose and forehead were moist with sweat, and her

shirt was sticking to her, but she was so relaxed with the women. Although some of the ladies only spoke Spanish, Clark did her best to communicate with them. I loved it.

Señora Gonzales noticed my admiration. She nodded. "A good woman, ay. Take care of her, you know."

"I will," I said, as we headed to the front porch to talk.

"She beautiful. How do you say?" Her eyes rolled in her head, as she tried to remember the cliché. "From the inside out. I don't know if you believe in spirits, but her spirit is pure."

She spoke as if she knew I had conflicted feelings. I nodded. "Yeah, she is pure."

"Good woman is hard to find."

I laughed, but I never doubted that. It was just weird how passionate she seemed about my stand-in wife. She was definitely a deep lady with a lot of wisdom. Maybe she knew more about Clark and me than even we knew.

When the students finished their briefing, I introduced myself to them and spoke with the group leaders. They were being driven around by a van service, and I stressed how important it was for them to stay together. When they all piled into the house, Clark came out. Tears were in her eyes.

"What's up?" I said, rubbing her shoulders.

"It's just so sad. Some of their babies died, or others are waiting to be tested. I mean, it's just so sad."

She tried to hold back tears. When I held her, she let the tears fall and continued, "It takes experiences like this to realize how blessed you are. I was so angry with God because I couldn't have a baby, and there are more problems in the world than the ones we complain about. Some of them have nowhere to go but here. This is the only place they can get health care."

"That's why we're here."

"Devin, I'm so proud of you."

"I'm more proud of you."

We stayed long enough to serve lunch and wash the sheets. Then we left the students to do the rest. Clark and I headed to the beach.

We lay a sheet out on the beach and Clark proceeded to take her shorts and top off, exposing her bikini. Her body looked like a perfectly shaped bottle of honey. She twisted her ponytail up and looped the rubber band around twice so her hair wouldn't be on her neck. She bent over to grab the sunblock from the bag, and I instantly got hard. *It's a shame what this girl does to me*, I thought. I took the lotion from her and put some into my hand and began to rub it on her. She returned the favor. It aroused me and I wanted to feel her that very minute. I told her to get on my back and we ran into the calm water.

There were no high waves, so we were able to walk far out. Once we were away from the shore, I put her in front of me and plunged my tongue in her ear. I reached my hand down her bikini bottom. Her hands held my face and she stared in my eyes. We kissed again. I dove in and pushed her up so that her legs were around my neck. The other people on the beach didn't exist as I pushed my tongue inside of her. I swallowed saltwater along with her sweetness. Finally, I took my dick from my shorts and wrapped her legs around my waist. I tried to glide inside her, but the water interrupted our movement. Finally, once I fought my way inside, her vagina clamped on to me and lubricated enough for us to make it work.

She whispered promises in my ear, and I did the same. Ours lips were glued together and her arms wrapped tightly around my neck. The cool, still water floating around us made me want to stay inside her warm pussy forever. And I nearly did, as it felt like hours passed before I came. She came several times and, finally, we walked out of the water exhausted and fell asleep on the sand.

36

CLARK

By the third day in Nicaragua, I was tempted to build a little hut and run away from it all, just Devin and me. We could leave it all behind for the peace and tranquility of this small island. We'd been just going to the outreach center and to the beach every day. There were no "bright lights, big city" to distract us from each other. All we heard was each other, and most nights we didn't even turn the television on. We loved each other in the rarest form.

As usual, we headed to the clinic after I had my morning coffee. Our driver pulled up at nine o'clock on the dot, and we hopped in the late '90s model Toyota Corolla. The air conditioner blew warm air, and the back window handles were broken. Devin and I both were soaked by the time we arrived, but we giggled the whole ride for no reason.

When we got out of the car, we heard a piercing yell escaping the house. Devin and I looked at each other and instinctively rushed to the house. Some of the students were rushing around, looking for warm towels. My heart dropped. They'd been saying since the day we arrived that Amina was due any day. She was the sweetest, thinnest seventeen-year-old girl that you ever wanted to meet. She had very little education and could speak only a little English, but from the moment we met, she clung to me. I often forced it to the back of my mind that she was dying of AIDS. I wondered how she got it and who gave it to her and why no one was here to take care of her.

The midwife arrived seconds after Devin and I. She put a sheet over Amina and checked her out. She warned Señora Gonzales that the baby was coming. Several people gathered near Amina, and the midwife asked us to back away. Amina was screaming and pointing. I was in the corner praying that everything would work out when Señora Gonzales said, "She wants you over here."

I was shocked. "Me?"

"Yes. Now come here, girl."

I rushed over, and Amina's thin fingers gripped mine tightly. I rubbed her hair to calm her down and began singing to her. Tears rolled from her eyes. After an eternity, the baby came out. She had given birth to a baby boy. The doctor handed him to me first. I cradled him in the thin little blanket he was wrapped in. He looked almost Asian, with a head full of straight, black hair. He was almost too adorable to be real. I stooped down beside Amina. "Your baby."

She wailed like she was still in pain. The midwife told her to calm down while she stitched her back up. Señora Gonzales asked me to walk with her. She explained that after they give birth a lot of the mothers experience some sort of guilt, because they don't know if the baby will be infected or will be able to grow out of it. Tears rolled from my eyes, because I didn't want to imagine this baby could possibly be infected. It was unfair that some of these women didn't have access to medications that would save their babies.

When everything settled, the midwife took a blood sample from the baby and said she would return with the results the next day. Amina lay in her little cot to recover. I pulled a small folding chair beside her bed and stroked her hair while she held the baby.

"His name?"

She smiled and pointed to Devin. *"Como se llama?"*

"Devin."

She nodded anxiously. I pointed to the baby. "His name."

"Si. Es Devin."

I called Devin over to tell him what she wanted to do. He spoke to her in Spanish, trying to confirm that was definitely what she wanted. Señora Gonzales said it was a great idea. Devin was the name, and Amina was happy.

Hours later, Devin and I were headed back to the hotel to get ready for the beach. I walked over to tell Amina that we were leaving. I rubbed her face and tears rolled from her eyes. *"Quiero tu tienes mi hijo. Comprende?"*

By the confused look on my face, she knew I didn't understand. She repeated. Finally, I called Devin over and he said, "She wants you to have her baby." He smiled at me. "She wants you to take her baby to the States."

I was overwhelmed, but I wasn't sure I could make that promise. Not at that very moment, at least. Devin said something else to her and she insisted. Señora Gonzales said something to her and then she turned to me. "Many of these mothers will not see their babies grow up. Amina says when she dies she wants you to take her baby. No need for pressure right now. Think about it. If you like, we will make sure that happens. If the baby is HIV negative."

My eyes shifted from Señora Gonzales to Devin to Amina. I didn't know what I should say. Clearly if Devin and I kept all of our promises, I would have loved to take little Devin home. But what if he stayed with Taylor and I stayed with Kenneth? I wouldn't be able to. I was a stunned deer as everyone flashed their eyes on me. I felt pressured, so I nodded. Amina said, *"Gracias! Gracias!"*

I hugged her again before leaving. It hurt not to know if I could keep my promise, although I felt a strong connection to that baby when I held him. When we sat in the car, I held Devin's hand and he wrapped his free arm around my shoulders.

He said, "We can come back and get Devin after the election. You know?"

"Devin, I'm not sure. What happens if he's positive?"

"Some of the babies are positive for antibodies for a while and they eventually grow out of it. So, they'll keep testing him. Why? Do you want to wait until the results are negative?"

I shrugged. A part of me wanted to take that baby home and love him one way or the other. Then, there was a part of me that felt like adding a baby into this already complicated mess would make things worse. But still another part of me knew I'd made a promise and somehow I had to honor it.

"Are we really going to be together, Devin?"

"Isn't that what we said?"

Devin spoke as if divorce was as simple as one two three, but I had seen Reggie and Sheena's divorce. They had fought over assets, custody, visitation, anything there was to fight over. It took a lot longer than either of them expected. Kenneth and I were so intertwined, and as much as Devin was sure he could do it, I wasn't so sure. The thought of walking into the house and telling Kenneth it was over frightened me. I wasn't sure he'd give in so easily. We always said divorce was not an option. What real grounds did I have to stand on?

Two days later, we got the results. Baby Devin was HIV positive and I found the courage to let Amina know that I wanted to wait until he got stronger before I adopted him. She understood. Señora Gonzales agreed that we should wait. She said you never can tell—either babies grow out of the disease or they die very fast, and she didn't want us to get attached and then lose the baby. Still, the results didn't prevent me from holding baby Devin all day long. He loved to be rocked to sleep and I loved doing so, after Amina fed him.

This was the first evening we didn't watch the sun set on the beach. Instead we went back to our room, showered, and made love. Around nine, we left to sit in the Jacuzzi. On our way, we passed the business center. Devin realized he hadn't checked his e-mail all day, and I'd completely forgotten about mine the entire week. We sat down at neighboring computers. When I opened mine, there were six messages from Teeny and five from Reggie. Each one had a subject heading that frightened me more:

Your Husband Is In Jail.

I will kill him.

Where are you?

Get Home Now.

I stopped breathing. I couldn't move. My brain deadlocked as I read the headline of an article Teeny included in her message: DIRECTOR OF MENTAL HEALTH CENTER ACCUSED OF HAVING A YEARLONG AFFAIR WITH AN UNDERAGE PATIENT.

This wasn't possible. My heart raced and I bit my nails as I scanned the article. Tears fell from my eyes. Kenneth was being falsely accused of having a relationship with a sixteen-year-old in my group home. All of the girls had been placed in other homes until the investigation was over. They couldn't disclose the young lady's name because she was a minor. And the article mentioned his wife being out of the country in an unknown location. I felt like I could faint—and apparently I did, because I awoke to Devin fanning me with a towel.

"Are you okay? What's going on?"

"I need to leave in the morning. I need to change my flight. Oh, my God! My husband is in trouble. One of my girls lied on him, claiming they had a yearlong sexual relationship." I screamed, "I know Kenneth would never do something like that! It's not possible!"

I needed to get home to see who the little heifer was that lied on him. I had to get out of Nicaragua before they tracked me down. Here I was making plans to walk out on him, and he was sitting in jail for someone living in my group home.

I started hyperventilating. Devin rushed out and grabbed me a bottle of water. When a group home gets a record like this one, it's usually over. I would have to reopen under a different name at a different location. God only knew if Kenneth could keep the center open, since we survived mainly on government contracts. Even if the allegations weren't true, which I was positive they weren't, they could still destroy everything we had built. As I expressed all this to Devin, he calmly said, "Let me know what I can do."

"We don't have a savings. We spent it all trying to have a baby. We're broke and we can't afford this. This is going to destroy everyone," I wailed.

There was no doubt in my mind that one of the girls did this to hurt me. There were only two sixteen-year-olds in therapy, Raven and Shatina. I flipped back and forth between the two and decided it could only be Raven. I sat there in anguish, stressed; Devin kindly began searching for flights back for me. He got me on a noon flight out of Managua, and I would arrive in Baltimore around nine in the evening. My bowels were loose, and I had to vomit. Devin held my hand as we walked back to the room. He didn't say much and I didn't need him to. I had to get back home and get Kenneth out of jail.

Reggie's messages stated that he refused to put his house up for a child molester. So, Kenneth had been sitting in jail for two days while Teeny tried to contact me. I felt like I'd betrayed him. I was cuddling in paradise while he was in a hard, cold jail cell. My guts spilled into the toilet. He definitely didn't deserve this. Devin asked, "Is there anything I can do to help?"

I kept saying no, but then I wondered how we planned to pay an attorney. How long would it be before they returned the girls to the group home? I could lose funding. The mortgage on the group home had to be paid.

"I'm going to need some financial help to get through until they bring the girls back."

"I'll transfer money into your account tomorrow. Don't worry. I got your back. Write your routing number and your account number down before you leave."

We turned the lights off and we lay in spoon position silently for hours. I cried and Devin wiped my tears. He was so gentle and understanding. I didn't know how to tell him that I wasn't sure I could break up with Kenneth until this was over. I owed my husband that much. Although he had evolved into an asshole, he was there for me when Devin had shattered my self-esteem. I would be cursed if I walked out now.

In so many words, I told Devin that when we got to the airport. He told me he understood, but it didn't mean it didn't hurt. He kissed me and said, "What if he's guilty?"

The plane was boarding and the attendant rushed me. My mouth hung open. I was appalled. Did he really think I could be married to a man capable of doing that? I pushed him away from me.

He said, "Go ahead, you got to get on the flight. It's okay. You just have misdirected anger."

I backed away from him. If I was angry with anyone, it was myself. I should have never been here, doing this. This was my punishment for disrespecting my vows. I climbed on the small plane and sobbed all the way to Managua. Somehow my life was always the one that got destroyed while Devin's kept on rising.

37

CLARK

There was so much turbulence when we began our descent into Baltimore. My jittery nerves didn't help. With every bump, I gripped the armrest and the couple next to me looked at me like I smelled bad. They had no clue what was going on with me. The second the plane landed, I called my mother.

She answered, "Teeny told me where you were."

"I know."

"So, what do you think?"

"I think that little fast girl is lying."

"I don't know," she said suspiciously.

I expected something different from her. My mother was Kenneth's biggest fan, but the uncertainty in her voice wasn't comforting.

"Why didn't Reggie get him out?"

"Number one, we didn't know where you were or if you already knew something. We just wanted to stay out of it. Reggie went out there and got all of Morgan's clothes. She's going to stay with us when she comes home next week."

My eyes watered again. It was a surprise that I still had tears, because I'd been crying nearly twenty-four hours.

"So you guys think he's guilty."

"Well . . ."

"Ma," I snapped.

"Well . . ."

"You know he would never do that."

"Well . . ."

People getting off the plane stared at me as I yelled into the phone. "Ma, you know Kenneth. He's never touched Morgan. Why would he want to do something like that?"

"Well, Clark. If it looks like dog, barks like a dog, chances are it's not a cat."

I felt dizzy as I stood up to get off. I couldn't believe my ears. So many advisors told me to get boys, because girls used the sexual-abuse thing too much and they could ruin your life. I refused to believe that and got girls anyway. I thought I could help them.

"Ma, let me go. I have to get my bags."

"Clark, just keep your eyes and ears open. You just never know. They don't arrest you unless they have strong evidence."

I hung up the phone. I couldn't take another second of it. Reggie had brainwashed her. I couldn't have been that blind. There was no way I could be married to a predator and not know it.

I called Teeny after I got my bags and headed out of the airport. When I got in the car, I began to be plagued with doubt, too. Teeny told me that Raven claimed that when she visited Kenneth for therapy sessions, they would have sex. It began merely with her giving him oral sex and then progressed to an all-out relationship. He supposedly gave her money to go out, and also bought her clothes.

As she rolled off the allegations, I said, "So what made her tell now?"

Kenneth had to cancel her session and she flipped out on his receptionist, claiming he was her man. The receptionist called the police on Raven, but Kenneth was the one they hauled away. Teeny warned, "You know it's typical for young girls to fall in love with their therapists. Right?"

I nodded, feeling strange.

"I'm thinking she's just obsessed with him. And not only that, Clark, Raven is obsessed with you. You know how she wants everything you have. That includes your man."

My heart plunged. Raven had seen me walk out of the room with Devin at the conference. Could it be that if she thought I was cheating, that would give her full rein on my husband? I started sweating. Just when I'd convinced myself that being true to myself wouldn't kill anyone, here it was my husband was about to lose everything, after years of grinding, after all the blood, sweat, and tears. Guilt consumed me. I had to get him out of jail and hold him until it felt better. This was all my fault.

The next morning, I took the deed to my house to the courthouse, and a few hours later I picked up Kenneth. He hadn't shaved, and he looked like he'd been crying the whole time he was in there. I got out of my car and ran to hug him. This man who never cries, rarely shows emotion, wept on my shoulder.

"Baby," he said.

"I know. I understand."

"I didn't do it. I swear."

That was all I needed to hear. I knew there was no way possible Kenneth could sleep with that on his conscience. "It's okay, baby. Let's go home. I'm here now."

He kissed my cheek. "Thank you so much, Clark. Thank you."

He didn't have to thank me. This was what marriage was about. My plans to run off and leave him high and dry were now a thing of the past. I had to focus on the future of my marriage. This was my obligation and, if nothing more, I vowed to be with him through this.

When we got back home, he wanted to talk about why Raven wanted to hurt him. I'd already concluded all these things. I told him that he didn't have to explain, that I believed him. End of subject.

When I got a private moment, I e-mailed Devin. We were on ice until further notice. I had to handle this situation, and at that moment I wasn't sure I could leave or even that I wanted to.

38

DEVIN

If you love something, don't fuck it up, because you may not ever get it again. Just when I had Clark on the right path, everything blew up. She felt more guilt than question. If this man was a molester, she should have been anxious to get out of the marriage. Yet she couldn't even wrap her mind around the possibility that he could be involved.

Beyond wanting to be Clark's man, I wanted the best for her, too. So I transferred twenty thousand dollars into Clark's bank account. The thanks I got was an e-mail telling me it was possible that our relationship was over. It wasn't as if I could do anything but wait.

By the time I arrived back home, I hadn't heard from Clark and I wondered if I should disrupt my home for something so unstable. When I got off the plane, I decided not to call Taylor. I wasn't sure what angle I was coming from yet. Instead, I sent Clark a text: HOW IS EVERYTHING?

When I sat in the car, I checked my phone and she responded: DEVIN, I LOVE YOU AND I ALWAYS WILL, BUT IT'S JUST NOT OUR TIME RIGHT NOW.

Clark had a way of hitting where it hurt. I was crushed as I reflected on all the plans we had made in Nicaragua, and now it wasn't our time. When the driver pulled up to the house, he got my luggage from the car, and I opened the garage door. Taylor's car was gone, and I was thankful I had a minute to gather my thoughts before I saw her.

I dragged myself into the house and turned on the light. I sat at the island in the kitchen and just stared into space. It was ironic because I was semihappy before Clark appeared, and now everything Taylor did was wrong.

Suddenly, I reverted to my ex–best friend, Jason: *You spoiled-ass, selfish motherfucker. You don't give a shit about anybody, as long as you get what you want.* That shit weighed heavy on me as I reflected on everything, how I'd abruptly left Clark and married Jennifer, how I'd ignored his request and not only dated Taylor but married her. Now I was considering leaving Taylor because the opportunity to be with Clark arose. What the fuck is wrong with me? I banged my fist on the granite countertop.

I looked at my cell phone and I felt like I wanted to call my boy, but I knew it would be the same as the other times I've tried—straight to voice mail. Was Clark really the solution to all the problems in my life? Could it be that the idea of Clark was just something I conjured up in my mind to justify my irrational behavior? Never enough. What if I finally got the chance to have Clark and I still wasn't happy? What then? Could I really afford that risk without looking like a damn loose cannon?

Taylor entered through the side door and startled me. I hadn't even heard the garage door. She said, "Hey, baby."

She hugged me and landed kisses all over me. Something seemed superficial about her love. "I missed you, honey."

That was hard for me to believe, considering she wasn't even home when I arrived. As I battled internally with her, she hugged me again tightly. I slightly pushed her from me. She looked confused. "Baby, don't act like that."

After spending the week with Clark, I knew what I was missing in my relationship. And maybe if she understood what I needed, I could abandon the thought of leaving her for Clark. Especially considering Clark was torn and convinced it wasn't our time. And after the way she bolted out of there, prepared to defend this man against all odds, I wasn't sure she'd ever be ready to let go. Clark was committed, and until someone hurt her she probably would never simply walk out. And I probably wouldn't even want her in that condition, so maybe, I thought, I should just be thankful for what I have.

I looked Taylor in the eye. "If this marriage is going to work, I need some things from you."

Her head snapped back as if she was surprised. I nodded. "Yes, if this marriage is going to work, I need you to be my wife. If I wanted a damn buddy, I would have stayed single. I need you to be supportive. I need you at fund-raising events. I want you to travel with me on my missions. I need you to connect to my emotions."

"What?"

"Taylor, I work with women all the time, and they always want to know where my wife is."

"But you liked that about me, that I never got in your business."

"That was when we were dating, Taylor. You're my wife. You're a part of my business now. Act like it."

She looked like she understood, and I wanted her to say something that made sense. Instead, she hit me with "Are you threatening me?"

I hung my head, because it was clear that words could not explain what I needed. Either it came naturally or it didn't. "No, Taylor I'm not threatening you. I'm pleading with you."

She stared out the patio doors for a few seconds. Finally, she turned to face me. "I'll do my best, Devin."

"That's all I can ask for."

I stood up and she stood up, too. She followed me up the stairs as I took my luggage into the room. When we got into the room, she asked me for a kiss. I gave her a halfhearted peck. She lifted my shirt and kissed on my chest.

"Taylor, stop. I'm tired. I had a long flight."

She pouted, walked into her closet, and changed into her pajamas. I went in the bathroom to brush my teeth and got prepared for bed. As I walked out, Taylor brushed up against me while coming in. She sucked her teeth. I didn't acknowledge her. She was offended, but I was in search of something greater, something to settle the hunger, something that made me feel like I felt when I was with Clark.

39

CLARK

The court date was scheduled for the middle of October. It would be five months of agony before Kenneth cleared his name. The money that Devin gave me wouldn't nearly be enough to carry us through the trial. I didn't know what we were going to do, but whatever had to be done, I guessed we would do it together, because everyone else had incriminated him. Teeny was probably the only person who believed him and that was because she worked with these girls. Like us, she knew they cause these types of scandals for attention. It was too bad that we both suffered. All of Kenneth's contracts had been stripped. He was forced to lay off his entire staff and so was I, because all of the girls had been removed from the home. We had nothing but each other.

Kenneth was talking to me again. He was forced to seek emotional strength in me. So I'd begun to remember why we fell in love again. Our love was different from Devin's and mine, but it was still love. It was that long-term, for-better-or-worse kind of love. I wondered if Devin would have even stayed through all my fertility issues. I wondered if Devin would love me on my bad days. Devin and I have hallucinating, breathtaking, addictive love, but I often wondered if it was real. Could it stand the test of time? I made the decision not to risk my marriage to see. This scandal was simply a wake-up call.

When Mia came home from school, she had already heard bits and pieces from Morgan. She kept asking me if there was something I wanted to say to her and would I tell her when she got home. On the day she arrived, I think both Kenneth and I were nervous. He didn't want to have to tell her and I didn't want her to have only my mother and Reggie's version of the story. It was around eight o'clock in the evening, but the sun hadn't set yet as she pulled up in the driveway, her small car packed to the roof. I stood in the living room, watching her. Her medium-length, dark brown hair was pulled into a short ponytail, and her long, thick brown legs were sticking out of a pair of very short khaki shorts. She wore a red Abercrombie & Fitch T-shirt and a pair of flip-flops. She slouched around to the passenger side, grabbed a large backpack, and headed in through the garage.

I walked through the house and into the kitchen. Kenneth was sitting in the family room, and I let him know she was on her way in. He looked at me like he was helpless, like he didn't know how to begin the conversation. I gave him a confident nod and smirk like I had it. Mia opened the door, and her big brown eyes looked into mine. She wanted to know everything. I gave her a hug and she said, "Hey, Ma."

"Hey, Mia-Mia."

She dropped her bag and went in the family room to hug Kenneth. They embraced for a long time and I heard them mumbling in each other's ears, but I couldn't make out what they were saying. I walked in to sit in the chair opposite the couch where they stood. When they pulled apart, I noticed they both had tears in their eyes.

Kenneth looked at me and I said, "Mia, I know you've heard bits and pieces of things from everybody and I know you just want to know what's going on."

She gave me her infamous *duh* expression, and I continued, "Well, I'm not sure if you remember Raven. She's only been in the group home for about a year and a half."

"Yeah, I know her."

"Well, she's the one. She's the one trying to say that your father molested her."

She looked at Kenneth. "Daddy, why is she saying that?"

"She's sick, Mia. She's a very sick girl. She's bipolar and has a host of other mental issues. I never touched that girl, and Clark knows I never touched her, so we're just going to fight this."

Mia dropped her face in her hands and finally looked up and said, "But it's your word against her word. What if you get wrongly convicted? Morgan told me that they found raunchy text messages between the two of you."

Kenneth's tone elevated. "Mia, look! I have never sent this little girl any text message. If anything, I may have left my cell phone unattended around her and she sent the messages to herself. I don't know."

Mia shrugged and looked at me. "Whatchu think, Ma?"

"I agree. Raven is very sick. She has a very sick obsession. That's what I think."

Mia looked like she trusted us. I walked over to sit beside them. I held both Mia's hand and Kenneth's, and I said, "We'll get through this like a family."

Mia joked, "So, Daddy. You want me to go beat her up?"

We laughed a little, but I knew Mia had no clue about our financial state. When she realized we might need her money from her summer job, which would eliminate her ability to shop, she probably would want to fight Raven.

There was no summer vacation, just Kenneth and me sitting in the house wondering how something so tragic could have wedged its way into our lives. I just wanted the nightmare to be over. Bill collectors had begun to call. Our lives were falling to pieces, one brick at a time. We were forced to put the group home up for sale because there was no way we could continue footing the bill. I prayed that it would sell in time to pay some of our legal fees, but the housing market was horrible. It would probably end up being foreclosed on. Reggie was helping me a lot financially, and I was beginning to feel too dependent. Not to mention, he'd been acting irritated about giving me money, primarily because he questioned Kenneth's innocence.

If my career in human services was over, I had to make some money somehow. I never thought I would have to do it again, but I began putting my résumé back out there for engineering positions. I knew that would pay the bills, but I was afraid that no one would hire me after I'd been out of the field for so long. As August approached, I started desperately posting my résumé on every career Web site available, because if I didn't get a job, we would be on the street by September.

40

DEVIN

A week after I told Taylor what I needed, she woke up and said, "Devin, maybe we should go to counseling. Before you, I hadn't had a real relationship. And I had to put all these things and activities in place so that I could still enjoy single life, and I guess I've never gotten rid of them. I was anxious to get married. But I think we missed a step. I was just becoming good at being a girlfriend, and the next thing I knew, I was a wife."

"Thank you. Do you want your father to do it?"

"Nah, I think another minister would be better."

We had a few sessions with a minister at the church, and he'd confirmed that I wasn't a basket case. Taylor was not being supportive, but it turned out that she resented how supportive her mother had been, sacrificing everything to be the preacher's wife, and Taylor refused to live in her husband's shadow. While I understood her issue, she had to understand this was a different form of support. I wasn't asking her to sit down and shut up; I wanted her beside me. Once we came to that conclusion, she agreed that she would do it.

As the weeks passed, our relationship was growing and I was the front-runner in the election. Thousands of Taylor's father's church members lived in District 4, and the race was scheduled to be a steal. My campaign was heavily funded, and we'd geared up to smoothly transition into the House of Representatives. The first week of August was when most candidates really began to air commercials and make themselves known. We took a head start and began flooding the airwaves on July 28. Everything was coming together.

Nicole had been with me for the entire summer, so I'd been able to spend a lot of quality time with her. It bothered me that she'd told me that she didn't like Taylor. Whenever I asked her why, she'd say, "It's just a feeling."

While it bothered me, it tripped me out at the same time. Nicole was definitely my child, because we acted on feelings and rarely on facts. I'd brushed it off since there was nothing she could pinpoint. I figured she'd grow out of it, assuming maybe it was just a slight rivalry, because Nicole had always been number one and now she shared the spotlight.

I stepped out of the car to grab Nicole from day camp. While I was in there for five short minutes, Curtis called nearly seven times. There was obviously something wrong. When I sat in the car, I called him on the car phone. Without greeting me, he said, "Dawg, tell me you didn't take your mistress to Nicaragua with you."

I looked in the rearview mirror to see if Nicole heard him or even knew what he said. She squinted slightly. Then, my stomach dropped as I pushed the phone button and held my phone to my ear. "What?"

"Ted Denorges is about to run a negative commercial, showing pictures of you and some chick in Nicaragua. Say it isn't so."

I sat in shock and said nothing.

Curtis said, "Devin, please don't tell me you're stupid enough to fuck the whole thing up over a piece of ass."

I felt like a complete asshole. Not only did I not have Clark, I was in jeopardy of blowing this election. No Clark. No Congress. Curtis yelled into the phone, "Say something, man! Shit! I gotta schedule a press conference like now to refute these claims."

Finally, I stepped out of the car. "Man, it wasn't just a piece of ass."

"What the hell was it?"

"I don't know, man."

"Look, you gotta be honest with me."

"Well, it was my old girlfriend and she wanted to come down to help out with the mission."

He chuckled nervously. "Devin, that sounds like bullshit. C'mon man. We're either going to blow this whole thing or we're going to come up with a strategy to combat it."

I huffed and paced in front of the car. Nicole hopped out. "Daddy, are you okay?"

I shooed her back into the car.

"Devin!" Curtis shouted. "What's the deal, man? You seeing the chick or what?"

"I saw her. She went to Nicaragua with me, but we're not seeing each other anymore."

"So it was a one-time thing?"

"Yeah, kinda."

"If you stand before the press with these half-ass answers, you may as well stop campaigning."

"We hung out a few times. I mean, she's married and I'm married. We decided it was best to leave it alone."

"From what I can tell, they don't have an ID on her. She's

wearing sunglasses in most of the photos. Do you think she'll come out?"

"Nah, I doubt it."

"We're going to take the route that you were in Nicaragua on a mission and a volunteer from the States happened to stay in the same resort as you and it was a one-time thing. You and your wife were facing some problems at the time. Okay?"

I kept wiping my face, hoping that somehow this would go away. More than myself, I worried about Clark. She would be shattered with this coming out now. I wondered if I should call her or try to contact her. Just as the thought crossed my mind, Curtis said, "Whatever you do, do not try to contact that chick in any way. No e-mail, no text message, and definitely no phone calls. We want to make sure she stays anonymous."

"I hope so."

"You need to come to the office to check out this commercial."

"I'll be down in a minute."

I wasn't sure I should take Nicole to the house first, because I didn't want to see Taylor before I had all the facts. So Nicole and I headed down to the office. When I walked in, some of the volunteers looked at me with disappointed expressions. I told Nicole to play on one of the computers and headed into Curtis's office. He was shaking his head. The commercial was loaded on his computer.

It opened with me talking about the school system and at-risk kids. Then a voiceover came on stating my slogan: "Devin Patterson, the voice of the people, the voice you can trust."

A cracked image of Taylor and me displayed and quickly

crumbled. Images of Clark and I hugging and kissing in Nicaragua piled rapidly on top of one another with a repetitive photo-snapping sound effect. The voiceover comes back. "How can anyone trust Devin Patterson, when his own wife can't?"

"Paid for by Ted Denorges for Congress. The voice people *should* trust."

That was a low blow, and I couldn't imagine why these images would surface three months later. Who took the pictures? Clark and I intentionally didn't take any pictures. My mind played tricks on me, and I wondered if Clark had a hidden camera and had sold these images.

"Who knew you'd be in Nicaragua? I intentionally told the media you'd be in the Dominican Republic."

I shrugged.

Curtis said, "It had to be someone close to you."

I didn't have any enemies that would want to destroy me in this way. As I sat and thought of the few people who knew where I was, my chest suddenly caved in. "Shawna Dillon had access to the foundation's intranet while we were planning the girls' conference—which would also give her access to the contact information of the student volunteers."

Curtis laughed. "Why would she do that?"

I blew out some hot air. She had probably never come on to him the way she came on to me. The look in her eyes on the day of the conference popped into my mind. And for someone so anxious to be a part of my campaign to simply fall off the face of the earth . . . surely she was involved. I wondered how much she paid the volunteer. I wondered how much they paid for the pictures. Some people will do anything for power, and my heart told me she was that person. Why didn't I listen to myself? I decided not to attempt to convince Curtis, because he'd probably think I was tripping. Not to mention, he was the one who brought her on board. The damage was done and it didn't matter who did it. What could I do to make it right?

"Maybe she didn't. Who knows? Maybe I'm just pulling at strings. What are we going to do?"

Curtis looked at me. "It will start airing at midnight. So I suggest you go home and talk to your wife. The press conference is scheduled for nine. Whatever you gotta do or say to get her here beside you tomorrow morning, do it. Let's go over the story again."

We got the story down. I met her in Nicaragua. My wife and I had a fight prior to leaving. We had a short affair and that was it. I was wrong. My wife and I made up. End of story.

When I walked out of the office, Nicole said, "Daddy, do you plan on feeding me anytime soon?"

I'd completely forgot that I hadn't fed the child. We rolled up to Chick-fil-A. After I ordered her food, she said, "Daddy, do you have a mistress?"

"What is a mistress, Nikki?"

"It's when you have a wife and a girlfriend."

"Who told you that?"

"I watch Lifetime with Mommy," she said.

"No, Nicole. I don't have a mistress," I said, half-laughing.

"Good, because nice guys don't cheat."

I looked at her through the rearview mirror. "Exactly."

When we walked in the house, Taylor had just come in from the hair salon. She wore a pair of plaid shorts and a T-shirt. Her flip-flops clapped on the floor and the happy pace of her steps saddened me. "Hey, honey."

"Taylor, let's go upstairs."

She frowned. She was still working on recognizing my emotions as she said, "Why? Let's chill down here for a minute."

I shifted my weight onto one leg and looked at her. "Taylor, we need to talk."

"A'ight, then," she said with a pout, and winked at Nicole like what's wrong with him. Nicole shrugged.

We headed up the rear staircase and my chest tightened with each step. When I cut the corner to enter the bedroom, Taylor said, "What is wrong with you, Devin?"

I took a deep breath and plopped on the bed, patting the space beside me. Apprehension and suspicion covered her face and I began to speak, "Taylor, you know I was very upset with you before I left for Nicaragua."

"Why you going back to that? We're doing better now."

"We definitely are, but I need to confess something. When I went to Nicaragua, I was really wondering if I wanted this marriage or not."

"I know, you told me." Suddenly, I heard fear in her voice.

"While I was there, I hooked up with a young lady and—"

"Devin, don't tell me you cheated on me."

I stared at the floor. "For that week, I did."

She shoved me and stood up in front of me. She pretended she was crying, but I didn't see any tears. "Devin, how could you do that to me? Why?"

"I was searching for something and I just didn't know how to tell you what I needed from you. When I got back, I felt guilty and I knew I had to tell you what I was feeling. Trust me, I could have just walked out, but I tried to find the words to make this marriage work."

Still, she acted like she was crying. I began to feel if she really loved me, she *would* be crying. I watched as she was tried to force an emotion that just wasn't there. "Devin, it's not fair. Have you talked to her? Who is she?"

"None of that matters. She is no one. It's over and I haven't spoken to her since I left Nicaragua. But someone sold some pictures to Ted Denorges's campaign, and they plan to start running a commercial tomorrow."

Suddenly, the tears she had been summoning fell from her eyes. It wasn't about me; it was the embarrassment that hurt her. I stood up to hug her and she fought me.

"I told you I didn't want you to run for Congress. See, we can't even deal with this in private. Now, everybody knows my husband cheated! Just drop out. Just drop out, Devin!"

I backed away from her. She didn't understand. I was in this thing until the end. It was the perfect out as she saw it, but I thought it was an opportunity to show perseverance. "Taylor, I will not drop out of this race."

"What are you going to do? The whole of DC-Maryland will know about my marriage." She draped the back of her hand over her forehead as if she wanted to faint. Then, she starting pacing. "Devin, if you cheat once, you'll do it again. I can't sit here and take this."

"Taylor, please forgive me. I told you that I didn't have any faith in our marriage when I left for Nicaragua. I'm sorry."

We went over and over the whole story. *Who is she and why did you cheat?* It lasted for almost three hours. Nicole knocked on the door several times to ask if I was okay. Finally, after I apologized and swore on the Bible that the woman was no one, she agreed to go to the press conference. She still wasn't sure if she planned to stay, but she felt she owed me the support.

* * *

We dropped Nicole off at the camp around eight-thirty and headed over to the office. Despite my confusion as to why she wasn't as emotional as other women whose husbands cheated, I was glad that Taylor looked like she hadn't lost a minute of sleep. There were no bags under her eyes and she wore that priceless smile when we entered the office. Curtis looked more stressed than either Taylor or me. That brought me a little bit of humor. We went into Curtis's office, because the press had already begun to arrive. I grabbed Taylor's hand and kissed it. "Thank you."

"Whatever, Devin."

I decided it would be best not to address her opposition. She was here, and that was pretty much all I could ask for. When Curtis came to get us, suddenly my neck cramped up and my hands got clammy. Taylor look at me. "You okay?"

"As long as you're beside me, I'm fine."

Her support kicked into overdrive, as she rubbed my hand and forearm. "You'll get through this."

We walked into the conference room together. I felt stronger with her beside me. We stood at the podium and cameras began to flash. Curtis opened the floor for questions. I followed the script as we planned. My wife and I had been through a difficult period. I had discussed this affair with her months ago and she had forgiven me. After thirty minutes of questions, it was a success. There were no arbitrary questions, and it appeared I'd squashed a lot of speculation. I looked at Curtis and he nodded, acknowledging that we were done. He said, "One last question."

He pointed to a female reporter, and she said, "Mr. Patterson, the young lady in the pictures—Mrs. Clark Anderson-Winston—is it true that you've had a ten-year on-and-off relationship with her?"

Taylor gasped and the shocked expression amplified through the microphone. Cameras snapped in rapid repetition to capture the surprised look on her face and the dumbfounded look on mine. I stumbled over my words. "I, um, I, um—"

Curtis stepped up to the mic before I incriminated myself. "The young lady in the photographs has not yet been identified and out of respect we'd like to leave it that way. Thank you very much. The floor is closed."

Taylor stormed out first. "You're a damn liar. I don't believe you," she screamed loudly as she headed to the front door.

I ran after her. "They don't know what they're talking about."

"They know something. They obviously know something!"

Several reporters and cameramen spilled out of the room, following and filming our tirade. When I realized we had an audience, I stopped in my tracks and watched her rush out the front door. They ran behind her and tried to ask me questions. I looked up and saw Curtis heading to his office. He'd given up, leaving me out there to survive among the sharks. I shoved the reporters out of my way and headed to his office. Taylor had given me all the reason in the world to go off with Clark, but Curtis had done nothing but bust his ass for me this entire campaign. I opened his office door and he stared aimlessly out of the window.

When he saw me, he started shaking his head. "It's over. We blew it."

"It's not over, man. It's just a bump in the road."

He threw a small canister of paper clips against the wall,

probably to avoid banging me in the mouth. "Why the hell didn't you tell your wife everything?"

"Shit, you told me to do what I had to do to get her here. I got her here."

"Now you look like a damn liar. Everyone knows you didn't tell your wife the truth!"

"And so what! People aren't voting for me because I'm faithful. They're voting for me because I'll represent."

"Who are you fooling, man?"

We both were yelling at the top of our lungs. Veins bulged from Curtis's head. I had not only destroyed my dream, I'd destroyed his, too. I took a deep breath, because I couldn't risk losing him, too. "Look, man. We just have to regroup. Even if I have to stand up there as a lying adulterer, we're going all the way."

"Get out of my goddam office."

"Curtis, you're just mad, man. I'm sorry."

"Devin, you're a fuckup. I quit." He pointed to the door. His nostrils flared. "Now, get the hell out my office while I pack my shit."

He was fuming, and his head looked like it would burst if he looked at me any longer. I got up and walked to the door. I rushed outside, prepared to struggle with the media, but they were all gone. I jumped in the car, and not until then did I realize Taylor wasn't in there. I called her over and over again. Still, no answer. I got out and walked around the parking lot. Where the hell did she go?

I sent her a text: WHERE ARE YOU?

She responded: GONE. COURTNEY CAME TO GET ME.

My next call was to Clark, and she didn't answer. I needed to warn her what was about to transpire. I left an urgent message. Then I called Jennifer.

"Jennifer, I need you to come get Nicole."

"You're supposed to bring her back in next week. What are you talking about?"

"Jennifer, I'm in the middle of a political scandal. I don't want Nicole to be in the middle of this."

"What happened?"

I wanted her to stop asking questions and to just come get her. I would explain everything later. But she continued to shout, "Devin, tell me what's going on."

"My opponent is airing a commercial showing pictures of me with another woman and calling me an adulterer."

"Well, are the pictures real?"

I gasped, loudly. "Jennifer!"

"Devin, I just want to know what's going on."

"Yes, Jennifer. They're real. I cheated on Taylor a few months ago, and it has come back to bite me in the ass. Will you come get Nicole for me, please? It's just not the place for her to be right now. I don't want her in the middle of this."

"Devin, I don't believe you. Who were you with?"

"Why does that matter? Don't ask me any more questions. I'm going through enough right now."

"Don't yell at me, Devin."

"Jen, c'mon. I really need you."

"I wouldn't be there for at least three hours, even if I leave now."

"Well leave now and I'll tell you all about it when you get here."

I drove around for a while before I went in the house. When I walked in, I searched the house for Taylor, but she was still missing in action. I left my cell phone on the kitchen table and went downstairs to the home theater to clear my mind. Sitting there in the dark, I yelled loudly. I was regretting everything, leaving Clark, marrying Jennifer, marrying Taylor, thinking I could turn back the hands of time.

41

CLARK

It took about two weeks before employers started calling me back. It seemed like once one company was interested, the interest became contagious. After the first call, I started getting multiple calls a day. Although I was reluctant about returning to the engineering field, I was happy somebody thought I was worthy. I spent several years in a project manager's position before leaving. Considering I've managed a group home for over five years, I guess a good manager is a good manager, despite the field.

So Kenneth and I spent a lot of time in the house fielding calls. The time off and sitting in each other's faces gave us the chance to get to know each other again. He had opened up and became more compassionate. He was now open to adopting. After I told him about the baby in Nicaragua, he promised me that we'd go get him as soon as this case was over. And of course, I'd have to change his name.

I had just made us lunch when my cell phone rang. After I put Kenneth's sandwich on the table, I looked at the phone. *DP* popped up on the screen and my heart sank. I quickly set the phone back down. Kenneth said, "Who is that?"

"Um, I think it's a company."

I wasn't sure why I said that, because my home phone number was on my résumé. He didn't question it, though. When it beeped, signaling a new voice mail, I nearly peed on myself. I missed Devin and I yearned to speak to him, but Kenneth needed me and I had to be here for him.

I put the phone in my sweatpants pocket and went upstairs, telling Kenneth I'd be right back. I rushed into my bedroom and the home phone rang and startled me. I peeped at the caller ID. It was a Prince George's County number, and I assumed it was an employer. I yelled downstairs, "Take a message for me, baby."

I stood in the middle of my bathroom and called my voice mail. "Clark," Devin sighed heavily. "I hate to tell you this because I know you're dealing with your own stuff, but your name was leaked in an attack on me. So just be aware and be careful. Don't admit anything."

He hung up and I was confused. How was my name leaked? What did they know? Oh, my God, how would this affect him? Without thinking, I called him back. Over and over again, his phone continued to go to voice mail. I began to sweat everywhere. It was hot. I fanned myself and paced the bathroom floor. *Please, Devin, call me back.* I needed to hear from him.

My phone rang, and it was another 301 number. I wasn't in the mood to speak to an employer. I was jumpy and anxious to know something. I waited for another five minutes. Finally I cleared my call log, left my phone in the bedroom, and headed back downstairs.

Kenneth stood in the kitchen like he'd seen a ghost. His eyes shot over to the large, sharp knife that I'd just sliced the tomatoes with. Mine followed. I was perplexed. It was as if

I was confronting a stranger. I sensed fear, so stepped back. "What's up, baby?"

His shoulders and chest inflated and he snatched the knife from the counter. He hadn't mumbled a word. I said, "Baby."

Like an angry lion, he charged at me. I rushed to the front door and tried to unlock it. My brain couldn't figure out why he was coming after me, and I yanked at the doorknob. It wouldn't open. I turned to face him, to plead with him. Before I could speak, his hand was around my neck and he lifted me off the floor. I tried prying his hand from my neck. He yelled, "You went to Nicaragua with Devin!"

I tried shaking my head. He said, "Don't fucking play with me, Clark."

He raised the knife and the point headed for my head. My life flashed before my eyes. I saw the knife darting toward me. Then a loud sound of it piercing through the door startled me as I looked at it from the corner of my eye. He let go of my throat and my body dropped to the floor. He yanked the door open and walked out. I got to my feet and hobbled after him. "Kenneth! Kenneth!"

"Go back in the house."

"Baby, please."

I grabbed his arm and he pushed me away, nearly knocking me to the ground. "Leave me the fuck alone."

"Let me explain." He looked at me. I felt his pain. "Please, baby. Let me explain."

He wiped the sweat from his face. "Explain what, Clark? You've been fucking him our entire marriage."

"No, I swear."

"You think I'm supposed to believe you? The goddam

reporter just told me y'all had an on-and-off affair for ten years."

"You have to know that's a lie."

"Why the fuck should I believe you? Tell me that—why the fuck should I believe you?"

I looked him in the eye. "Because I believed you. I never once asked you if what Raven said was true, because I know the man I married. And you should know me."

"Marriage doesn't mean shit to you, Clark."

He headed back toward the house and I stood there and watched him stroll back down the street. Tears rolled down my face. I didn't know what to do or say. I followed him down the street and before I made it to my house, the door slammed. When I tried the door, it was locked. I banged frantically, before realizing that I could just enter the code into the garage. When the door rose, my heart pounded. I wondered if I should go in or just stay on the steps. I didn't have keys or a purse or a phone, but I wasn't sure it was safe to be in there with him alone. I walked back to the front of the house and sat on the steps. My head rested in my hands, and I wondered if I had willed this to happen. I wanted adventure. I wanted exhilaration, but it wasn't worth it. I wanted to go back to a stiff, regular life.

As I sat there, crying uncontrollably, Mia's silver Hyundai Accent swerved into the driveway. She jumped out of the car and ran to me. "Are you okay, Ma? Taliah called me and said y'all were fighting outside."

Taliah was a girl across the street. I was slightly embarrassed, but I couldn't focus on that at the moment.

"What's going on?" Mia asked.

I shook my head. I didn't want to talk about it.

"Did that girl do something else?"

"It was me this time, Mia. It was something I did."

She adjusted her teeny-weeny denim shorts and sat on the brick steps with me. "Whatchu mean? What happened?"

It pained me to say it. I couldn't find the words, so I just shook my head.

"Where's Daddy?"

"He's in there, but he's very angry."

She looped her arm through the Louis Vuitton doctor's bag that I'd handed down to her and stood, pulling her keys out. I jumped up. "Mia, you shouldn't go in there."

"He can't be that angry."

She put her key in the door and I stood behind her. The door swung open and I crept in her shadow. I wanted to be sure the coast was clear. She walked into the family room and called him hesitantly before I peeked around the corner. He had yanked the phone out of the wall. She trotted over to him and I stepped into the kitchen to see his response.

She hugged him. "Daddy, are you okay?"

He wept in her arms, exposing a side of him that I'd never seen. "Mia, my life is fucked up. I don't have anything. I've lost everything."

She kept repeating, "It's okay, Daddy. It's going to be okay."

"We're going to lose our house. I won't be able to pay for you to go to school. We have nothing. All I have is you, Mia."

"Daddy, Mommy's here. She's not going to leave you."

"She's not your damn mother! How many times do I have to tell you that?" he snapped.

My heart shattered and I couldn't believe my ears. I knew he was angry, but the way he said it let me know they'd had this conversation in the past. *Not her mother.* Mia's biological mother left her with Kenneth when Mia was five and went off to marry some guy and then some other guy after that. She had only been a casual presence in Mia's life. From the beginning of our relationship, I had been there day in and day out: her first period, her first boyfriend, her first everything.

I walked closer to him and tears fell from my eyes. "How could you say that?"

The emotion in the room forced Mia to cry, too. "Daddy, please."

"Please nothing. Ask her, Mia. Ask her! Ask her to tell about how she's been fucking somebody else our entire relationship."

She gasped and I looked at her apologetically. "Mia, that's not true."

"Daddy?"

"Check out the *Washington Post*. It's all in the paper today."

Mia glared at me. I shook my head, but her expression told me she believed him. I didn't get the benefit of the doubt she'd given him. I guess blood *was* thicker than water. Kenneth slouched back into his seat and dropped his head in his hands. Mia's deep-set eyes pierced through me. Her chocolate skin was red with anger, as she and I stood face-to-face. She was not my daughter and I was not her mother. I was just a woman who had hurt her father.

"Mia, listen to me. I never meant to hurt him. I love him. We've been having a really hard time and I did something I shouldn't have done."

"What did you do?"

"I had an affair."

"What are y'all doing to each other?" she yelled, as she stormed out of the house in tears.

I went to sit beside Kenneth, rubbed his back, and poured my heart out. "Kenneth, you have to believe me. I never meant to hurt you. This was a one-time thing and I broke it off. I believe in you and I believe in our marriage. You have to know that. You haven't lost everything, because I'm not going anywhere. I'm here for you, Kenneth. I'm here for you."

He leaned back and looked at me and I didn't know how to interpret his expression. Finally, he spoke. "I believe you."

I hugged him tightly and he halfheartedly hugged me back. "We'll get through this. All of this. These things make relationships stronger."

I probably should have packed up and rolled out, but I didn't. His emotions had just gotten the best of him. He would never hit me. It was just what he was dealing with that had forced him into that rage.

I wondered about Devin and how his wife handled the news. If the media were blowing up my phone, surely they were parked outside of his house.

Kenneth stroked my hair. "How did we get here?"

"I don't know."

"I just want it to be like it used to be."

I nodded on his chest. "Me too."

Kenneth was out of control and it was killing him. He'd always been the one with all the answers. Now he was a victim in need of therapy. He was off balance and angry at the world. We turned the television off and lay down on the family room floor in silence, like we were waiting for the earthquake to pass.

42

DEVIN

Jennifer called me three hours and fifteen minutes later. "Devin, do you want me to come to the house?"

"No, there are reporters camped outside. I'll give you directions to the day camp."

"Wow, Devin. It's that bad?"

I laughed it off. "Real bad."

"I'll see you in a minute. Give me the address. I'll plug it into the navigation system."

I felt slightly choked up as I gathered Nicole's things. I owed her a more stable life. This just wasn't fair to anyone. When I pulled from my driveway, reporters snapped pictures of me, and I just couldn't understand why they wouldn't let us deal with this in private.

Curtis called just as I was driving off. "Why the hell haven't you been answering your phone?"

"I thought you quit."

"Man, I'm not going to let you drive off the cliff alone. I believe in you and I'm working with a publicist that's excellent with damage control. Don't talk to any reporters—and more importantly, don't call that woman."

"I won't."

"Let me smooth this situation over."

"I'm sorry, man."

He laughed. "Shit, if you win despite all of this, I can manage any campaign I want."

"Yeah, man. Look on the bright side."

We shared a few laughs in the midst of the turmoil, because at the end of the day, I would either win or lose. Really it was that simple. The press was just a bunch of nosy-ass, inconsiderate-ass people trying to break a bigger story than the next reporter. It had nothing to do with the race or me; it was just a job.

When I pulled into the parking lot of Mitchellville Christian School, Jennifer was sitting in her black Porsche Cayenne, typing on her BlackBerry. I took Nicole's bags from my trunk and walked over to the truck. I tapped on the passenger-side window, and she unlocked the door. I climbed in and she looked at me. Her long, curly, dark brown hair was pulled back into one ponytail. Her pale cheeks were flushed and her large almond eyes dimmed.

"Devin, you'll get through this. You always do."

I often kicked myself for abruptly divorcing her. I blamed her for losing Clark, but it was no one's fault but mine. The least I could say about Jennifer: she was one constant in my life.

"I know. It's just crazy."

"Politics is hard," she said.

"Yeah, I messed up."

"As long as I've known you, I've never known you to be a cheater. You usually walk out before you cheat."

I smiled. "You're right. I've never cheated on anyone until now."

"Why now? In the middle of your campaign."

"It was Clark."

She looked away from me. "Why did I know that?"

"I don't know."

She folded her small lips tightly and shook her head. "While I was driving down here, I told myself that the only woman that could deter you from your path would be Clark."

I looked at her and she looked at me. Tears formed in her eyes. "I'm so sorry, Devin. I was so young and dumb. My parents told me to go to law school and snag the man with the most potential and I did."

"Yo, Jennifer. Don't start blaming yourself for this."

"You had something very special with Clark. You loved her instinctively. You know?"

I took a deep breath. She had summed up those feelings that just wouldn't go away. If I had control, I would have let this shit go a long time ago.

She continued, "Is it over? Is she still married?"

"Yes and yes."

"So, what is Taylor saying?"

"She found out at the press conference that it was Clark, and she pretty much stormed out in tears and hasn't answered her phone since."

"Damn, Devin. I don't know. It's harder for women to get over cheating when they know you really love the other woman."

I leaned my head back on the headrest, ran my hand down my face, and sighed. "I know."

"What do you want?"

"I'm not sure."

"You know what you want. You're just not sure it's the right thing, that's all."

We walked into the camp together. Nicole looked as if she wanted to cry when she saw Jennifer. The look in her eyes upset my stomach, but she was cool enough not to fuss or fight. She looked at me and said, "It's okay, Daddy. I'll see you when you come to New York."

I kissed them both. They headed out of the parking lot, and I was left to sort out my mess.

It wasn't until I walked into the house and saw that Taylor had trash bags full of her things that I half-knew what I wanted. I didn't want her to walk out. Not yet, anyway. We could get over this. I stepped around the bags and rushed through the house.

"Taylor!" I yelled, as I ran upstairs.

She frantically threw clothes and shoes and jewelry in huge trash bags. I looked at her and asked, "What are you doing?"

"What if we were wrong about each other? What if you were really made for me?" she yelled.

"What!"

She hurled a shoe at the closet. "Motherfucker, that's what you said about her the very first day I met you." She shook her head. "I knew then that you weren't over her. And I should have listened to my intuition. I always knew."

"Taylor, there is no way you could have known anything. It was something that happened and was over very shortly after."

She walked to the closet door. "Devin, you may have had a short physical affair with her, but you've had an emotional affair with her for a long time. She's your one that got away, Devin! She's the one that got away!" She started crying. "You never get over that person, and you wait your whole life for them to forgive you. Remember all the talks we had when we first met? They were all about her. You've spent your whole life wanting her forgiveness."

"Taylor, I want *you* to forgive me. I don't want *you* to be the one that got away. Clark is committed to her marriage. You don't have to worry about her. She's not leaving her husband and I have no plans to leave you."

"Devin, I don't want to be second-best. I'm not that girl. I can't stay here. I gotta go," she said, shaking her head. "I'm leaving you."

"You can't just quit on marriage."

"You did before, so why wouldn't you do it again?"

"Because I learned my lesson and I know marriage takes work."

She pushed clothes down in her bag. "What if you found out that Clark left her husband? What would you do?"

I took a deep breath, wishing I could plead the Fifth. When I lifted my head to speak, she looked disappointed and said, "Exactly what I thought."

I wanted to tell her she was wrong. I wanted to console her, but all I could think about was all the plans Clark and I had made in Nicaragua, and how we both had settled for the next best thing. It was for a good reason, but, nonetheless, neither of us could have what we really wanted. I stood there, feeling like a damn failure.

She tied the bag and bumped me as she passed. "I'll be staying with Courtney."

I walked behind her. "Are you sure you want to do this?"

"Are you sure you *don't* want me to do this?"

"Yes."

She stopped at the bottom of the stairs and looked me in the eye. "No, you're not."

My wife piled her bags in her car and pulled off. I stood

in the garage, embarrassed and downright tired. As I walked into the house, the melody to Babyface's "What If" played in my head. I poured a glass of Crown Royal Reserve and the words of the song got louder: *What if we were wrong about each other? What if you were really made for me?*

43

DEVIN

Curtis nearly flipped when I told him that Taylor had walked out. He frowned. "Man, tell her she's gotta come home. We need her by your side."

I shrugged. "Man, what am I going to do? Force her to stay?"

"Do *something*, man. Why are you so nonchalant about this?"

"Man, let's just focus on what we got to focus on."

"Fool, do you realize that the majority of your vote are church folk, and her father has an influence on all the churches in the damn district?"

"So you think if she stays with me, they'll vote for me?"

"Your wife can make you or break you."

It had been nearly twenty-four hours since I spoke to Taylor. The one thing I knew for sure was that when her mind was made up, there was no changing. Curtis urged me to remove emotion from this matter and focus on the image. He basically said, "Who gives a shit if you're in love with the other woman? For the sake of this campaign, you are the doting husband that made a damn mistake."

I listened intently to his advice and I partially agreed.

Curtis may have been short with me, but he was relentless. Damn if my emotions would sabotage his plans. After I didn't respond to some of his advice, he snapped, "Don't act like a bitch, Devin. Handle your business. Go get your damn wife back."

I wondered if Curtis had to ever go get anyone back after they'd been publicly disgraced. This shit was no trivial task, but clearly something had to be done. Otherwise, I would have wasted everyone's time and effort, and my parents' money.

When I left the campaign office, I went to Taylor's father's church. It was the middle of the day and he was usually there. When I pulled up and saw his Cadillac outside, I suddenly got cold feet. Pastor Jabowski did not marry divorced people, but because it was Taylor, he had performed our ceremony. Initially, he refused, but his wife made him do it. She told him that his daughter had to be an exception to the rule. Before we got married, he asked me over and over was I sure about this, was I sure about Taylor? And I promised this 350-pound man that I would take care of his daughter until death. He was the only person Taylor listened to, and if I was going to make this right, I had to go through him.

I knocked on the door of the executive offices and, surprisingly, Pastor Jabowski answered. My heart dropped. I half-smiled at the wide, dark-skinned man standing stoically in front of me before reaching out to shake his hand. He gripped my hand tighter than usual, like he wanted to crush my fingers. "Devin," he greeted me.

"Bishop."

He turned to walk toward his office and I followed. He said, "I was wondering if you'd come talk to me."

"Yeah, I didn't know where else to turn."

He held the door to his office open and I walked in to sit down. After he sat in his office chair, he removed his glasses and wiped the invisible sweat from his wide nose. His expression lacked compassion, but could I really blame him? I'd hurt his daughter. Still, he was a man and I had to appeal to his manhood. He stroked his mixed-gray goatee impatiently.

"How many times did I ask you were you ready to marry my daughter?"

"A lot."

"Why do you think I asked you so many times?"

"You just wanted to be sure."

He chuckled. "Is that what you really think?"

"I don't know. I guess."

"Actually, this marriage never sat right with my spirit. My wife swore you were the one she prayed for, but I didn't think so. God has never lied to me, because I know His voice. You know, women can guide you in the wrong direction, in a different direction than you heard your Father tell you to go."

"Bishop, listen. I made a mistake, and you know for yourself Taylor and I got counseling after that affair. I knew that cheating wasn't the answer and I wanted to make it right. I'm still human."

"That's a cop-out, Devin. I don't entertain folly. Being human means you have a conscience and you have reason. You know when you're doing wrong. There is no logical excuse to go lay up with another woman. You seek counseling before you resort to that, and men of the world resort to that alternative. Weak men seek that alternative. Men who don't have the words to express their needs and desires to their wives resort to that. Which man are you?"

I smirked, because I didn't identify with any of the above.

"Tell me. Which one are you? Weak, worldly, or word-less?"

Man, this appeared to be going nowhere. I readjusted in my seat and mumbled, "I guess worldly."

He nodded, as if he agreed. "So what do you want from me, worldly man? Are you seeking religious counsel, or do you just want me to tell you, 'I understand, people make mistakes'?"

"Actually I was hoping that you and Mrs. Jabowski would talk to Taylor about working it out."

"And why would I tell my daughter a silly thing like that?" He laughed.

"Because I am her husband."

He rested back in his large executive chair, and springs that had been pushed to the limit screeched. "Really?" he said sarcastically. "Well, Devin, nothing in the Bible is new. And the answers are all in here. Women are instructed to stay with their husbands no matter what."

"I know, and I—"

He interjected, "But the one thing she is allowed to divorce for is adultery. Don't you think what you did was adultery?"

"Yes, sir."

"And ironically, I don't think you're a worldly man. I think you're a wordless man. You speak so eloquently on the political scene. You even have me convinced. You can communicate on concrete topics, but emotions are too intangible for you. You can't measure, divide, or define them, and you struggle with that. Until you get that right, you'll be skipping from one marriage to another."

I hated to think that I was that person. I'd always been able to express myself. This was about regret and less about communication. But how could I tell him how much I loved this other woman?

"Bishop, I'm telling you, I love Taylor and we were having problems and I took the wrong approach. And no, I didn't get counseling beforehand and I should have. Unfortunately, I didn't. I know better now, and since we had counseling our marriage was better until this came up. You know?"

"Look, I advised Taylor not to marry you. Number one, you didn't come through me first. Number two, like I told you, I didn't feel it. Still don't, but Taylor has always done it her way. Since I never blessed the marriage from the beginning, I don't think it's my place to get it right. It's yours. I'm sure you know where to find her over in North East."

I appreciated his little bit of help. He was trying to let me know she was with Courtney, though I already knew that. When I stood up to shake his hand, he stood, too.

"Thanks for your help, Bishop Jabowski."

"I'll pray about this and see how God leads my spirit." He walked around the desk and opened the door. "I let my Father tell me what I should and shouldn't do. So you never know, He may tell me I'm trippin'."

I nodded irritably, because I wasn't going to get anxious about the possibility only to be disappointed. He patted my back. "All right, Mr. Congressman."

With a smile, I said, "Yeah, thanks a lot."

When I left the church, I considered heading to Courtney's house. Instead, I headed home. Taylor would call when she was ready. I decided I should stop harassing her. It wasn't getting me anywhere. I was out of get-her-back tricks. This shit was for the birds. One thing I did agree with Bishop

Jabowski about was that cheating was for weak men. Damn if I have the energy to convince a woman to take me back.

Seven hours later, I sat in the family room, letting the television entertain me, eating a peanut butter and jelly sandwich, flipping through my iPod, blasting all the old-school songs that reminded me of Clark through the speakers. Sisqó's song, "Incomplete." His voice elevated, and I felt emotional as he yelled, "Without ya, girl. Without ya, girl."

When the song ended, I heard Taylor's footsteps. "Devin, you're pitiful."

I looked up to see her standing poised and unemotional in the kitchen. She didn't look like she had lost any sleep. In fact, she appeared relieved. God was on my side and had advised Bishop Jabowski to talk to her.

I stood up and walked toward her. "Thank you for coming here, Taylor."

"I don't know why you're thanking me. I came to get the rest of my stuff."

I reached out for her arm and she pulled away. As she backed up, I took several steps toward her. "Taylor, listen. You didn't have to move all of your things out of this house. You can stay here. I'll move."

"Why would I want to stay here? Why? I don't need this big house just for me. This is your house. I don't want any part of it, any part of the lie."

"I never lied to you."

She smirked. "You're absolutely right. You never lied. I lied to myself. You told me what you were, who you loved, and I told myself that being with me would help you get over her."

"So what are we going to do?"

" 'We' are no longer an item. I want out."

We now stood on opposing sides of the kitchen island, debating our cases. "Are you sure?" I asked.

"I'm positive."

"So after one mistake, it's just over."

"Baby, it's not one mistake. You don't get it, do you? You have a problem with me. You're always complaining that I don't show you enough attention. I don't help you. I don't rub your back when you get home. And I'm trying my best and still you cheat. Maybe I'm not what you need. Maybe she is."

"Taylor—"

"And maybe you're not what I need. I'm tired of thinking. I'm tired of trying. You've cheated on me, all of this, in the first year of marriage. I will not sit around for years and let you destroy my self-esteem to the point I just accept this kind of shit."

My shoulders sagged, and she continued, "I won't do it. I just won't do it. If I'm not what you need, let me get back on the market while I'm still young enough to snag something else or before you get me knocked up."

"It's that easy for you?"

"Wasn't it easy for you to be all up in Clark's face? It's just that easy for me to walk out."

"Taylor, I need you."

She shifted her weight and rolled her eyes. After taking several deep breaths, she said, "Do you need me because you love me, or do you need me for your campaign to front as if I care?"

I looked at her. I considered lying, but at the risk of being smacked, I said, "I love you, I do. But I'll be very honest, I don't know about the future of our marriage. We have a lot of structural problems. I mean, anytime you marry someone as fast as we got married, you'll have those problems, and it takes a lot of hard work to make it right. I just don't know, but right now a divorce would not look good. I'll lose this race if you leave me."

"You know, Courtney and I have gone back and forth about this. She actually told me I should support."

"She did?"

"When I look at you, Devin, I see myself a few years ago. I know how it is, wanting someone that you hurt to forgive you. You just want one more chance with them to make it right. I know how strong that desire can be. You end up abandoning all your morals just to correct one mistake. It hurts to be the girl on the other side of the game, and I hate—I mean, I despise the way you made me feel. But at the same time, I understand everything you're feeling. And that's why I can't take you back. I know where your heart is, and I know that I'm worth more than second place."

My mouth hung open. She smiled, "Fix your face, because I plan to support you and I don't know why. I just feel it's the right thing to do."

"Are you serious?"

"Yes, I'm serious. Courtney and I talked all night and we both concluded you're a good person in a bad situation. If I hadn't been through this before myself, it probably would be harder for me to understand."

"Thank you."

"You better thank Courtney. This is what she told me I should say."

I smiled. "Are you serious?"

"Yeah, if it wasn't for Courtney, I would have probably burned the house down."

"Tell Courtney that I really appreciate her."

"She really believes you can win this election, and she didn't want this to ruin your political future. I told her I'd only do it if you were honest with me and if you could look me in the eye and tell me that you needed me to win." She clapped. "So, Congressman Patterson, you passed the test. Any woman can respect the truth."

I wanted to run to Courtney's house and shower her with gifts. She continued, "And not to mention, I can support you now that I don't have to be the doting, humble wife."

"That's busted."

"Devin, let's be real. You sprung everything on me so fast. One day we were dating, the next day we were married, the day after that we were a public power couple. I mean, I was just overwhelmed."

"So you feel like I pressured you."

"No, you shocked me. I didn't expect you to ask me so soon, but I'd been on the market too long to say no, and I loved you, but I thought it was fast."

"So we were set for failure."

"Not necessarily. I mean, when we got married, there were no problems. You had no demands. You were partially in New York, but when this became every day, all day, your needs took precedence, and I found myself feeling pressured and overwhelmed and forced to be something that I didn't want to be."

"A wife?"

"No, Devin. A wife in the limelight."

"I told you I wanted to be a politician."

"I thought you'd change you mind."

I laughed. "So you got bamboozled?"

"Basically. And I didn't have the heart to just walk out

because of that. I tried to do better. I really did. And it's crazy because a part of me wanted you to win, because I care about you. But the selfish side of me hoped you wouldn't so we wouldn't have to live under a microscope."

"I feel you."

She walked around the island and sat on one of the bar stools. "And ever since you put in your application to run, I've been complaining about living under the damn microscope. What the hell would make you think you could get away with cheating?"

"I don't know. I really don't know."

"Devin, that wasn't smart at all. Actually, it was quite dumb."

"Who you telling?"

"Well, I got your back. I'll be by your side until we get you into the House of Representatives."

"Can I get a hug?"

She stood and reached out her arms. "Of course you can."

We held each other tightly and rocked side to side. "Taylor J, you're one in a million."

She pulled away. "I know."

"You're a trip."

"No. I'm just confident."

"And you should be."

If nothing else, I knew I wasn't too wrong about Taylor. She just wasn't really interested in being a politician's wife. After this big scandal, I wasn't sure I blamed her. Unfortunately, my desire to be a politician hadn't changed, so maybe I'd see TJ next lifetime.

I poured us each a glass of wine, and we ended up knocking out a bottle and a half before nine o'clock. She told me she was leaving because she didn't want us to get into a compromising situation, but I couldn't let her drive like that. So we lay together fully clothed in the bedroom. She told me that I should go get Clark and I told her that would never happen. And, surprisingly, she slurred, "And you need to call Jason."

It was weird that she mentioned him, because this week's events had me thinking a lot about that expression on his face when I slammed the door. It was a look of hate, almost as if he damned my existence. Maybe his wish came true.

44

CLARK

One split second can change your entire life. Finally, after about a month, the phone calls about Devin stopped. Each time the phone rang, I was reminded of Devin and how happy I had been with him. My heart would flutter the same way it did when I was with him. So I often just took the phone off the hook. I didn't need those feelings corrupting me. I just wanted to forget they ever existed.

The trial was approaching and I had to focus on clearing Kenneth's name. I was working every day, and the tension in my home had increased, because I would come home groggy and tired. I wasn't cooking dinner and he wasn't used to it. He was stressed that this little girl had destroyed our lives. He promised never to work with troubled kids again. So he'd flip back and forth on whether we could really adopt. What I knew for sure was that I had no money or plans to try fertility again.

When I got the job, I didn't expect to despise it so much. I hadn't worked in the corporate world in so long, and I immediately understood why. I missed my connection with people. I missed making a difference in someone's life. Nothing mattered to me here. All the systems could have crashed and I

wouldn't have cared. I should have showed a little more interest, but I just couldn't. It was like there was so much more
to do. I couldn't wait until the trial was over and I could get
my group home back.

I sat at work, bored, so I decided to surf the Internet. For
some strange reason, I looked for articles on the scandal with
Devin and me. I gazed at the pictures on my screen; Devin
and I looked so happy. I shook my head, wishing things
could be different. Then I found recent pictures of him and
his wife. They were working things out. Trying to get the
bitterness off my chest, I closed the browser window. Then I
decided to sync my BlackBerry calendar onto my work computer. The progress status bar popped up for each component. For some strange reason, maybe just for entertainment,
I started looking at my scheduled task. I reminisced on having meaningful things to do with my day instead of sitting
in a damn cubicle all day and going home.

Suddenly, a date from nearly eight months ago stood out.
Kenneth came in at 3 a.m. My heart sank. Could that have
been the same date that Raven claimed they went to Atlantic
City? I shook my head. Why was I tripping? How had I let
these allegations start making me doubt him? I called Kenneth's attorney, but he didn't have any exact dates. Raven had
just rattled off a bunch of fictitious or fantasized events. My
stomach began to ball in knots and I had to pee. Maybe the
boredom had gotten the best of me. I couldn't allow myself
to believe this bullshit.

I scanned my calendar day by day, searching for any in-
consistencies, scratching my brain, wondering where all this
uncertainty stemmed from. It had been months since she
had made the claims, but I never once questioned him. Why
today? Why was I feeling a pit in my belly? I rushed to the

bathroom. Quickly covering the seat, I plopped down and tears rolled from my eyes. Was this conflict stemming from the picture I saw of Devin and his wife? Did I inadvertently want Kenneth to be guilty so I could run off with Devin? I just wasn't sure. Devin and his wife looked in love to me. My head was pounding, my heart was racing, and I couldn't make sense of it. The trial began in seven days and I wasn't sure I wanted to sit there and listen to all the evidence.

I cried out loud, because it hurt. Everything was just wrong. I wasn't happy about my situation. I just wanted to run away and forget about everything. To hell with the house and everything. Just go. Just run. I sat on the toilet losing my mind when I heard someone come in. I wiped my tears and tried to get it together. *If there is something to be known, Lord, please let me discover it before the trial.* I couldn't be publicly disgraced twice in less than a year.

I went home and Kenneth wasn't there. He'd gone fishing on the Eastern Shore because he claimed he needed to free his mind. I walked into the house on a mission. I rummaged through his office drawers, looking at credit card bills and dates. Then I moved to the coat closet, searching all of his pockets and even checking his inner soles. I just felt like something was calling my name. I went upstairs and began pulling his suit jackets from the rack. I went through all his pockets. My heart broke into a million pieces and I couldn't believe my eyes when I pulled a pair of pink lace panties from a pocket and the crotch was crusted with bodily fluids. "No!"

I had bought several of the girls similar panties for Christmas. I knew they were hers.

I frantically ran out of the room and down the stairs. I paced the floor, because I didn't know what I could do with this. I knew I couldn't stay bottled up in that house until he got home. I rushed out and hopped into my car, because I was going to wherever he was. I called him and I called him until he finally answered.

"Kenneth, you fucked her."

"Clark, what's wrong with you?"

My mind raced. "You fucked that little girl. I know you did."

"Calm down, baby."

"I'm not your baby." I held the panties balled in my hand. I wasn't even conscious of the fact that they were contaminated with someone else's bodily fluids. "Who's fucking panties are these? Whose fucking panties are these?"

He calmly said, "Clark, I think you're having anxiety again."

"Fuck you. Don't try to preach that shit to me."

I was angry. I was mad. I felt betrayed. Raven was no longer a disturbed teenager. She was my husband's mistress. I couldn't understand. My heart didn't understand. Why would he want a child? Then I began to think like Reggie. I slammed on the brakes in the middle of the street and headed toward my brother's house. I didn't want to be in that house with him if he was a child molester.

I rushed into the house, crying. I was nearly hyperventilating as I told my mother what I found. She said, "Are you sure they are Raven's?"

"I'm positive, Ma. I bought the panties myself."

"What are you going to do?"

"I don't know, but I don't want to see him. I might kill him."

"Clark, don't talk like that. You need to stay here with us until the trial is over."

I'd been fooled. I'd been played and I should have known. I let guilt blind me. Because of what I had done, I thought Raven was just trying to hurt me. I felt sorry for her. I wanted to find her and apologize for what he'd done to her. I didn't know how to go on with a molester as a husband.

Ms. Teeny came over to Reggie's house and all of us sat there, backtracking and wondering how long it had been and how we'd been so careless. I felt the system had failed Raven. I had failed her and I had failed myself.

45

CLARK

Kenneth pleaded his ignorance up until the day of the trial. Mia called me a million times asking me how could I abandon her father when he needed me most. Ms. Teeny and I showed up at court together. Mia had driven down from school, and she was right there by her father's side.

I looked at him sitting there, defending his name. Several of his employees took the stand to attest that he was a good man and could have never harmed this little girl. But when they were cross-examined and asked about the nature of his relationship with Raven, they all suggested that it was weird. My heart was pounding throughout all the testimonies. I'd already assumed his guilt, but I hoped I was wrong, just for my sanity. If I judged Kenneth wrong, it was possible that I was just a bad judge of character. I beat myself up as I tried to understand how this could happen under my nose.

Raven glanced back at me and my eyes caught her eyes. She looked like she wanted me to save her from all of this, like she wished she hadn't said anything. Who knew where she was living now? I wanted to give her a hug.

When I took the stand, the defense attorney asked me questions about Kenneth's character. Though I was convinced he'd done this, I answered honestly. Basically, I let them know he was a good man and a good father, and he believed in the overall good of people. When I was cross-examined, the attorney made me question everything I thought I knew about Kenneth, even suggesting that Kenneth preyed on me when I was his patient. He made him out to be this monster who blew his top when he didn't get his way. I sat there wondering if I'd been married to a man with multiple personalities. I reflected on our relationship. I was so vulnerable and needy when we met that I did whatever Kenneth wanted me to do. I thought he was so smart that I could follow him anywhere. It wasn't until I started standing up for my rights that I noticed a change. Kenneth hadn't changed. I had, and it explained why he would deal with this little girl. He had a need to control his relationship. The prosecutor painted me to be one of his victims, and I stepped off the stand convinced that she was right.

When Raven took the stand, Kenneth had a nonchalant expression on his face. He looked in a different direction as she spoke. After she stated her name, she began to cry. She was an open book, and the emotions that she displayed on that stand confirmed there was something between them. She even shouted out, "He told me he loved me. You told me you loved me."

She wept loudly as she tried to get Kenneth to look at her. His reluctance to face her confirmed my suspicion. The pain in her voice shattered me, and I broke down as she went into vivid detail about their relationship. She opened her diary and read the dates and times they had sex. And, the most hurtful news of all, she claimed that he told her that she was more woman than his wife, because I couldn't have kids.

Ms. Teeny wrapped her arm around me and I cried on her

shoulder. I had heard enough. I owed him nothing else. There was no other way Raven could have known this. I didn't care if he rotted in jail. Still, it was technically his word against her word. To seal the case, the prosecutor read a few text messages from the transcript. She stated the dates and times. There is no way Raven could have been sending messages to herself from Kenneth's phone at the stated times. I felt like I had diarrhea, because the wording was so familiar, so Kenneth. He was telling her that he loved her and when she was eighteen, he planned to take care of her. Teeny looked at me and her eyes were watery, but I was just stunned. Finally, we decided it was best to leave the courtroom. Neither of us could take it anymore.

The jury deliberated for less than an hour before they returned with their verdict. The judge ordered that Kenneth go to jail while awaiting sentencing. He would not be returning home until it was all over.

We went straight to my house, only to discover that he'd changed all the locks. Teeny called a locksmith and he opened the house up for me. I went in there and packed up all of his shit. Mia could stay with me as long as she wanted, but I wanted every other memory of Kenneth out of my house. I wished I would have stayed in Nicaragua and left his ass in jail. Now it was too late. I'd messed this thing up big-time.

Morgan called Mia and she claimed she didn't want to see me. She asked Morgan to meet her at the house so that she could get all of her things. She was driving back to school and she didn't plan to ever come back to Maryland again. My motherly instinct kicked in and I called her repeatedly, but she didn't answer.

*   *   *

Kenneth was sentenced to three years and would likely serve a lot less than that. I went to visit Kenneth one time with divorce papers in hand. There wasn't really a whole lot I needed to talk about. When he came out to the visiting room, his head hung down. I held mine high.

He sat in front of me and thanked me for coming. I said, "Don't thank me. I'm here to handle business."

"Clark, I'm sorry."

"It doesn't matter. You're sick."

"I've been a therapist for twelve years and I have never dealt with anyone underage."

"Why Raven?"

He took a deep breath. "Clark, you have to believe me. She was so aggressive, and I guess I was just being weak. We were having problems and it was just easy. I'm stupid."

"I'm glad you know that. You're stupid as shit. I just came here to give you these divorce papers. If you want to contest it, they'll bring you to court. But hopefully, you're not even considering that."

"No, I'm not. All I want is that you will take care of my Mia."

I shrugged. "Mia hasn't answered my calls. She's angry with me because she thinks I betrayed you."

I felt sorry for him, but I didn't know what I could do to help him. It was over. I stood and he apologized again. I walked out and cried my eyes out. I was on my own again and my marriage was a big joke. I never wanted to do it again. I didn't know if anyone was worthy of my trust.

46

✦

DEVIN

As the days before the general election approached, I asked
Jennifer to bring Nicole down so she could be a part of the
momentous occasion, win or lose. I wanted my parents, Jennifer, Nicole, and Taylor beside me. It would have been too
much to ask for Clark, but deep down I yearned for her to
be there, too. Jennifer and her husband, Aaron, came in on
Friday night. My parents flew in on Thursday night. I hired
a chef to prepare meals for the weekend.

My mother had always been a fan of Jennifer's and if she'd
had it her way, we would still be together. They sat at the
table on Friday night, breaking down my mistakes and how
I'd always loved Clark for some strange reason. Over the past
few months, I had become a love cynic.

Taylor and Courtney waltzed in around eight. By that time
the chef was serving up his appetizers. Taylor gave hugs as
she chomped on the seared scallops. It was her favorite. She
beamed and everyone was glad to see her; glad that she was
such a good woman. If she were egotistical, even if she didn't
want me, she could have made me suffer for my indiscre-
tions. I loved her for that, and so for many days I wondered if
she would reconsider being with a politician. But ever since

we'd been apart, she looked like a freed bird. I think Taylor thought she wanted to be married, but she was a single girl at heart. I used to think it was cute that after we got married, she still called me her boyfriend, but I think that was all Taylor ever wanted.

On Saturday, we held a rally. My complex family gathered. Taylor spoke a little about the man I was and how I shouldn't be judged by my mistakes but rather my sacrifices. She moved the crowd. Her speech was tear-jerking and powerful. I watched in awe. She probably would be a great politician's wife. Finally, I stepped up to the podium and rambled off my plans and promises. People cheered. They believed in what I had to offer.

The same chain of events took place the next day at Taylor's father's church. I was slightly nervous about speaking there. Initially, he told Taylor it wasn't appropriate for him to support an adulterer. That would give his members the wrong message. She had a way with her father; she was the one of his three daughters who wasn't scared to stand up to his reign. Before long, he agreed.

Taylor stood before the congregation and talked a little about herself and how she'd done some things; but that churches should embrace sinners, not shun them away. "It's about forgiveness and love. It's not about who's right and who's wrong. Good people do wrong things, just as bad people do good things. This man"—she smiled at me—"is a good man. The voice of the people, Mr. Devin Patterson."

She got a standing ovation and I had to calm the crowd as I stepped up to speak. Her words were fire and she didn't even know. She was clearly her father's daughter. I stood at the podium clapping while watching her take her seat. A fleeting thought passed: *Maybe if I lost we could start dating again*. Taylor was convinced that I was worth nothing to no one except Clark. I stood up and greeted the congregation. My eyes scanned the church, trying to connect with them. My words disappeared when I saw Jason in the crowd. I smiled at him and I looked back at Taylor to see if she'd seen him. She clapped anxiously. I felt empowered and at peace. At least my life had returned to some state of normalcy. I wasn't sure what inspired Jason to come through, but that was my boy and I wanted to apologize for stealing the girl he loved. I was inconsiderate, which was why Taylor and I weren't together now. His presence damn near brought a tear to my eye, but as Taylor would say, *I'm too cool for that*.

"Thank you for giving me the opportunity to speak to you today. You can hear from me and not my opponent who I am. You get a chance to connect with me and not with the naysayer message. I am a man. Not just any man, one who believes in justice and prosperity for all mankind, especially my kind."

The church members nodded and clapped. I looked at my mother, who often felt my blackness was too intense and I should tone it down some. My purpose on this earth was to change things for my people, and why should I try to disguise that? I was proud, and I injected pride in the church as people stood on their feet, holding on to my words and my plans. By the time I sat down, I was sure that I had sealed the election. Bishop Jabowski's sermon was the icing on the cake. *The Chosen One*. I could go home and rest and enjoy my family.

When the service was over, Bishop Jabowski prayed over me. He prayed that my scars would be healed and I could go on and live my purpose without all of the demons that possessed me. He spoke as if I was wicked. Damn, I was just unlucky in love. I wasn't the devil. Still, I thanked him and walked into the vestibule where they had set up a table for me.

People came up to me to talk and shake my hand. Some even asked for my autograph, and a few of the younger women slipped me their numbers. Why do chicks love bad boys? Didn't they see how much trouble I was in for chasing ass? Unfortunately, they were the furthest things from my mind, so that was a wasted effort. I had to get my life in order, and I didn't plan to mask things with another woman. I never believed in piling problems on top of problems. When I looked up and saw Jason, I walked around the table to shake my man's hand.

"Whatchu doing here, man?"

He shrugged and with a silly grin said, "I'm still registered to vote in this district."

"Yo, that's why you my man."

"I just wanted to say the way I carried things was real busted."

"Naw, dawg. That was me. I should have left her completely alone when you asked me to, but like you said, I'm selfish." I laughed. "I *was* selfish."

He smirked. "Whatever, yo."

"For real, man." Suddenly, it dawned on me that he probably didn't know. "Man, you know Taylor and I aren't together anymore. She just has my back through this. You know."

"Yeah, I heard all about you and Clark." My chin drooped as I nodded. "What's up with that?" he said anxiously.

"Back with her husband."

"Whoa. Yeah, sometimes it's like that. You ain't always going to be with the one you love."

Just as he said that, Taylor cut the corner. In seemingly slow motion, she said, "Hey, Scooter."

Scooter was her childish nickname for Jason. He leaned in for a very distant hug. "Hey, Taylor. How's everything?"

It was as if she negated the positive energy flow. I wondered if he was still a little bitter about everything. It seemed like he should be over the situation, but then it hit me: I still wasn't over my girl, why should he be over his? Taylor obviously sensed the tension she'd caused and kept on moving.

Jason and I started recapping. He and Akua got married. She was expecting their first child. They were still at Yale. He was now an attending physician and Akua was still completing her surgery residency. They moved to a big home right outside of New Haven. I was proud of Jason. He'd made it work with his runner-up and I was still running after the winner. Something had to give. My eyes shifted to find my runner-up, and at that moment I couldn't fathom making it work, because she'd always be Jason's winner. I knew I wouldn't be able to sleep if one of my boys was married to Clark. There were multiple reasons why Taylor and I were irreversibly done. Things we should have taken into account before we walked down the aisle were completely overlooked.

Jennifer and Nicole burst through the crowd. Nicole's piercing voice yelled, "Uncle Jason!" as she bolted toward him.

He hugged her and stroked her hair. "Hey, Nikki, what are you up to?"

"Everything," she said, rolling her eyes.

We all laughed. Jennifer reached out for a hug. Looking at me, Jason joked, "See, man, I told you that you wasn't happy unless you had it all."

Jennifer said, "That's my baby daddy."

We looked at Jennifer and laughed. Jason talked to Nicole and Jennifer for a minute before my parents came over to speak. Jason became the guest of honor. No one had seen him since he was a no-show at the wedding. They didn't know the whole story, and I never planned to tell them. Before Jason left, I told him to answer the phone when I called. He laughed. "Yeah, man, I will."

"That was real gay."

"Let's not get started with that," he said, raising his eyebrow.

I raised my hands in a defenseless manner. "A'ight, dawg. You right."

Shortly after, we all began piling out of the church, headed home to Chef Damon's lobster tail and filet mignon dinner.

47

DEVIN

I could barely sleep the night before the election. Ironically, around two in the morning, Nicole appeared in my doorway. "Daddy," she said.

My head popped from my pillow. "What's up, baby girl?"

She climbed into my bed. "If you win, does that mean that you can't come see me as much as you used to?"

"No, why would you say that?"

"I don't know. It just seems like everybody is making a big deal out of this."

I pushed her hair from her eyes. "Because it *is* a big deal, baby. You know how I tell you to always follow your dreams?" She nodded. I continued, "This is my dream. It's been my dream since I was your age."

"Daddy, I'm proud of you."

I hugged her. "And I'm proud of you."

"So, is Ms. Taylor ever coming home?"

"I don't think so, Nikki. It's hard for a lot of women to deal with the limelight."

"Why did you cheat on her?"

"Why do you think I cheated on her?" I asked.

"Um, because she wasn't in love with you."

I held the side of my head and propped my elbow up on the pillow. I'd questioned how she knew it was true that I cheated on Taylor, but she answered a different question. Nicole had fresh eyes and a lot of wisdom. I wanted to lie to her and explain that I was no cheater, but clearly she knew for sure I'd cheated. Surely, she'd probably researched it on the Internet. So I talked to her like the little lady she was. "You think she wasn't in love with me?"

"I don't know. It was just something about her that . . . I don't know."

I didn't press her for more, because she'd said enough. In her own way, she tried to tell me this before I married Taylor. Of course, I didn't listen, because what could a nine-year-old know about relationships? Obviously, she knew more than I imagined. One thing for sure, I didn't regret having my little girl in my life.

"It's okay. You don't have to explain."

Nicole sighed. "Daddy, I hope you find somebody like Mommy again."

"I hope so, too. For now, I'll just be happy with you."

"That sounds good."

Finally, I was able to rest my eyes. It seemed like only minutes passed before the clock buzzed, letting me know it was seven o'clock. I shook Nicole and she squirmed irritably. Then I decided I would leave her there until I got out of the shower. I walked through the house waking everyone who planned to accompany me to the polls.

By the time the car arrived, Taylor was there. My parents, Taylor, Nicole, and I piled into the car and headed to the voting polls. When I stepped out of the car, photographers snapped pictures and asked me questions. Nicole held one hand and Taylor held the other. When we left, we attended a breakfast hosted by some volunteers. Jennifer and Aaron met us there.

After we left breakfast, I stopped at several voting stations to show my face and let the voters know I was down for them. Later, we headed to the facility we'd rented out for all of our supporters. Amazingly, by five-thirty the place was packed. They passed hors d'oeuvres and wine. Music played, but we were on pins and needles. The race was very close. The later and later it got, the closer it got. An hour after the polls closed, we were dancing around and celebrating, praying for a victory. Before the scandal, I had my opponent by a much larger margin, but that situation really hurt me. Finally, I got the call from my opponent around ten-thirty, congratulating me. I won! It was almost unbelievable. I had begun to believe it was over. I'd thought I would just try again in four years. I stood there stunned as the balloons and confetti fell from the ceiling. Tears came to my eyes and as much as I wanted to resist, I let them fall as I rushed to the stage to make my victory speech.

Just before I spoke, Curtis announced that Barack Obama was the president-elect and that right after my speech we'd turn the big screens to Grant Park. The crowd cheered and shouted with joy. I wiped my face, but I couldn't stop the stream of tears from rolling. I needed to compose myself, but I couldn't. As I stood at the podium and looked into the hopeful eyes of people who for the first time felt they had really made a difference, I was humbled.

"DP, DP, DP, DP!" the crowd chanted. And I got filled up more. I tried to calm them with hand gestures and they continued: "DP, DP, DP!"

"Thank you! Thank you!" I waited a few more minutes

and finally they gave their attention to me. "This race was never about me. It was always about us, our people. And I'm glad that we were able to stand up and rebuke those vicious attacks. No path to success comes without roadblocks, but perseverance always prevails. My people, our people, we are determined to overcome. We are determined to have our voices heard. Thank you for entrusting me to speak on your behalf."

They cheered more, and it was obvious they weren't going to allow me to finish my speech. I said, "I would like to thank all of you! For your support and prayers on those rough days." I gripped Taylor's hand and looked at her. "And to my wife, words can't express what I feel for you. You are an amazing woman."

The crowd clapped loudly. I sniffed to hold back the tears. I'd done enough damn crying in public. "You are a queen and I am a better person because of you."

Everyone clapped and chanted my name. When it came out we weren't together, people would think this was all an act, but I meant every word. Taylor's cooperation made the difference in the race. Her ability to be completely honest about her feelings made me want to be a better man. She hugged me and we kissed onstage. Cameras flashed rapidly. This was the best night of my life.

Finally, I said, "Now, let's get this party started!"

The music came on and Taylor and I danced together onstage. I leaned in and said, "Stay with me tonight."

I couldn't imagine sleeping alone after this victory. I wanted to hold somebody. She obviously had a few glasses of wine. "No, Devin. If I go home with you, we may end up back together."

"Would that be so bad?" She shrugged. Our foreheads

were together and I asked again, "Is that the worst thing in the world?"

"It's not the worst thing, but it's not the smartest thing." She huffed. "To hell with it. How can I let your fine ass go home and sleep alone? You're still mine until the ink is dry."

I laughed and we kissed again. I wasn't sure what we were doing or if it even made sense. All I knew was that I needed her and I wanted her that night. We'd hash out the particulars in the morning.

48

CLARK

Almost a month after the trial, Mia's number popped up on my caller ID. My heart dropped, because I didn't know if she was calling to fight or if she was ready to forgive me. I picked up quickly. She sniffed a little. "Hey, Ma."

"Mia-Mia?"

"Yes. I just wanted to tell you I was sorry. I didn't want to believe that Daddy could do something like that, but you just never know."

"You're right, Mia."

"I'm sorry he hurt you and that you hurt him. It's just sad. I never thought things would be like they are. I don't even know where to come home to. What am I supposed to do for Thanksgiving?"

"Mia, this is your home and don't you forget that. I can't love and support a man who molested a child, but I will always love a child that I raised."

She sniffed again. "Thanks, Ma."

"Mia-Mia, I'll always be there for you, okay? Don't let anyone tell you that I'm not your mother. Okay?"

After her phone call, I was at peace with everything. Well, almost everything. I wanted to talk to Raven. I contacted her social worker after the trial to see if we could have a supervised meeting, but she didn't think it was a good idea, at least not so soon. So that was an open wound that I would have to let heal in time. And maybe one day I would get my opportunity to apologize to her.

The group home had been foreclosed. Ms. Teeny and I were planning to reopen under a different name, but we would have to go through the entire proposal and certification process again, which could take upward of a year. In the meantime, I continued to work and make the best of my upside-down world. Maybe there was a message in all of this, but I had yet to figure it out.

As the general election approached, I thought more and more about Devin. I wanted to call him, but I didn't. I wanted to see him, but I didn't. It wasn't so much that we'd been exposed, but more because I was embarrassed. I wondered what Devin thought of me. How could I be stupid enough to think that Kenneth was innocent? Maybe a part of me wasn't ready to fully take that next step with Devin. Maybe I would always think he'd hurt me like he did the first time. It was just easier to support Kenneth and run away from what I felt with Devin, but who could I run to now?

Ever since the trial, I'd been coming straight home from work, curling up in my bed and watching movie after movie.

On the night of the general election, Reggie invited me over so that we could have drinks and celebrate. We were certain that Barack Obama would win the election, but I preferred to stay home. I wanted to see if Devin Patterson would win, too, and I didn't want anyone reading too deeply into my emotions. I had a bottle of wine and my remote control to keep me company. I flipped back and forth between MSNBC and the DC and Baltimore local news channels. I needed to know if Devin won. Even if he couldn't be mine, I wanted him to win and I wanted to see him. I wanted to see the expression on his face.

When they announced that Barack Obama would be the next president of the United States, I leaped from my bed with excitement. My phone rang off the hook, but I turned up the television to hear the reporters. I would call Reggie and Teeny back shortly.

When I switched back to the local news to hear what they had to say, I nearly fainted when the cameras went to Devin Patterson's victory party. He'd done it. A part of me was proud, but then there was a part of me filled with rage. How did he manage to come out on top all the time? My heart sank when Devin finished speaking and turned to kiss his wife. He stroked her face like he was so in love. Why did I feel betrayed and jealous?

My phone seemed to be ringing like crazy: text messages, phone calls. Everyone was excited—everyone except me. I covered my ears with a pillow and let tears run down my face. I didn't bother to wipe them. Visions of Devin and his wife upset me to the point that I was shaking, wondering if he would have really left her and whether I'd be sitting here alone anyway. She was beautiful and elegant, and they looked perfect together.

My body was numb. It just wasn't fair. I wanted Devin. She didn't deserve him. I did. I should have been there. I should have gone to meet Devin when he called me days before I married Kenneth. I was thirty-five years old, back on the singles scene, back working a nine-to-five and digging myself out of debt. I didn't know how to pull all the pieces back together. I went downstairs and grabbed another bottle of wine. I didn't bother to grab a glass. I planned on taking it straight to the head.

49

✦

DEVIN

I rolled over and looked at the clock: 6:07 a.m. I patted the other side of the bed, and Taylor wasn't there. My head popped up and I got out of bed. I walked through the house. Jennifer and Aaron were packing their car to leave. When they saw me come down the stairs, they looked shocked. They'd told me they were leaving early so Nicole could make it to school in time. Obviously there was a baffled look on my face, because Jennifer said, "Taylor left a few minutes ago."

I was slightly embarrassed, because I didn't realize anyone knew she'd stayed the night. "Oh, yeah, she fell asleep. She told me she was leaving early."

Nicole sat in the family room, bundled in her coat, pissed that she was up at the crack of dawn. I walked in and kissed her on the cheek. "Have a good day, Nikki."

She nodded and looked extremely agitated as I walked her to the door. When they left, I quickly called Taylor. When she answered, I said, "So is that how we do it now? You come get a piece and leave before sunrise?"

"Look, Devin. We aren't doing anything. I came to keep you company last night because you deserved it, but I don't plan to just be getting a piece from you," she said with conviction.

"But I've offered you more."

"And I've declined."

Her words stung and would have offended anyone who had any feelings for her. I wondered when all this anger surfaced. It just didn't make sense. I said, "Taylor, what's wrong? Why are you acting like this?"

"Your phone is in the bathroom. Check your text messages." She hung up.

I rushed upstairs and into the bathroom and looked at my text messages. C Winston had left four new messages through the night. The first one read: BRAVO DEVIN! The next one: DID YOU EVER REALLY LOVE ME? The next: I'M SICK WITHOUT YOU. And finally: IT'S JUST NOT FAIR THAT WE NEVER HAD OUR TIME.

My heart sank. What the hell was she doing up all night sending these messages? I called her, and she didn't answer. I called nearly ten times before my parents got up and began moving around the house. A part of me wondered if I was interrupting her home, but the other part didn't care. She was hurt and missing me the same way I missed her. We'd bypassed each other enough on the road of life. An hour or so later, my parents' car came to take them to the airport, and it wasn't even eight o'clock yet. I didn't have to be anywhere until ten. I needed to see Clark.

When I called back again, she answered the phone groggily. "Hello?"

"Clark."

Her voice perked up. "Devin?" She sounded surprised to hear from me.

"Yes, Clark. It's me. Yes, I've always loved you and I'm

more sick without you and whatever time you want to be our time, let's make it happen."

She sucked her teeth and I could hear her moving around in her bed. "What?"

"I'm responding to all the messages you sent me last night."

She coughed and laughed. "Devin, I was so drunk."

"A drunk man's words are a sober man's thoughts. But I'm sober as shit right now. My words and my thoughts are the same. I've spent almost ten years missing you, regretting every relationship because of you. I can't do it anymore. Our lives have grown together; despite all the time we spent apart. Let's stop fooling ourselves."

"Devin, how can you just make that decision today and you were telling the world how much you loved your wife last night?"

"Clark, my wife and I are separated and we plan to legalize it next week."

She sniffed, and I continued pouring my heart out. "You deserve me. You deserve a good man that loves you." She started crying, and I kept going. "And I deserve you. We are supposed to be together, and I don't care what anyone thinks about it."

"Devin, I'm getting a divorce. My husband really did have a relationship with that girl."

For some strange reason, I never doubted that he was guilty. Clark deserved a better life and I wanted to give it to her. I felt as if God had given me another chance, and I promised not to mess it up this time.

50

CLARK

I met Devin at his condo in DC the day after the election. When I walked in the door, he said, "Would you move into a house that I lived in with an ex-wife?"

"I was your first wife, Devin, and from the looks of things, your only wife. Why wouldn't I?"

"I hoped you'd say yes. I want you with me."

We haven't left each other since that day. Devin gave me an astronomical budget to redecorate his home and make it my own. We stayed in his DC condo until the renovations were done. Then we moved to our home in Mitchellville. It was all I ever dreamed my house to be.

I sold it all, *everything*. This was a fresh start and the promise of the life I always wanted. The house sold for way below market value, and I barely broke even because of the second mortgage on the house. Devin settled all of my outstanding debt. That was the least I could do for Kenneth. When he got out of jail, at least he'd be starting with a clean slate. I wasn't sure what he planned to do, but that was no longer my problem. I took on Mia's tuition, because she was still my child. Our relationship was outside of Kenneth.

Devin and I opted to be life partners and not taint our

bond with marriage. We were committed to each other, and we wanted to wake up every day and reaffirm that commitment. We didn't need any legal papers to force us to be together. Our union was totally at will. I didn't fear him leaving and he didn't fear me leaving. We'd been married spiritually for a long time, and we had nothing to prove to anyone.

My new job as director of programs for Love My People has been adventurous and rewarding. My purpose would spread around the globe, helping black girls and women everywhere. It was my responsibility to organize high-society charity events to raise funds for our programs. That was probably what I loved most. Ms. Teeny is my well-paid assistant director, and she loves getting the opportunity to travel and look at all the fine black men this world has to offer.

She wouldn't be accompanying Devin and I when we headed back to Nicaragua to pick up our baby, Devin. Amina had passed away about a month before, and Señora Gonzales contacted Devin to ask if he and his wife were still interested in adopting the baby. We never thought twice. Instead, we began handling things and making sure the paperwork was processed correctly.

When we got on that little plane from Managua to the Corn Islands, I held his hand tightly, still the bumpy ride I recalled, but this time I wasn't afraid. I was excited about life. Our life together and the life of our new baby.

When we arrived at the outreach center, Señora Gonzales was glad to see us. We hugged and she told us how Baby Devin was doing. He'd tested negative before he turned nine months.

Señora Gonzales wanted to have a small going-away party for him. He was such a happy baby and even sweeter than

I recalled. We stayed the night and took Baby Devin to the hotel with us. I had expected him to take a moment to adjust, but he fell right asleep in the Pack 'n Play we'd rented from the hotel.

Before we left the next day, we said our good-byes to Señora Gonzales. We promised her that we'd be sure Baby Devin knew his heritage and we'd bring him back as often as possible when we were doing our outreach work. We decided to tack *Patterson* on the end of his name, and not change his last name in case he ever wanted to know more about his biological family. Señora Gonzales looked at me as we were about to leave. "You have something to tell me, no?"

"Huh?"

"I can look at you and see something."

Devin smiled and said, "Yes, we're expecting a baby, too."

"No!" she said dramatically. She yanked me and hugged me. "God bless you."

My eyes shot at Devin. We'd agreed to keep it under wraps until my second trimester. I guess we were merely a week away. So it was no harm. Yep, on our first try, the IVF worked. Devin and I were biologically created for each other. When we told people that we were adopting a baby, those who knew we were trying to conceive thought we were crazy. We were just making up for lost time, and I'd never been more happy and fulfilled in my entire adult life.

READING GROUP GUIDE

1. Did you feel that Clark had lost herself in her marriage? If so, what could she have done differently?

2. What do you feel was Devin's motive for marrying Taylor?

3. Did you get the impression that Taylor was in love with Devin? Why or why not?

4. Did Kenneth seem to resent Clark? Where did it seem to stem from?

5. What were your initial thoughts when Clark decided to reach out to Devin? Was it wise?

6. Do you think Clark would have made the first call if her marriage was more stable?

7. Do you think that Clark and Devin were realistic about their feelings for each other after so much time had passed?

8. Would you have been able to trust Devin if you were Clark?

9. Would you have been able to support Kenneth during his dilemma? Why do you think Clark did?

10. How do you think Taylor and Devin's marriage would have played out without Clark in the picture?

11. Did you have any compassion for Kenneth in the end?

12. Did you think all the characters got what they deserved?